Sting of the Scorpion

by

Earl Underwood

A Detective Jack Storm Mystery

Shoppe Foreman Publishing
Oklahoma City, Oklahoma, USA

Copyright © 2016 by Earl Underwood. All U. S. and international rights reserved. No part of this book may be reproduced in any form or by any means without the prior written consent of the author, excepting brief passages used in reviews.

Cover image of scorpion by johnaudrey ©

**Published by
Shoppe Foreman Publishing**
Oklahoma City, Oklahoma, USA
www.ShoppeForeman.com

See last page for place and date of printing.

ISBN-13: 978-1977949356
ISBN-10: 1977949355

Dedication

I know that I always dedicate my books to my wonderful wife of nearly fifty years, and for good reason. I can't imagine my life without her, nor would I want to. For a couple to stay together a half a century and still love one another is a major accomplishment. So once again, *this one's for you, kid!*

Acknowledgements

Throughout the course of a lifetime, most of us acquire many friends, usually through our work or our career of choice. I've had the good fortune to have been in a career where I was able to make many good like-minded friends. True friends can go many years without speaking to one another, but that doesn't diminish the capacity of the friendship. If we're lucky, we will have one or more that could never be replaced. I have several such friends, and I never take them for granted.

During my thirty-two-year law enforcement career many people entered my life and made an impact. Some are now gone but not forgotten, but most are still here. I now take this opportunity to thank some of those friends and co-workers who have been a part of my life.

Captain John Duncan was one of the first detectives I rode with when I was assigned to the Hialeah Detective Bureau. He and his partner Richard Kelly left many lasting impressions on me during my first weeks in the Bureau. Alex Whitmore and I were with him when he made his first ever hole-in-one at Doral Country Club. We played many, many games of golf together and shared some great times. In his memory I have used his name in this book.

Barry Krane and I both worked on the Hialeah Police Department but seldom together in the same unit. That didn't stop us from becoming friends, and we still are to this day. Barry consented to my using his name as one of the characters, and I thank him for it.

Daniel Bucciante and I have remained friends since I was in the Bureau when he worked in Auto Theft. We still converse by phone every couple of weeks or so and reminisce about the good old days. I hope you enjoy your character Danny.

Linda Ward, you know I still love you like a big brother.

Al Strawberry, my friend and neighbor across from my vacation home in Maggie Valley, North Carolina, is another who allowed me to use his name in this novel. Thanks, Al. I think I did you good!

A shout out to some of my best friends – Earl Dedrick, Jim Heath, Mike Reich, and Ray Oetting. Gil Mugarra, I haven't forgotten you, partner. Rest in peace, Gil – we were a great team.

Of course I can't thank my editor and publisher Larry Forman enough. I truly appreciate all the work he puts in to make me look good in print. I'm looking forward to many more years working with him.

On one last note I have to mention none other than my High School Principal, Leon McLean, who is currently residing in North Carolina with his wife Janice. When I began writing several years ago, I sent him one of my first published books, my autobiography/memoirs. His review and comments encouraged me to continue my writing and ever since I have sent him each new novel as it was released. He is one of my biggest fans, and the respect I have for him knows no bounds. Garland High was such a long time ago, Mr. Mac, but sometimes it seems like only yesterday. God bless you and Janice.

Once again thanks to Shaunie and Adria.

Chapter 1

El Scorpion

WITH THE FAINTEST HINT OF A SMILE gracing his face, the target loomed larger than life in the Scrome LTE 10-power scope. The crosshairs were aliened on an area slightly above his right eyebrow. The magnification was great enough that his head nearly filled the scope, affording *El Scorpion* an optimum shot. The man was totally oblivious that he had been targeted for assassination and was mere seconds away from instant death. He was standing on top of the steps outside the massive main doors of the recently completed Milander-Soto Convention Center, shaking hands and speaking with several dignitaries.

The scope shifted ever so slightly, highlighting others in close proximity to the target. It lingered on an attractive female who had the bearing of an undercover cop, despite her attempt to mask it. She wore white slacks complimented by a beautiful pale peach colored blouse, accented by low-heeled black shoes. No weapon was visible, but he knew she was, at the very least, security of some sort, which meant she was also armed somehow. Her eyes never stopped moving, looking at everyone and everything, missing nothing. Standing next to her was the target, a man who appeared to be above six feet in height, lean but muscular and exuding his own aura of authority. There was a persistent breeze which insisted upon blowing his thick mane of hair askew, and he unconsciously kept brushing it back with his free hand. It was apparent that he was being diplomatically patient with the gathered dignitaries as he was exhibiting subtle signs indicating he was ready to leave.

The Scorpion relaxed, slowing his breathing and then exhaling his breath ever so slowly as he refocused the scope on his intended target. The activity below indicated that he needed to act now, so he gently began to squeeze the trigger, his hands as steady as a surgeon, his breathing totally under control. It almost seemed as if he was caressing the trigger with the tender touch new lovers were prone to give each other, gentle, sensual and loving. In a farfetched way it actually was as if he were caressing his lover since he thought of his weapon in similar but obviously nonsexual terms. Both mentally and physically relaxed, he was subconsciously prepared for the recoil of the deadly Russian Dragunov SDV rifle once the round escaped from its barrel. There were many other and definitely much better sniper rifles now available on the market, but he had begun his profession with the Dragunov and saw no reason to change now. It had served him well over the many years he had used it, always accurate and always deadly.

Sting of the Scorpion

* * * * * * * * * *

The projectile, called a 7N1, 7.62mm round, was designed by the Soviets for hair-splitting accuracy over a half a century ago. The bullet was developed with a steel core and a hollow spot in the nose of the round with a lead knocker behind it. Upon impact into a target the knocker would move forward into the hollow spot, destabilizing the bullet and causing it to begin a deadly tumble into whatever it struck. Almost ninety nine percent of the time the bullet would result in immediate death. This was the deadly round the assassin would be utilizing today. The oppressive Florida humidity in tandem with the current breezy conditions would almost certainly affect the flight of the bullet as it flew towards its target. The sound suppressor attached to the barrel could also affect the flight, but not very much. The assassin had already allowed for those specific conditions, performing the necessary calibrations needed to adjust for what would be an altered and slightly higher trajectory. In a perfect scenario he would have already fired at least one shot to warm the barrel, but the timing, exposure and circumstances today wouldn't allow for it. A bullet traveling down a cold barrel often misses its target, no matter how proficient a shooter you are. This particular shot could be considered overkill by professional standards, but he needed to make sure the target would be killed on impact. Those were the terms set forth in the contract if his substantial payment was to be forthcoming.

* * * * * * * * * *

Earl Underwood

The Scorpion had patiently sat motionless on the makeshift seat in front of the windowless opening of the uncompleted building for some time now. The earlier shower had only enhanced the humidity once it had passed. It would be almost impossible for anyone on the ground to spot him in his perch fifteen floors up. He had stationed the seat back far enough from the open window that he would be ensconced in the shadows of the room. He was currently enjoying the slight rain-cooled breeze that managed to waft into the empty room, giving some respite to the stifling heat in the enclosed and unfinished area. The oppressive humidity was comparable to being slapped in the face with a hot rag. The sweat soaked his hair as if he had just climbed out of a swimming pool. It ran in rivulets down the back of his neck, almost akin to a small tributary attempting to locate its mother river.

He had been stuck in this town for three long days now waiting for the target to return from his vacation. Now, the target was back, and the call he had been waiting for had come. He had made sure he arrived early, giving himself the necessary time needed to set up his roost and prepare to wait for the opportune time to fulfill the contract.

* * * * * * * * * *

His birth name was Juan Castro and as far as he knew, or so he had been repeatedly told by his family, he was not related to Fidel Castro. His eye peered through the scope mounted on the Dragunov sniper rifle, as it had for the last twenty minutes, give or take a few. For now he had kept his eye about an inch away from the scope, prepared to quickly press it to the rubber cup once he was ready to take the shot. The deadly weapon was mounted on a small tripod, an accessory he usually didn't employ. Today was different because of the breezy conditions and the necessity for success. The tripod would maintain complete stability of the powerful rifle.

When he had been approached with the contract for this hit and provided with the pertinent details by his broker, he had immediately declined, without any hesitation whatsoever. The high profile of the target along with the guaranteed uproar following his death would potentially put a gridlock on any escape plans. Juan had several standing rules involving contracts which would raise a red flag and allow him justification for turning down a contract. No children or women would ever be targets, no heads of state, and never where there was the slightest possibility of not having a good escape route. He hadn't survived in his chosen profession this long by being careless. He meticulously considered every aspect of a contract before he would accept it, and he had turned down many worth a cumulative total of millions of dollars. That would be a healthy sum – hard to refuse for some in his profession, but not all could command such a fee. But then again, he had made many millions more than he had ever turned down. So he could now afford to be selective, and he was. It had not always been a career as lucrative as it was now. Many years ago he had started down this path and worked for only a few thousand dollars a hit. His reputation, discretion and success rate over the intervening years had elevated him to a stature where he was in de-

Earl Underwood

mand and could command the fee he charged these days. He had changed his name many years ago to Victor. That was the name he used when he wasn't on a job where he needed an alias, of which he had many.

His broker, one of many who dealt in these types of unsavory criminal activities, had sent him another encrypted email, his first choice of communication. He never worried much about getting caught through his emails since he always eradicated them after each use. His broker knew to simply add the next letter and number in the alphabet to the existing email after each contact.

He had opened the new email and noticed that the offer had now doubled, from one million to two million dollars if he would take the contract. In his email reply, he attached a phone number that was connected to a throwaway cell phone, called a "burner," and pressed the send key. Once his broker called him and the conversation had ended, he would destroy the burner. He answered the call when it came in and listened patiently as his broker explained who the target was, the generous fee and the location where the hit was to be carried out. When the broker had finished with the details the Scorpion patiently explained to him that there wouldn't be enough time for him to properly canvas the location of the execution, plan his escape route or arrange for the necessary weapons. After all, he couldn't just hop on a commercial airplane with a sniper rifle and ammunition and expect everything to be overlooked. Still, he considered the deal for a very long minute before finally advising the broker there was only one way he would accept the contract on such short notice and because of the notoriety of the target. He would need one million dollars deposited in his numbered Swiss account, and it would be absolutely *non-refundable,* whether he succeeded or not.

In addition he would expect another two million dollars deposited upon successful completion of the contract. If the client couldn't agree to these terms, the broker was not to call back with any type of counter-offer. His terms were not up for negotiation. The following day, almost twenty-four hours exactly, he received the next sequential email from his broker and was given the green light. Also in the email was the name of an underground weapons dealer for him to contact once he arrived in Hialeah, Florida, in the United States. The locale from where he was to carry out the job would be up to him to establish once he arrived. The Scorpion checked his Swiss account and was pleased to see that the non-refundable one million dollars had been deposited only hours earlier, the client already assuming he would take the deal.

Following usual protocol Victor hadn't been furnished with the name of the client and hadn't expected to be. Almost always a broker was used as an intermediary to present any deals and arrange for payment. Never was the client's name disclosed. It didn't surprise him in the least; it was common for all parties in his line of business to remain anonymous. Not knowing the name of the client was beneficial and healthy for all involved. It also wasn't unusual for a client to put a hit out on his own contractor, severing any potential ties that could possibly connect the client to the crime. Included in the email was an attachment that included several photographs of the designated target. Once he had committed the photos to memory, he used a specialized computer program to completely and permanently erase the emails and photographs from the hard drive. There would be no "ghost" images for the FBI or any other high tech agency to find if his laptop ever happened to fall into their hands.

Victor was only a few months shy of fifty-two years of age now, but he was still fit and strong, due to diligent and stringent workouts. His mind was still sharp. He was getting weary though, tired of the killing and tired of always having to look over his shoulder. He was especially tired of wondering if today would be the day when a client made the decision *he* was no longer needed, for whatever the reason and made arrangements for *his* demise. He had been seriously contemplating retirement for the last few years and those plans were instrumental in his decision to take this particular contract, although against his better judgment. There was something about it that gnawed at his gut, something telling him he should change his mind and not take it. He ignored the gnawing and silently vowed that this contract would definitely be his last.

He had over thirty-three million dollars in various banks in Switzerland and the Caymans, and even a couple in Germany. With this contract and the hefty compensation he could reap, he would never have to worry about his financial security. He could finally disappear and begin living out his life in comfort and style with his wife. Juan was no man's fool. He knew he would still be forever looking over his shoulder, wondering if someone would be coming after him for whatever reason. Still, he felt confident it would work. *No, he would make it work,* he thought to himself. Yes, he was definitely tired of the killing and hiding. In the beginning his first few hits had excited him, giving him a feeling of exuberance and power. Now with wisdom, age and scores of contracts fulfilled, it had become merely a job to him; nothing more – nothing less and definitely nothing personal. The thrill of the kill had faded over time, an indication that it was indeed a good time to retire. Too many in his field had become greedy and not lived to enjoy the fruits of their labor.

Chapter 2

Juan Castro

Juan Castro was born in Matanzas, Cuba, in 1964, less than a hundred miles from Havana. From an early age he had worked the sugar cane fields with his parents. He had made friends with many kids his age during those years, and the life of poverty they lived was the same for each of them. It was the only choice they had, a society where poverty was endemic and corruption was an expected aspect of any form of authority. Like kids everywhere they played games and dreamed big. In Communist Cuba those dreams were nearly unattainable, yet they still dreamed on, never stopping, never giving up hope.

Upon reaching his seventeenth birthday, he and a few of his friends around the same age were taken to the PNR, National Revolutionary Police Force, in Matanzas. It was mandatory that all male citizens be conscripted into a period of police work upon reaching their seventeenth birthday. When Juan was in his second year of police work, he was approached by agents of the DI, the Intelligence Directorate. Several complex situations in which he had been involved had revealed a level of intelligence not found in many of the other officers or friends in his unit. His investigative skills and detailed report writing stood out starkly above all others. His many exploits and commendations had ultimately caught the attention of the local DI agent-in-charge. He was soon asked to join the DI, and he immediately accepted, aware of their reputation and the elevated status they enjoyed. At nearly nineteen years of age he was one of the youngest DI agents in training. He continued to excel in all fields of his training and most notably on the firing range. It wasn't very long before he became far more qualified in firearms than the other recruits, and even some of the instructors. He seemed to have a natural talent, maybe even a gift, for firing weapons, especially with deadly accuracy over long distances. A target hit from a quarter of a mile was seemingly easy for him and even as far as a half a mile was in his range, under the right conditions.

He had barely three weeks of training under his belt when he was selected for a specialty, the DI Sniper Squad, a group that was only mentioned in hushed voices. Their reputation and exploits were well known, and to the true Cuban patriots they were very high on a pedestal, almost superheroes.

After the DI command could see that his potential had virtually no limits, it was decided he would be sent to Omsk, in the Soviet Union, a staunch ally of Cuba, for advanced intelligence and weapons training. He was envied by most of the other recruits, but his true friends, and especially his family, were deliriously happy for him. They all knew that he was going to have a much better life than they ever had.

After he arrived in Omsk he was loaded into a military vehicle and whisked away to a military base about ten miles from the outskirts of town. He was housed in a run-down building with other trainees, the majority of them Soviets. The barracks were clean and organized inside, due to the strict orders that the trainees would keep them so.

Juan was placed under the specialized training branch of the GRU, the Main Intelligence Directorate in the Soviet Union, after he was given a preliminary qualifying weapons course. The Soviet instructors, almost never prone to exhibiting emotion, were extremely impressed with his shooting proficiency. His exceptional IQ enabled him to quickly grasp the rudimentary basics of the Russian language, at least enough to understand and converse with his instructors to a passable degree.

The advanced intelligence training he received enhanced his deadly skills, and the elite sniper training program propelled him to the top of his class. A different type of reaction was expressed by all of the recruits now, and it was one of awe and a lot of respect. The entire class was impressed and to some degree, almost afraid of his prowess. Juan had never allowed himself to get very close to the other trainees, keeping mostly to himself.

After nearly six months of intensive training, he was told he would be returning home to Cuba, his training now mostly repetitive. There wasn't much more he could be taught to enhance his deadly skills at this facility. From now on it would be the experience he gained in the field that would further his knowledge and sharpen his skills. He never heard it himself but the class of Soviet students discussed behind his back his total lack of emotion and the subsequent fate of any poor soul who ever ended up in the sights of his rifle.

Juan now had no intention of returning to Cuba if there was anything he could to do about it. He wanted more out of life than the drab existence that awaited him at home in Matanzas, Cuba. Shortly after his arrival in Omsk he had spent many hours pondering how he could possibly stay in the Soviet Union or any place other than Cuba. He knew that the Soviet Union was totally out of the question because of their strong ties and alliance with Cuba. If the Soviet authorities even caught a hint that he was planning to defect, he would immediately be put in shackles and sent home where the Cuban authorities would probably at the least incarcerate him for a long time.

After being flown the nearly fourteen hundred miles from Omsk to Moscow, he boarded a Llyushin Il-62 airliner at Aeroflot. The plane was scheduled to make a stop in Cartagena, Colombia, before continuing on to Havana, Cuba. It was in Cartagena where he seized the opportunity to escape a life of squalor and the depressing poverty that surely awaited him in Cuba.

When the portable stairs were pushed up to the plane for the departing passengers, he deftly and calmly blended in and deplaned, walking casually past the stewardesses along with the other departing passengers down the portable stairs. He forced himself to remain calm and use the evasive training techniques he had been taught. No one had paid any undue attention to him, and he quickly entered the terminal unhindered at Rafael Nunez International Airport, keeping pace with the departing passengers.

He realized he had to find a way to get past customs if he was to make good his escape. Getting caught now would result in his being deported to Cuba in handcuffs and certainly not to a hero's welcome for sure. Walking slowly, he lagged behind the other passengers ahead of him, his mind racing, trying to figure how he was going to get through customs. Suddenly he espied a janitorial closet off to his left. Instantly he realized he had just possibly found a way to get past the customs officials undetected and out into the main terminal. He was also aware that this might be his only chance other than running full out and hoping to get away. The Colombian police were visible everywhere, patrolling in pairs with their rifles slung over their shoulders, so running was not an option.

Once he saw that no one was paying any attention to him, he quickly sidled over to the wall by the janitorial door and silently prayed to himself that it would be unlocked and uninhabited. Casually scanning the area and seeing that still no one was paying undo attention to him, he tried the door to the closet and to his relief found it unlocked. With one last furtive glance around, he slipped through the door, hoping no one was inside, and closed it behind him.

The room became pitch black once he closed the door, but running his hands over the wall he found a light switch. Flipping it up the dim light bulb instantly illumi-

Sting of the Scorpion

nated the cramped room, revealing the carts and cleaning supplies used by the janitorial staff. He spotted a dark blue denim work shirt hanging on the back of the door with the name *Carlos* stitched in white over the breast pocket. Juan was astute enough to know that he would also need a photo ID card to clip onto the janitor's uniform shirt. If he found one, he figured that it would be hard to compare any facial features from a distance. He searched all around the room but couldn't find one anywhere. He hadn't really expected to see one if the attendant was on duty now, since he would have to be wearing it. He decided to take his chances as he quickly slipped the work shirt over his own – luckily it fit him fairly well. He spotted a worn, stained ball cap lying on a shelf with the name of some janitorial service emblazoned on the front. The heavily sweat-stained liner gave him pause, but he put it on. He had to readjust the strap on the back of the cap to fit his head snugly. The cap's bill would hopefully help shield his face somewhat from inquisitive officials.

Finally he gripped the handle of one of the only janitorial service carts inside that was stocked with cleaning materials and pushed it from the room, casually closing the door behind him. He took one of the dust cloths on the cart and draped it over his shoulder, concealing the area where he assumed an identification card would be clipped. He kept the nametag partially visible just in case one of the patrolling officers looked his way.

He was keenly aware that there was a real possibility that most of the airport personnel knew Carlos, and therefore his actions would be thwarted before he had any chance to exit the terminal. But he had to take the risk –

he had already fully committed himself and there was no turning back now.

He forced himself to push the cart at a leisurely pace, not wanting to appear in a hurry, keeping his head lowered to avoid anyone realizing he was not Carlos. He had an inclination to push the cart faster, but he forced himself to maintain control over his impulses. Moving faster while pushing a cart could draw unwanted attention and that would possibly be enough to end his chances of freedom.

He could now see the spacious open terminal just ahead, the milling of hundreds of people akin to cows in a pen, the taste of freedom so near and so sweet on his tongue. Only the narrowing of the gates manned by the customs agents created the sole obstacle to his freedom. There were hundreds of people in the terminal with many dozens in line awaiting their turn to pass on through. He silently prayed that all the attention would be focused on those in line, keeping him invisible for a few minutes longer.

As Juan neared the long line of noisy travelers waiting to be cleared through customs, he could feel sweat beginning to slowly trickle down his back and his heart rate quickly increasing from the sudden rush of adrenalin coursing through his body. Still resisting the urge to increase his pace he utilized his training and kept his head down, controlling his breathing and slowly pushing the cart, appearing distant to the agents.

After what seemed an eternity his cart slowly rolled past the line of travelers and customs agents. Then he was out into the open main terminal. He couldn't believe how easy it had been. The customs agents hadn't given him a second glance. He quickly sought out and found a rest room halfway down the vast terminal. Pushing the cart inside and thankful there wasn't another attendant present, he began wiping a sink while waiting for the two individuals inside to finish their business and leave. He then entered a stall and took off the uniform shirt and hat. He balled them up and tossed them into a trash receptacle on his way out the door.

Once he was in the main terminal he quickly blended into the maelstrom of travelers, becoming just another person heading home. He had left the janitorial cart inside the rest room parked by the door, leaving no other clue he was ever there. He briefly considered going to the luggage carousal and grabbing a piece with the hope there would be some clothes his size. He quickly dismissed that idea as too risky – he needed to leave the airport before his absence on the plane was noticed and an alert was issued to security.

From that day forth he had spent the rest of his life in Cartagena. Only occasionally did he think about his family in Cuba. He had never been very close to his father, but he really missed his mother. He could still remember what his younger brother and sister looked like, but their faces were becoming harder and harder to picture.

He eventually married a Colombian woman, Marta Bustos, and although they had tried many times, they were never able to have children. It was probably for the best considering the line of work he was in and the many trips he would be away for weeks on end. He was blessed with a wife that loved him and understood he had to be gone so much in order to give them a good life. The only thing Marta knew about his job was that he took many trips out of the country on business. He had told her when they first met that he was a representative for a manufacturing company and had to visit other countries to set up operating accounts, conduct efficiency tests and interview managerial candidates. She never once questioned him, and they had a normal, happy upper middle class lifestyle. As an only child and her parents deceased, she had no one to meddle in their family life.

For the first several years there had been many attempts by DI agents from Cuba to find Carlos, but always without success. Eventually they seemed to have given up looking for him, but he knew he still had to remain cautious and keep his guard up. He changed his name to Victor Mendez as soon as he had entered Colombia and started his new life. He had changed his appearance by growing a neat beard and changing his hair color.

Using the skills and tradecraft he had been taught to near perfection in the Soviet Union, he soon found a master forger and convinced him to make a set of identification cards allowing him to pass as a Colombian citizen. He had made an arrangement with the forger to pay him double his fee once he was able, after being honest and up front with him about his defection. The forger had accepted the agreement since he sympathized with his plight and had no doubt he would be paid in due time. Over the following years Juan honored his promise and paid the fee in full, with interest as he had promised.

He spent his first year in Colombia living on the dangerous back streets of Cartagena, becoming a petty thief

Sting of the Scorpion

to survive and becoming quite adept at it. The street gangs, territorial thugs and everyday hoodlums learned the hard way to steer clear and leave him alone. He had many altercations over that first year, resulting in severe injuries, some to him but most to his foes. Even death had come to some who had dared test him in his first year on the back streets and alleys. Soon the word was out that he was more than capable of killing a man in seconds. Eventually he was left alone, respect and some fear following in his wake.

Juan, now using the name Victor, carefully made it known throughout the underworld that he was the man to go to when someone needed a permanent solution to a problem. His reputation grew with each successful contract, and soon his skills were in high demand, not only in Colombia but other countries as well.

With each success came money, lots and lots of money, and the independence which allowed him the option to choose or deny any particular contract. There had been a few contracts he had absolutely refused to consider for purely personal reasons. Most involved unnecessary risk, but a few violated his steadfast rule against killing women or children, whether they were collateral damage or not. If there was any chance during a mission that a woman or child could be injured or killed during the execution of the contract, he turned it down cold. He was well aware that he couldn't control the inadvertent incursions of Innocents during the execution of a contract, but so far he had never accidently harmed a child, although he had killed a woman. The thought of killing an innocent child would haunt him the rest of his life, so therefore the reasoning for his strict rule.

With the vast and varied assortment of connections he had cultivated over the following years, he had accumulated over two dozen authentic looking forged passports, all with corresponding photo identification cards. At a secreted storage locker downtown he had a cache of emergency cash, the passports and a huge assorted array of weapons. He was now using one of the fake passports for his trip to Hialeah under the name of Francisco Vega.

Sometime in his past he had acquired his nickname, El Scorpion. One of his former clients had made the statement, "When Victor is in town, someone's going to feel the sting of the scorpion," and the name had stuck with him ever since. He actually liked the moniker Scorpion and never objected to anyone referring to him by it.

Chapter 3

Contamination

VICTOR WAS A VERY LONG WAY FROM HOME and now in downtown Hialeah, in South Florida. He was hunkered down on the fifteenth floor of one of several new condos under construction two blocks due east of the Convention Center. He had chosen this site and specific floor because the line of sight was unobstructed and he had a near perfect view of the front doors to the Milander-Soto Convention Center.

He had parked his non-descript rental car in front of a bank a little more than a block west of this location, at Palm and Forty Ninth Street. When he left here he would be heading back towards the carnage he would be creating but he had little choice. He was in luck when he selected this tower as the workers were concentrating on completing another one several buildings away. There were no workers in or around this particular building, so he had no problem slipping through a fence and onto the construction site unseen. Diligently scanning the site for any security personnel and seeing none, he slipped into the unfinished building. His luck was still holding out because the elevator was operational – he would have been cutting it too close having to climb stairs fifteen stories and then descend those fifteen stories once he had taken his shot. It would have really been cutting any chance of escape much too close, if not making it impossible. Now he only had to make a quick jog to the bank, get his car and work his way south to Okeechobee Road. From there it was clear sailing to Miami International Airport, which was only a fifteen to twenty-minute drive. A piece of cake, but only if everything fell into place as planned, and his luck continued to hold.

* * * * * * * * *

Once he completed the pull on the trigger and the floating firing pin struck the round in the chamber, the kick from the recoil was instant and hard against his shoulder. Even with the sound suppression device affixed to the barrel the muffled report echoed throughout the room which was devoid of walls.

Peering through the scope, he watched as the fired round almost instantly found its target, the head exploding like a dropped melon on pavement. Almost in slow motion he watched a spume of gray brain matter and dark red blood pelted and splattered on those unfortunate enough to be in close proximity of the victim.

A confused look of shock and total surprise suddenly registered on the Scorpion's face. Before the body of the target had completed its fall to the tiled floor, he realized

Sting of the Scorpion

that in the split second he had pulled the trigger someone had inadvertently leaned in front of the target. It was only a nano second, but it was enough for a miss. He had missed the target, and he had failed! He knew he didn't have the luxury of taking a second shot – the scene would be mass pandemonium now.

Quickly he stood and made preparations to head for the elevator. He swiftly and expertly broke down the sniper rifle, collapsed the small tripod and stowed both in a nondescript black case. He had worn tight thin surgical latex gloves to avoid leaving any prints in the room. He quickly stripped them from his hands and pushed them deep into his pocket. He was well aware of how latex gloves could be turned inside out and prints possibly lifted.

He took one quick look around for any damning evidence he might be leaving behind. Seeing none, he sprinted to the elevator, the case in his hand. When he had reached the fifteenth floor earlier, he had blocked the door to the elevator with a wheel barrel he found nearby, locking it in place and keeping it readily available for his descent.

Now the only thought on his mind was getting to his car without detection, to the airport without incidence, and then out of the country as quickly as possible. He had missed his target and it galled him to no end. But what was done was done, and he didn't have a lot of time to dwell on it now. He walked fast to the bank where he had parked the car. After placing the gun case in the trunk, he was soon on the road. He turned east on 103rd Street and when he reached LeJuene Road he turned south towards

Earl Underwood

Okeechobee Road.

As he drove south, his mind racing a mile a minute, it hit him. For the first time he had failed to retrieve an empty shell casing. When he looked around the room he hadn't seen it but it was there, somewhere, and he was sure the police would eventually find it. He brushed it off since the weapon was untraceable and the serial numbers had been etched clean with acid. Still, they would be able to determine what kind of round was used and pinpoint the location he took the shot from. He would have preferred finding the shell, but it would be a fool's errand to return and try to retrieve it now. Time would not be on his side in such a quest.

Chapter 4

Timing is everything

Two weeks earlier.

AFTER A RELAXING WEEKEND with his beautiful bride of nearly three months, Jack Storm, "Stormy" to his friends and co-workers, was not ready for it to end. When he was with Shaunie the torrid world of criminals, thugs, crime and killings were non-existent. Police work was the career he had chosen, but there were times he grew weary of it. He loved his work, at least the investigative aspect, but there were instances that the everyday contact with the scum of society grated on him, giving him doubt as to how much longer he wanted to be exposed to it.

He and Shaunie had taken their time and leisurely driven up the west coast of Florida, both enjoying the getaway from the everyday grind of work, the hustle and bustle of South Florida, and content just being with each other. Their time was spent in the small picturesque towns scattered along the west coast of Florida, visiting art galleries and quaint antique shops, keeping an eye out for that one special piece which would compliment any room in their home.

After spending the night in Cedar Key, they arose early and had breakfast before driving the short distance east back to I-75, where they began the long drive back to Miami. With the top lowered on the BMW convertible, the warm Florida sun softly beat down on their heads. It was not really that uncomfortable as it was only the beginning of June. The weather forecaster had said there was very little chance of rain for the weekend so they decided to return home with the top down.

They were not in much of a hurry to return home, but both needed to be back at work Monday morning, whether they liked it or not. Shaunie had her own company to run and had an important meeting scheduled the first thing Monday morning with a new client. Jack needed to get back for a deposition at the States Attorney's office.

Three months earlier Jack Storm and Shaunie Marie Kelly had gotten married. By mutual agreement the wedding wasn't overly huge and only selected guests had been invited. Gil Torres, Stormy's former partner and good friend had been the best man. He had delayed a vacation trip to South America just to do Stormy the honor of being his best man. Among the invitees were Captain John Paradis, Miami Police detective Leo Sharp, Stormy's new partner Dakota Summers, Lawrence Foresman, Bill Murphy and Major Aramas also of the Miami Detective Bureau. Several other detectives Stormy worked with were also in attendance. In disguise and carefully maintaining his distance from the main body of guests was Pablo, Stormy's friend and confidential informant of many years. Jacks parents were deceased, having died in a plane crash many years earlier, so with no brothers or sisters he had no immediate family present. Shaunie had her closest friends in attendance and immediate members of her family were present. Her father had proudly walked her down the aisle, his watery eyes not going unnoticed by the wedding guests. Her mother, whom everyone said could have been her sister, was her maid of honor.

After the wedding, Jack and Shaunie had taken a cruise for their honeymoon. The Royal Caribbean *Oasis of the Seas* had been their home for seven glorious days. It was one of the largest and most opulent cruise ships of the Royal Caribbean fleet. The cruise took them to several Caribbean islands, all the way out to St. Lucia. The trip had been tremendously therapeutic for Shaunie – the ordeal she had suffered at the hands of the murderer Rolando Fuentes several months earlier was still fresh in her mind. Although she hadn't been seriously hurt, she still experienced occasional nightmares stemming from the incident.

Rolando Fuentes had been Jack's new partner for only a few days when it was discovered that he was responsible for several murders in the Miami area. It had been an act of revenge against those he felt were responsible for the death of his father many years earlier. His father had been a Miami undercover officer and was falsely convicted for a crime after being set up by a notorious crime boss. In Rolando's twisted mind he felt justified in committing the murders, garnering revenge for the death of his father who was murdered in prison. Cornered, Rolando had escaped capture when he had fallen overboard in the dark of night from a freighter on the Miami River, after being shot by Stormy. He had been holding Shaunie captive on the abandoned freighter in an attempt to lure Stormy to him. He placed the blame solely on Stormy for thwarting his vengeance killings. His intention was to kill Stormy on the freighter with Shaunie watching the heinous act. With the help of his friend, Miami Detective Leo Sharp, who was nearly killed in the rescue, the plan went awry and came to an end when Stormy cornered Rolando and shot him. Rolando's body was never recovered from the river, and to everyone's surprise he was found dead weeks later in a small apartment on Bourbon Street in New Orleans during Mardi gras. The cause of death was listed as an apparent heart attack, but Stormy had lingering doubts. His death had closed out the numerous murder cases in the Miami area that were tied to him. For months now Stormy had a deep-seated feeling that his long-time friend and confidential informant, Pablo, knew more about Rolando's death than he was telling. Stormy had no intentions of pursuing the matter since Pablo had almost died after being shot point blank in the head by Rolando. Besides, underestimating Pablo and his connections was something no one should ever do.

* * * * * * * * *

Monday morning at the Hialeah Detective Bureau was no different than usual. There were dozens of reports tak-

Sting of the Scorpion

en over the weekend by the road patrol officers. These were now being assigned to detectives for follow-up. Some of the older detectives were already busy working the phones, trying to close minor cases in order to lighten their load. The usual innocuous horseplay by the junior detectives was in evidence at the rear of the squad room. Most involved ribbing about various football games that played out over the weekend.

Stormy took a seat at his desk after pouring a cup of coffee, which was fresh and exceptionally robust this morning. He leaned back in his chair gingerly holding the hot cup of steaming coffee and looked over at Dakota sitting across the desk from him.

Taking a sip from her cup and peering at him over the rim she said, "You look downright content this morning, Stormy."

"I am, Dakota. I surely am. I had a wonderful weekend, albeit much too short." He blew softly on his coffee, took a sip then set the hot cup down.

Dakota turned up her nose at her cup and placed it back on her desk. "I really hate cold coffee. The cream separates, and it tastes like crap." With a teasing smile on her face she said, "A great weekend huh? Just what have you and Mrs. Storm been up to?"

"Do you want all the up close and personal details?" Stormy asked. He began laughing heartily as Dakota began to blush.

With a grin she said, "No, you can spare me that. I'll just use my imagination."

Ruffling through the reports on his desk Stormy said, "Actually we went for a little drive."

Her eyebrows arching a little she asked, "All weekend?"

"Yep, we took a drive up the west coast, picked up some artwork for the house and just simply enjoyed ourselves."

"I never pictured you being an art aficionado." Picking up her cup she headed to the back of the squad room, intent on refilling it with some fresh *hot* coffee.

Calling after her, Stormy replied, "You would be surprised at what I'm into."

Before she could respond with a clever remark, Captain Paradis walked up to them and asked, "You two have anything pressing this morning?"

"We have a deposition at eleven. Other than that, nothing really pressing," Dakota responded.

Turning and walking back to his office, Captain Paradis said over his shoulder, "When you return from your deposition stop in and see me...and make that after lunch."

Continuing her trip to the coffee pot Dakota murmured, "Wonder what's up?"

The two of them worked quietly at their desks, occasionally breaking the monotony with a phone call to a victim or witness relating to a case. Occasionally a case could be closed with a simple phone call – the victim declining to press charges or for a myriad of other reasons. This was the most boring part of the job for Stormy. He wasn't crazy about being stuck at a desk doing paperwork for hours on end. He felt he was at his best in the field, investigating, making arrests – anything but here.

At about ten o'clock Stormy put his work away and

told Dakota it was time to head for the States Attorney's office for the deposition. She tidied up a few things on her desk, retrieved her weapon from a drawer and after clipping it onto her waist band, followed Stormy out to the parking lot.

Stormy revved up the Charger and backed out of the parking space at the rear of the station. When he finally merged into traffic on LeJuene Road and was heading south for Miami, he began to feel better, freedom from being chained to a desk. He suddenly thought about the weekend and the fantastic night he had spent at Cedar Key with Shaunie. He couldn't suppress the smile that suddenly appeared on his face.

Glancing in his direction and watching the smile suddenly appear, Dakota asked, "What are you grinning about, Stormy?"

"What? Can't a guy smile for no reason?"

Dakota snorted with a laugh, "No reason? Get real, Stormy. You never do anything without a reason."

"It's a private thing, okay?

Still laughing at his discomfort she said teasingly, "But I'm your partner, your buddy, your dear old friend, and lest we forget, trusted confidant. You can tell *me* anything."

Laughing heartily Stormy said, "I'll remind you of those very words the next time *you're* in a weird mood."

For the remainder of the drive they continued to make small talk. They talked about the upcoming hurricane season and how the forecasters were again predicting a more active one than usual. It seemed like only yesterday that hurricane Alice had barreled through Miami, but its fury was mostly spent after crossing the state from the Gulf. They talked football, pending cases and a multitude of other things. In fact, they were soon discovering they had more in common than they had realized.

Stormy was comfortable with Dakota and felt he could say about anything around her and it would never spill from her lips unless he wanted it to. They had been through a lot in the few months since they had become partners, and he already felt he could trust her implicitly, and that was saying a lot for Stormy. Shaunie also liked her, and the feeling was mutual. She and Dakota had even gone on a couple of shopping trips together. Yep, things were good now, and he hoped they would remain that way. It seemed the older Stormy got the more he resisted change.

After about thirty minutes or so driving in moderately heavy traffic, they arrived at the State Attorney's office and parked in the lot reserved for on-duty police personnel. They were about thirty minutes early, so they had to wait for a little while, in fact almost an hour. About eleven fifteen they were called in, one by one. It didn't take long before both of them had given their depositions.

On the way out they killed a few minutes chatting with other officers and detectives they knew. Finally they returned to the car and began the drive back to Hialeah. It was close to noon, so they decided to make a quick stop at a small popular Cuban café on the way and grab some lunch. They were expected in the Captain's office around one o'clock, so they had plenty of time. After sharing a large and delicious hot pressed Cuban sandwich and draining the last drop of their Café Cubanos, they re-

Sting of the Scorpion

sumed the drive back to Hialeah.

When they arrived and entered DB, the Detective Bureau, they were told by Adria that the Captain was back from lunch and waiting for them.

As they walked through the open door to Captain Paradis' office, Stormy asked, "You wanted to see us, Captain?"

Terminating the call he was on, Captain Paradis said, "Yes, take a seat please."

Picking up a manila folder from his desk once he had cradled the phone, he handed it to Dakota. She reached for it across the desk, puzzlement clearly showing in her eyes. Before she could open it, Captain Paradis said, "No need to open it now. I'll tell you what's in it."

Placing the folder on her lap, she looked at the Captain, no visible expression on her face now, but a little concern starting to gnaw at her gut. Sensing her apprehension the Captain smiled and told her, "No need to worry. It's just your promotion to Senior Detective."

Turning and giving her arm a squeeze, Stormy said, "Congratulations, Dakota. You deserve it."

"Now you need to head out to City Hall. The Personnel Department needs you to sign some papers for the promotion to update your personnel file," Captain Paradis said.

Stormy and Dakota rose from their seats but before they could leave the Captain said, "Stormy, I need you here. You can get with Dakota later."

Stormy gave Dakota a smile and returned to his seat as she left the room, a huge smile plastered on her face. He was truly happy for her and really thought she deserved it. He had turned down promotions himself for sergeant, twice, both times over the protestations of his Captain. He just didn't want to give up being an investigator and being sergeant would effectively do just that. He had never regretted those decisions and knew that if he ever changed his mind the Captain would try to make it happen. Now he turned his attention back to Captain Paradis, wondering what he had planned for him.

"Stormy, Detective McLean is out on leave for a few days. He has some personal problems that he needs to take care of, something to do with an inheritance he said. He was working on a special case for the Wells Fargo Bank by the mall and was supposed to be there to meet with their security team today. I know you don't work white collar crimes, but I'll need you to sit in on the meeting in his stead, take notes and when McLean returns, go over with him the notes you took."

Stormy replied with a knowing grin, "Well, for one thing, Captain, I never knew that an inheritance was a problem, more like a blessing I would think. But I'll attend the meeting and take notes for him."

"Don't be a wiseass, Stormy. I don't know what his problem is, but it's really none of our business," Captain Paradis said, without a hint of rancor. He and Stormy had a good relationship and had even been out socially on occasion. He was used to Stormy's sense of humor, although sometimes he didn't really get it.

"What time is this meeting?" Stormy asked.

With a mischievous grin the Captain said, "Three o'clock sharp and the Chief Operating Officer for the security division of Wells Fargo out of Iowa will be there to

Sting of the Scorpion

chair the meeting. His name is Alexander Krane and you will be expected. I took the liberty of notifying their office that McLean is out on emergency leave. Instead of cancelling the meeting they asked if I could send someone to take notes for McLean, and I volunteered you. You can thank me later."

"Exactly what type of investigation was McLean conducting?" Stormy asked.

"It involves identity theft, actually a well organized ring in Hialeah proper," the Captain began. "Normally the Security Division of Wells Fargo would investigate this, but McLean received a tip from his informant naming the head of the ring and his location. He began digging into the background of his suspect and decided what he had unearthed was enough to make contact with Mr. Krane and fill him in."

"Let me guess, he was asked by Krane to work the case with them. It would only make sense since McLean has the informant and the name of the ringleader."

"That's correct, Stormy, and McLean was responsible up to now with uncovering the names of several other operatives for the ringleader in South Florida. He was to meet with Mr. Krane today and make arrangements for obtaining arrest warrents for those individuals. I don't expect *you* to try and obtain the warrants, just take down the information McLean will need when he returns. Do you have any further questions?" Captain Paradis asked.

"Nope, I think I have all the info I need for now."

Stormy glanced at his watch and saw that he had about an hour before the meeting. He decided to make a few more calls on some cases before leaving. Once he had

35

completed several of the more pressing calls, he glanced at his watch and saw it was time to go. Grabbing his coat and slipping it on, he headed for his car. Pulling out into traffic he headed south to Forty Ninth Street and then west to the Westland Mall area. The Wells Fargo Bank, a two-story office complex, was directly across the street from the mall, and he arrived at his destination with fifteen minutes to spare.

He parked in the back of the bank lot near the rear door which the bank employees used, although he walked around to the front entrance. When he entered, and mostly out of habit and his police instinct, he mentally observed about a dozen customers, some in line at the tellers' windows, a few sitting at desks with bank officers and others waiting their turn.

He sauntered past the teller cages and over to the directory which was affixed to the wall next to the sole elevator. He scanned the listed office numbers until he found the one for the security office. As he reached to push the elevator button, the door slid open with a whisper and several women stepped out, some giving him a little more than friendly glance. He smiled back and entered the elevator, punching the button for the second floor.

Exiting the elevator on the second floor, he walked down the newly carpeted hallway and quickly found the door marked *Director of Security* on his left. He knocked softly and heard a female voice call out for him to enter. He walked in, and the administrative assistant sitting at the desk inside the room asked his name and who he was there to see. He told her, showed his identification and then took a seat at her request.

Sting of the Scorpion

He only had to wait approximately five minutes before the assistant told him to enter the room on his right. Stormy opened the door and entered a modest conference room of sorts. There were four people sitting at the rectangular table with piles of folders and paperwork spread out in front of them.

The man at the head of the table stood and extended his hand, flashing a warm smile. "You must be Jack Storm. Captain Paradis told us to expect you. I'm Alex Krane out of the home office, but just call me Alex, no formalities here today. Please, take a seat Detective Storm."

Stormy observed that Alex was maybe an inch over six feet in height, average weight and had an engaging smile. His dark hair was thick and neatly combed, but with a slight overhang on the forehead. He was dressed impeccably, and there was no doubt his suit, obviously not off the rack, cost much more than any he owned.

"Please, call me Stormy, most everyone does."

Once he had taken his seat he was introduced to the other three men at the table. They were the security personnel for the bank and all were very young, younger than him. So much for the older and more experienced security officers he was expecting.

As if Alex could read his mind he said, "These guys have had some serious and extensive training and are among the best we have at Wells Fargo, Detective Storm."

"I'm sure they are, and it's a pleasure to meet all of you." Stormy replied, smiling at Alex, slightly surprised at his astute perception.

37

"We'll get right down to business, unless you need to be brought up to speed, Stormy," Alex said.

"No, Captain Paradis filled me in, so I'll just take notes to pass on to Detective McLean."

For the next hour they went over the information McLean had given Alex and in the end decided that they would give McLean the green light to secure the arrest warrants. Based on the information McLean had gathered, it was evident that there was more than enough probable cause.

They ended the meeting and Alex walked with Stormy out of the room and to the elevator. They made small talk on the way, and Stormy shook hands once again before taking the elevator to the lobby. He had taken a liking to Alex, admiring his reasoning and willingness to cooperate with local law enforcement. *He was no slouch when it came to reading people either*, Stormy thought to himself.

Stormy left the elevator and as he began walking across the expansive lobby, he noticed there were still about the same number of people in the bank, although some were not the same ones from before. He was almost halfway to the front door when he heard his name called out. Looking back he saw an old neighbor of his standing in line at a teller's window. He remembered the first name but the last escaped him.

"Hey, Stan, how have you been?"

"Doing great, Jack. Loving the new house and the neighborhood is just perfect for raising my kid," Stan replied.

He remembered now: Stan Kowalski had been his next door neighbor when he had first moved into the house in Miami Lakes. About a year later he had decided to buy a new house in Palm Springs North. He wanted to raise his children in a more family-oriented neighborhood, one where his kids could go out and play without much traffic and where neighbors kept an eye out for each other's children. That had been about two years ago if he figured correctly.

"Well, tell the wife hello for me, Stan. It was good to see you again. I have to run. My partner is waiting for me at the station," Stormy said as he turned and headed for the door.

Before he could take another step two masked men burst through the front entrance brandishing automatic weapons, AK 47's to be exact. One raised his and fired a short burst into the ceiling, yelling for everyone to hit the floor. As plaster rained down from the ceiling, the security guard attempted to draw his weapon but was gunned down immediately by one of the robbers before he could clear his weapon from its holster. Both of the men wore flesh-colored masks covering their faces.

Several women began crying and some screaming. The man who had fired into the ceiling swiftly turned and aimed his weapon at them, shouting, "Stop that screaming or I'll make sure you won't ever be able to again. Now shut up and get down on the floor…DO IT NOW!"

Stormy slowly began to push his jacket back in order to pull his weapon but the armed men were standing behind several of the customers, forcing them to the floor. He quickly made the decision not to intervene just yet – too many innocent people were in his line of fire. Slowly he lay down on the floor, his head turned in the general direction of the masked men so he could watch and hopefully get the chance to disarm them. He glanced over at Stan who was on the floor staring at him, expecting him to do something. Stormy looked hard at him and put his finger to his lips, silently urging him to keep quiet about him being a cop. Stan must have gotten the message as he slowly nodded his head.

On the second floor the shots were heard by all, even though they were muffled. Alex Krane, recognizing the sound for what it was, quickly pushed the alarm that went directly to the Hialeah Police Department. He also called the police department via landline and advised them of what was happening and about hearing the gunshots. He started herding the upstairs employees into the conference room and designated several of them to barricade the door with the conference table and chairs. Once he saw them springing to action, he left and closed the door behind him. He sprinted to the stairwell and slowly descended the steps to the ground floor. He was unarmed but he needed to determine if there were any casualties. Also he wanted to see how many perpetrators there were so he could call the police department back and advise them. If there were any visible casualties he would need to make a call for EMS. He was well aware of the need for stealth, especially since he was unarmed. He was not a fool – he knew he wouldn't be any help if he were shot. His main concern was for the safety of the customers and employees, and he intended do what he could.

As one of the robbers forced the tellers behind the counter to stuff the money into a duffle bag, the other kept his eyes on the people lying prone on the floor, watching

Sting of the Scorpion

for anyone who wanted to try to be a hero. Stormy kept his eyes on the robber guarding the people on the floor, not able to see the one behind the teller cages. His brain was racing, trying to figure out how he could turn the tables on the two men, without endangering any innocent people. For now he knew he had to restrain himself from taking any action. There was simply nothing he could do at the moment, and it frustrated him.

Suddenly sirens could be heard in the distance. They were closing fast. The two men turned and looked out the large plate glass window, and at a nod from one, the other cautiously inched his way to the window in order to get a better look. As he reached the window he saw several marked police units arriving, taking up positions in front of the bank, some driving on around the building. The officers exited their cars and used the open doors as barricades for themselves. If they had known about the AK 47's they wouldn't have been so eager to use the car doors as shields. Those rounds would penetrate the car's thin metal like butter. All of the officers now had their weapons trained on the front entrance. The man looking out the window turned and scurried quickly back to his accomplice, relaying in detail what he had observed.

"You watch everyone on the floor. Get all of those tellers out here and down on the floor with the rest," the man who appeared to be in charge said. Leaning down he grabbed a middle-aged woman by the hair and yanked her up on her feet. She was visibly terrified but went without much resistance as the man held her in front of him, moving towards the front door of the bank. They disappeared around a wall that separated the door's alcove from the rest of the bank. He yelled back to his accomplice, "Just keep everybody covered. Anyone moves, shoot 'em."

It now appeared to Stormy there was probably going to be a standoff of sorts. He had to figure out something, and he had to do it fast. These men wouldn't hesitate for a minute to shoot any of the hostages, which they had already exhibited by shooting down the guard. The man hadn't stirred once since being cut down, still lying in a pool of blood, which had slowly stopped spreading out across the tile floor.

As Alex Krane peered through the small window on the stairwell door, he could see customers lying on the floor, their hands on their heads. He could see one masked subject standing near the teller cages and another armed subject walking a woman towards the front door. From his angle he failed to see the security guard lying in a pool of blood on the floor. He turned and raced back up the stairs to call in what he had observed.

Chapter 5

Eduardo San Peron

EDUARDO, KNOWN AS "CRAZY EDDIE" to his friends, was the only child of Antonio and Isabella San Peron, a local businessman and purported crime boss. He grew up a privileged child, never wanting for anything because of his family's wealth. His parents adored him unconditionally but when he was fifteen his life changed drastically. His mother passed away from breast cancer and in his anger at God for taking her, he gradually withdrew from his friends, even his father. His father was convinced that it was grief and that he would eventually get over it. He never did. Instead he turned to petty crimes resulting in several arrests, which his affluent father always managed to take care of using his connections.

Eduardo began hanging out with new friends, mostly children of parents who came to Florida during the Mariel boatlift. These were the kids that managed to coax him deeper into a life of crime. After all, his father was infamous for his criminal activities, a fact he discovered on his eighteenth birthday, so why not live up to the family tradition.

Although he had embarked on a reckless path of crime, his father continued relentlessly in his efforts to change him. Eduardo often promised his father he would change, but he never made an honest attempt. He continued to wallow in self-pity over his mother's death, blaming everyone and everything except the deadly disease which was the real culprit. Years earlier he had blamed God and totally pushed religion out of his life. He was a walking disaster and destined for a life in prison, or possibly even death.

His best friend, Alberto "The Snake" Nunez, was twenty-seven, a little over six years older than him. Eduardo and Alberto both seemed to have an affinity for nicknames, thinking that would elevate them in status around the neighborhood.

They had become inseparable and looked down with disdain on most of their friends. They felt they were smarter and above the petty criminals who tried to hang out with them. Most of the crimes they committed now were serious felonies. They had long ago graduated to burglaries and a few mom and pop robberies. They were beginning to get not only greedy, but also dangerously reckless. The lack of planning for the crimes they carried out began leaving telltale trails of evidence, and it wouldn't be long before the authorities connected them to the burglaries and other criminal actions. They thought they were unstoppable, immune to capture, and so they were becoming dangerously brazen.

It was a hot humid night in Hialeah, and the usual sea

Sting of the Scorpion

breeze was noticeably absent. The bloodsucking mosquitoes were in abundance, and the heat overly sweltering. The mosquito spray trucks were prevalent throughout the city, their thick fogs of repellent stinking up the still night air, but they didn't seem to be making much progress. The persistent buzzing around his ears was a clue that the mosquitoes were winning the battle.

Eduardo and Alberto had driven to West Twenty Ninth Street to the Crazy Parrot, a bar they frequented often in one of the many strip malls lining the street. No one ever paid much attention to them, and they would occupy a table for hours, nursing their *Cerveza* and planning their next caper, all without interruption.

On this muggy night they were still on their first beer, bored and pensive. They glanced up as a tall, dark, and slender man entered the building. He didn't stop at the bar. Instead he continued on until he reached the table where Eduardo and Alberto were seated. Eduardo slowly leaned back in his seat, looking up at the stranger intruding his space, his cold eyes boring piercingly into the others eyes. No one said a word for several seconds. Finally the stranger asked, "*Puedo tomar asiento?*"

"First of all, *amigo*, we speak English at this table. So if you don't, then take a hike, vamoose."

Not sounding apologetic at all, the stranger said, "Of course I speak English, sorry for the lapse."

"Second of all, since you can understand me, take note that this is a private party," Eduardo spat out.

The stranger spoke softly, something about his demeanor unsettling to Eduardo, "I think you may want to hear what I have to say."

Eduardo slowly turned and looked at Alberto, who was quietly taking in the exchange between the two. Alberto looked over at the stranger and asked, "I suppose you do have a name?"

"My name is of no importance to you. If you're not interested in what I have to sell, I'll go elsewhere."

Now Eduardo's curiosity was piqued. He glanced once again at a bemused Alberto, and sensing no objection, he gestured for the stranger to take a seat. Once he settled in, the stranger said to Alberto, "You can call me Mister J., if you feel the need to have a name."

"Oh, so now we're playing the secret agent game?" Eduardo snorted.

Mister J. responded softly, his voice almost a whisper, "No games here, *amigo*, strictly business."

"I think I need to teach you some manners, *amigo*," Eduardo said with bravado and beginning to stand.

"Sit down right now. I won't hesitate to pull the trigger."

"What trigger, Mister J. What trigger?" Eduardo asked sarcastically, pausing in his attempt to stand.

Mister J.'s dark eyes never left Eduardo's face as he said, "The one on the gun aimed at your *cojones* beneath the table."

Eduardo stared intently at Mister J., noticing the stranger's left hand out of sight under the table. With uncertainty he slowly lowered himself back in his seat, never taking his eyes off of the man. *I'll deal with this smug punk later. He has no idea who he's messing with,* he thought to himself.

"You've made a very smart move, Eduardo. I didn't

really want to make a mess in here nor do I wish to harm you," Mister J. said, keeping his hand under the table.

Raising his eyebrows in bewilderment, Eduardo said, "How do you know my name? I've never met you before. I've never even *seen* you before."

"I have my sources. A few weeks ago you were asking around about where you could buy some AK 47's. With a little research I became aware of your various exploits, your burglaries and other petty endeavors. Why you need weapons that powerful is beyond me, but I'm in the gun business and I could care less what you intend to do with them. They're clean, not registered, and brand new. Are you still interested?"

Eduardo's mind began racing as he replied, "I may be…depends on how much you're asking."

About a month earlier he and Alberto thought it would elevate their status even more if they were able to pull off a robbery using weapons. Alberto expressed how he had always wanted an AK 47. He and Eduardo had made inquiries around town, but no one could or would provide the weapons. Either none of the people they asked trusted them or they weren't connected enough to find the right people, the real professionals. Soon they quit asking and moved on to other things. Now, completely out of the blue, the weapons were being offered up to them.

"I want four thousand apiece for them. I'm even willing to throw in a few boxes of ammo to close the deal. This is a onetime offer, so you need to decide now. I don't trust you two as far as I can throw you, and I *don't* think you are as proficient in the crime business as you think you are. I *do* think that the direction you are moving in now will be your downfall, sooner or later. You're too careless, too inexperienced and poorly organized. But, that being said, I'm willing to make the sale tonight, that is if you're still interested."

Eduardo was having trouble controlling his anger at the scathing words directed at him and Alberto. No one talked about him and his best friend in that manner and got away with it. But two factors kept him from killing the man outright. One, he wanted the weapons and two, having a gun aimed at his privates was a deterrent, to say the least. He was armed, but he wouldn't be able to pull his weapon before Mister J. fired a shot. He would swallow his macho pride for the time being, but if he ever crossed paths with this man again, the outcome was going to be a lot different, that he guaranteed.

"Well, do we have a deal or not? I have other things to attend to," Mister J. said, almost with indifference.

They were being humiliated and treated like amateurs and Eduardo was close to the point that he didn't care about the weapons. Alberto knew the signs of his friend exploding and reaching over, laid his hand on Eduardo's arm in an attempt to keep him from doing something rash. Eduardo finally calmed down and slowly nodded his head, accepting the deal. His face was still flushed, and his anger had not totally abated.

"Where can we see the guns?" He asked through gritted teeth.

"Meet me tomorrow morning ten o'clock sharp at Amelia Earhart Park. Take the dirt road through the strand of pine trees until you reach the lake. I'll be there waiting for you, but you won't see me until I'm ready. Make sure you come alone, just the two of you and be unarmed. If I see anyone that even looks as if they are with you, I'm gone, and there will be no second chances. Stand by the water's edge, lift your shirts and turn around slowly. Then walk back to the edge of the trees. I'll be waiting… and oh, yeah, don't forget to bring the money, in a plain paper bag."

"We'll be there, and don't even think of trying to rip us off," Alberto said.

"Rip you off? Don't be ridiculous, I'm strictly a businessman. Once we're finished I don't expect to see either of you again, ever," he replied, a disgusted grin appearing on his face.

Oh, I think we'll be seeing you again, my friend. You can count on it, Eduardo thought to himself. He definitely had a score to settle with this hotshot, and he planned to have him followed once the buy was done. Yes, he was going to teach this guy a lesson about treating people like him with respect.

Mister J. rose from his seat, slipping his left hand into his pocket as he stood, in such a manner they couldn't see if he had a gun or not. They watched as he left the bar, his hand still in his pocket, never once looking back.

"Do we have that much money available?" Alberto asked, pushing Mister J. from his mind for now.

"Yes, but it'll cut us short. But I have plans to replace it a hundred times over, very soon."

"Were you going to fill me in on those plans anytime soon?"

"Now is as good a time as any I suppose," Eduardo replied with a smile.

For the next several minutes he went into detail about his plans for robbing the Wells Fargo Bank by the mall. He went into great detail as to how they were going to carry it out. He explained why he hadn't said anything about the bank before now. He had been trying to secure some weapons suitable for intimidating the bank employees. Now that the weapons were within their grasp the plan could commence.

"I don't know, Eduardo. You think this is a good idea? We've never tried to pull off anything this big before."

"Don't go all chicken on me, Al. I've done my homework, and it'll go down like clockwork, and besides, we'll have a ton of money." Eduardo laughed and patted Alberto on his shoulder.

"What about your father? Is he going to go ballistic on you?"

"My father has his own life, and it's not that much different than ours. Besides, he won't know it's us, we'll be wearing masks and I don't intend to tell him," Eduardo responded with his mind already set.

* * * * * * * * *

The following morning at nine-thirty, Eduardo and Alberto drove to the Amelia Earhart Park on Sixty Fifth Street. It only took them fifteen minutes. The car carrying two of their friends was parked just inside near a picnic table. They were assuming that Mister J. was already inside the park, so they stopped next to the picnic table.

"Yo, Hector. You guys ready to follow this dude?"

Sting of the Scorpion

Eduardo said to the two in the car.

"We'll be all set once we move the car outside of the park. We'll wait for your call telling us what he's driving." Hector replied.

"Don't screw up, Hector. I really want to know where this guy lives."

"Don't worry, Crazy Eddie. We've got this."

Eduardo drove the car further into the park and headed down the dirt road through the strand of pines. Before long they were at the lake and following directions, they exited the car and walked to the water's edge. When they were close to the water they turned and lifted their shirts, showing they had no weapons on them. Try as hard as he could, Eduardo couldn't see anyone in the tree line, although he had no doubts that Mister J. was there somewhere.

Eduardo and Alberto left the lakes grassy shoreline and walked to the edge of the woods, looking for Mister J. When they reached the tree line and still hadn't seen him, they continued walking further into the lightly wooded area. The trees were sparse and other than four-wheeler tracks, they didn't see a car or Mister J.

"I do believe we've been stood up, Alberto," Eduardo said, pausing and looking around.

"I don't trust that guy. Let's get the hell out of here, Eddie."

"I don't trust him either, but I really wanted those guns. We'll head back to the car and if he still doesn't show, then we'll leave. But make no mistake about it, I'm going to be really pissed off."

They began walking back to the car and just before

they stepped out into the opening, Mister J. stepped from around a large tree trunk. Alberto gave a small gasp, startled when Mister J. popped up right in front of them. Eduardo stopped short and faced him, noticing he had his hand in his pocket again.

"You know, pal, you're starting to creep me out with that hand always in your pocket," Eduardo said belligerently.

"Get used to it. It's the way I operate and until I get to know someone, it'll always be that way. Besides, I told you, I don't plan to have any further dealings with you after this. Did you bring the money?"

"It's in the car. Where are the guns?" Eduardo asked.

"Nearby, let's go get the money first, and then I'll take you to the guns."

"Let's not, I'm tired of playing your secret agent games. Either you want to do business or not, just make up your mind," Eduardo said with his patience at an end. "I did everything you asked, and now I'm losing my desire to do any business with you. Produce the guns right now, or we're heading back to the car and leaving."

"If you understood how many times clients have tried to rip me off you would understand my precautions. Very well, the guns are in a box buried in the sand behind the tree where I was standing. One of you can dig up the box and check them out while the other goes to your car and retrieves the money. Does that work for you, Eduardo?"

"That works. I'll dig, and Alberto can go retrieve the money."

As Eduardo walked around the tree he espied a small shovel, actually a collapsible military spade that had been hastily covered with pine needles but with part of the blade exposed. He looked at the base of the tree and saw that the sand was disturbed, having been smoothed over by hand. He bent down and picked up the shovel and began scooping away the soft sand, slowly at first then with increasing intensity.

When he was down about two feet in depth he struck the box, the shovel jarring his hands as it struck the wooden chest. It sure seemed like a lot of precautions were being taken but then he realized that the box may have been placed there well before hand, with the presumption he was going to buy the weapons. Eduardo still hadn't seen a vehicle that Mister J. would be driving, which made him wonder. *Had he placed the box here earlier and walked in today, leaving his car elsewhere?* That would sure throw a kink in his plans for Hector if he couldn't describe the car they were to follow. As he hauled the box from the shallow sandy pit, Mister J. walked up with Alberto, the bag containing the money in Alberto's hand.

The box had been lightly nailed shut so Eduardo used the edge of the shovel blade and pried open the lid. The AK 47's were wrapped in a heavily waxed paper and packed in straw and looked new. He unwrapped one of the weapons and glanced around to see if any bystanders were present. He saw none and commenced to pull one of the weapons out of the wrappings.

He had never held an AK 47 but he pretended to know what he was doing as he slowly looked the weapon over carefully. He held the weapon out and sighted down the barrel, playing with the trigger briefly. Finally he placed the gun back into the box, tapped the lid in place and turned to Mister J.

"Give him the money, Alberto," he said without taking his eyes off of the man.

Alberto passed over the bag, and Mister J. shoved it down his waistband. He gave a mock salute to Eduardo and turned to walk away.

"You're kidding me, *amigo*. All of this cloak and dagger stuff and now you're not even going to count the money?" Eduardo asked.

"I wish I could just say I trust you, but that would be a lie. I know how to find you, so I'm sure it's all there, or else it better be for your sake," Mister J. said with a grim look on his face.

"It's all there, *amigo*, and I would love for you to find me sometime," Eduardo replied with a sarcastic smile of his own.

"As I said…our business is done, and so I bid you a good day gentlemen."

"We would be happy to give you a ride to your car…that is if you can trust us." Alberto laughed.

Mister J. didn't bother to respond. He just pulled a pack of cigarettes from his pocket, tapped one out and lit it with a zippo lighter. He smiled at the two, exhaled a puff of smoke and then turned and walked into the woods, soon lost from sight, disappearing as easily as he had emerged earlier.

* * * * * * * * * *

"Are you going to follow him?" Alberto asked.

"Nah, I'm done playing with him. Maybe someday we'll meet again, and then I'll have my chance."

They both grabbed an end of the box, although it wasn't that heavy, and carried it to the car, putting it inside the trunk and covering it with a blanket. As they slowly drove out of the park they kept trying to spot Mister J., but he had totally disappeared as if he had never been there. When they were on the road and headed home, Mister J. had already begun to fade from their minds. Now they were going to familiarize themselves with the guns by testing them in the Glades. Soon they would carry out the plans for the bank robbery.

"What about Hector? Are you going to tell him to forget about the tail?" Alberto asked.

Quickly dialing Hector's number he told him to forget about the tail and that he would get with him later to settle up. *Yeah, like that was going to happen*, Eduardo thought.

Chapter 6

Deadly standoff

As soon as Captain Paradis heard of the standoff at the bank he immediately called Captain Chandler in patrol.

"Captain Chandler, have you dispatched SWAT to the scene yet?"

"Yes, they are en route as we speak. Why do you ask John?"

"Please make contact with the SWAT commander at once. One of my men, Detective Storm, is more than likely still in the bank. Dispatch received only one phone call from the bank, from an Alex Krane. He's the Director of security for Wells Fargo and is in town for a special meeting. Detective Storm was in the meeting with him. He wasn't able to give any information about Storm or his whereabouts, only that he had left the meeting several minutes before the gunfire erupted. We haven't heard from Storm so we have to assume he's still in the bank and unable to contact us. I don't want your guys ending

Sting of the Scorpion

up shooting him by mistake," Captain Paradis said with some concern.

"If Detective Storm makes contact with you let me know as soon as possible. Uniform patrol has the bank covered now and the suspects are still in the bank. I think you may want to respond to the scene, so get with me once you arrive," Chandler said.

"I'm heading that way as we speak. Do you need any of my guys to respond also?"

Captain Chandler said, "No, not just yet, I'll know more once I get there and confer with the SWAT commander."

For a moment, Captain Paradis considered not sending any of his guys to the scene, but he changed his mind and made a decision: he would have two of his detectives proceed towards the bank but hold up about a block away. They were to await his order to move in and only when he gave the order. He respected Captain Chandler's decision to not use his detectives at this time, but, on the other hand, he had a premonition they might be needed.

Captain Paradis called out to the two detectives, "Duncan, Whitaker, come with me."

On the way out the door he explained the situation and what he expected of them. He made sure they understood that they were to stay at least a block from the scene until he called for them. They assured him they understood and then sprinted to their car. Once the Captain was in his car and rolling, he radioed dispatch and advised he was enroute to the bank and that Detectives Duncan and Whitaker would be standing by a block from the scene.

When Paradis arrived at the bank he observed the

placement of the marked units, noticing that there were cars in front and at the rear of the bank. The SWAT team was also just pulling into the parking lot, coming to a stop behind one of the units. He parked his unmarked car behind another unit and exited, searching for Captain Chandler.

"Captain Paradis, I'm over here," Chandler called out.

Looking in the direction of the voice he spotted Chandler standing beside the SWAT van, out of any line of fire from the subjects inside the bank, his team members forming a semi-circle in front of him. He bent over slightly at the waist and swiftly made his way to the van.

"Any contact with the suspects yet?" he asked.

"No, but they've moved several of the hostages to the windows and they now have their hands pressed to the glass. It makes it kind of hard to see anything inside," One of the SWAT members replied.

"Do we have a hostage negotiator on site yet?" Paradis asked.

"He's just now pulling up. I'll have him meet with us here. The van will provide ample cover while we brief him," Chandler replied.

The hostage negotiator, Sergeant Vance Mitchell, carefully made his way to the SWAT van and joined the group assembled there. Captain Chandler apprised him of the situation and told him about the hostages that were placed at the windows. The negotiator glanced around the front of the van to survey the scene. He saw the hostages at the window, but he couldn't see any of the suspects.

"Do we know how many perpetrators there are inside?" he asked.

Sting of the Scorpion

"We have no idea at this time. A security officer called the station, and said he could see two perps but there could be more."

"Do you have the phone hook up for the bank ready inside the van?"

"Yes, we have it set up to make the call whenever you're ready, Vance," Chandler replied.

Entering the van through the side door Vance took a seat by the phone, as he turned on the recorder. He donned the headphones and dialed the number for the bank then sat patiently as it rang, and rang. No one answered, but he let it keep ringing for another minute or so before breaking the connection.

"Evidently they're not going to pick up the phone, so I'll have to use the bullhorn," he said. "I assume you have a flak jacket for me to use?"

One of the team members procured a vest from the storage bench and handed it to him. Vance carefully put on the jacket, making sure the crotch flap was in place and then asked for a helmet. When he was sure he was as protected as he could be, he asked for the bullhorn. Stepping out of the van he could see the SWAT sniper with his eye pressed to the scope, prone on the pavement under the edge of the van, aiming at the bank door. Even with the flak jacket on, he attempted to protect himself further by standing behind the fender of the van, resting the bullhorn on the hood as he prepared to address the armed men inside the bank.

"Attention inside the bank, this is Sergeant Mitchell of the Hialeah Police Department. We have the bank surrounded so you have nowhere to go. Let's end this peacefully and without harming anyone. Open the door and throw your weapons out. If you come out with your hands behind your head, I promise you will not be harmed."

Suddenly the door to the bank opened partially. A woman standing in front of a masked man was framed in the doorway, obviously distressed, shaking and crying. As if he knew the sniper was out there the masked man made sure he was completely concealed behind the woman, the barrel of his weapon resting on her shoulder.

"You, Mister Mitchell, can save your breath until all of these police cars are gone. I have over a dozen hostages inside and if my demands aren't met I'll start killing them, one for every hour you are still here," the man yelled out.

Sergeant Mitchell responded through the bullhorn, "You know I can't do that and you certainly wouldn't want to compound the problem by killing innocent people. Let's begin by sending out the hostages, and we'll work it out from there."

"Are you not hearing me? Do I look stupid to you?"

"I hear you, but it will take time. In good faith while we work it out send out at least one hostage."

"Not gonna happen, pal. This ain't a TV show. You heard my demands, and believe me, I'll do exactly what I said."

Without turning his head Mitchell moved his mouth from the bullhorn and asked the sniper, "Do you have a clear shot?"

"No, sir, he's too tight behind the woman and besides, do we know if there are other gunmen inside? It might set them off."

"Yeah, you're right. We need to determine exactly how many suspects are inside."

Raising the bullhorn to his mouth again, Mitchell spoke to the gunman. "Why don't you at least let some of the hostages go? They haven't done anything to you. It would be a sign of good faith, and we can begin to negotiate."

"You're not listening to me. I'll say it one more time – one body per hour and the clock just started *ticking*!"

Chapter 7

Stormy takes action

THE CHILLING WORDS Stormy had just heard yelled out to the police negotiator convinced him he didn't have an abundance of time before he needed to make a move. The woman the gunman held tightly at the door was becoming hysterical, her heavy sobbing spilling inside the lobby now for all to hear. At that very moment the second gunman walked in front of Stormy's outstretched body and paused, listening to his partner yelling at the police presence outside of the bank. Stormy saw his chance, one that he would have to take now because there might not be another opportunity anytime soon.

The second gunman took a step towards the front entrance and without hesitation Stormy made his move. Quickly reaching out with both hands he grabbed the ankles of the gunman in midstride, causing him to begin falling to the floor. The gunman held on tightly to his weapon as he fell, grunting in pain as he landed on the weapon, the air spewing from his lungs in one big gush.

Sting of the Scorpion

Stormy was up in a split second and on top of the gunman before he could regain his breath. He pulled his weapon out and slicing through the air, struck the man in the temple, rendering him unconscious almost instantly. Wasting no time he cuffed the unconscious man's hands behind his back, picked up the AK 47 and began cautiously moving towards the front door, motioning for the customers to stay down on the floor and remain quiet.

As he approached the still body of the bank guard lying in a pool of blood, he stopped and checked for a pulse. After confirming the guard was dead, he gently placed the AK 47 on the floor next to the wall. He would need both of his hands free to control his own weapon in order to subdue the gunman. Attempting to carry the AK 47 *and* his weapon would be too much of an encumbrance. When he reached the alcove he knelt down and quickly darted his head around the corner, gauging how close he was to the man holding the woman. He saw that the gunman was only several feet away and had his back to him, still holding the woman close, his body concealed from the police presence outside by hers.

Stormy stealthily made an attempt to sneak up behind the man, his weapon drawn, but his actions must have been sensed. The robber began to turn his head in Stormy's direction, almost as if in slow motion. Stormy wasted no time; he rushed the gunman as the man began to bring around the AK 47, allowing Stormy no option but to fire his weapon. The first round caught the man in the side of his neck, and grunting in pain and surprise he released his grip on the woman. Still, he continued swinging his weapon around in the direction of Stormy. The second round caught the man in the forehead, about two inches above the bridge of his nose, almost dead center. Stormy stood with a two handed grip on his weapon, the smell of cordite permeating the air.

The AK 47 clattered noisily to the floor as the man's muscles suddenly relaxed, the weapon slipping from his now lifeless hands. Almost as if he were about to pray, he dropped to his knees and sat posed there for a second or two, his open eyes blank, bewilderment written on his face. His brain finally accepted the fact that he was indeed dead.

Without further resistance he slowly succumbed to gravity and toppled over onto his face, the thud from the hard tile floor echoing in the alcove. A small rivulet of blood slowly began flowing from his head, painting the white tile floor in an abstract depiction, separating into more rivulets and framing his head in a halo of red.

During the altercation the distraught woman had run out the door once the gunman had released his grip on her. With the woman safe and the threat from the gunmen neutralized, Stormy quickly walked back into the bank lobby, the rising murmur of scared voices greeting him. He urged everyone to calm down and stay on the floor with their hands outstretched because the SWAT team would be entering the building soon. He also yelled for the hostages with their hands on the front window to get down on the floor with everyone else. Quickly he explained that the police had no way of knowing if any of the gunmen were still in control so anyone standing would be considered a threat to them.

Stormy worked his way into the middle of the customers lying on the floor and then dropped to his knees. He placed his weapon on the floor beyond his reach. Taking his badge from his belt, he clutched it in his hand and faced the doorway, his arms held high over his head. He wasn't sure if any of the SWAT team members would recognize him, so he took all of the necessary precautions. He wasn't too worried about them throwing flash bangs into the bank – there were just too many civilians, and they wouldn't go to that extreme except as a last resort. A couple of the men lying on the floor attempted to stand with a little false bravado but quickly lay back down when Stormy yelled at them.

They didn't have to wait very long. Within a few minutes of his shooting the gunman at the front door the first of the SWAT team entered the building, holding a Plexiglas shield and carefully poking his head around the alcove wall. Then he slid along the wall allowing more SWAT members to enter the lobby. When they saw Stormy on his knees, holding out the badge, two of them carefully sidled over to him. The second SWAT team member quickly recognized Stormy and said so to the others. Stormy stood and pointed out the first gunman he had taken down and handcuffed, while at the same time retrieving his gun from the floor. It appeared the first gunman was still unconscious as he wasn't moving at all. *I must have struck him too hard*, Stormy thought to himself.

Kneeling and finding the man was still breathing, Stormy emitted a sigh of relief. The gunman was simply down for the count, basking away in la la land. He advised one of the SWAT team members to call for EMS

Earl Underwood

and have them check the gunman out before attempting to move him.

"Stormy, are you okay?" Captain Paradis called out as he walked into the crowded lobby, concern evident in his voice.

"I'm fine, Captain. How is the lady who was held at the front door?"

"EMS is checking her out as we speak, but she seemed to be okay. Naturally she's freaked out from her ordeal, but otherwise she should be fine."

The SWAT team helped all of the civilian hostages assemble at one end of the bank lobby. As soon as it could be arranged they would all be ushered into the nearest conference room, one by one, to be interviewed before they were released. The bodies of the bank guard and the gunman whom Stormy had shot were covered while awaiting CSI and the homicide investigators. Measurements, prints and videotaping would have to be carried out before the bodies could be removed.

Stormy felt the presence of someone at his back and turning saw Stan, his former neighbor, standing behind him.

"Detective Storm, I just wanted to say how much I admire the way you handled this robbery. You definitely saved a lot of lives here today with your actions."

"I want to thank you also, Stan, for understanding why I needed you to stay silent about me being a cop. By doing so you probably saved a few lives yourself, including mine."

"I appreciate that Detective Storm, but you're the real hero here today, and I can't wait to tell my wife all about

Sting of the Scorpion

it."

"I was in the right place at the right time if you think about it. Just doing my job, Stan, and please, tell your lovely wife hello for me," Stormy said, turning back to the Captain, effectively dismissing Stan.

"Stormy, I'll need your weapon and badge. You know the procedure: FDLE will be conducting an investigation to make sure it was a good shoot," Captain Paradis said, holding his hand out.

"I know, Captain. I've been through enough of them in the last few years, in fact, too many," Stormy replied, reluctantly handing over the weapon and badge.

"Then you also know that you will be put on administrative leave until they clear you for duty."

"I expected that also. I guess Shaunie and I will take a little vacation, unless I'm to stay in town," Stormy replied, an understanding smile on his face.

"No, you can leave, but keep your cell phone with you in case they need to speak with you," Captain Paradis said. "Also you know that you'll have to visit the Department shrink before you can return to work."

"I know too well, having been there a few times in the last few years. It's always the same questions, almost like a script, but I understand the need," Stormy replied.

"Who are you going to assign this case to?" he asked.

"I suppose detectives Duncan and Whitaker, since they're waiting for my call," the Captain replied.

"You need to make your report for them. You want to do it here or at the station?"

"I'll do it here I guess. I'll see if Alex can find me an empty office to work in. Have Duncan find me when he arrives."

"I'm calling them now, and I'll tell Duncan you'll be doing your report here."

"Thanks, Captain. I'm going to find Alex and get started," Stormy replied, heading for the elevator.

As he began walking to the elevator he noticed the CSI supervisor, Linda Ward, enter the lobby with her team. He gave a smile and waved to her as he entered the elevator, which she returned as she continued walking to the crime scene.

When Stormy reached the second floor of the bank he sought out Alex. He didn't have to go far as he spotted him at the door to the conference room where he had been only an hour earlier. He was watching as the other security officers were putting the furniture back in place. He turned when he heard Stormy call his name.

"Hey, Stormy. I heard about how you saved the day downstairs."

"I just happened to get lucky. The gunmen split up, giving me a chance to take them on one at a time," Stormy replied, brushing off the compliment.

"Well, anyway, good job. You may have saved some lives and for that Wells Fargo is appreciative."

"Unfortunately the bank guard wasn't so lucky."

"I heard, and I'll make contact with his family if you like," Alex said.

"That would be great, Alex. I really appreciate it. Those are the calls I really hate to make. Can you also make arrangements for an empty office for me to use. I need to type up my statement."

"No problem. You can use the manager's office since

Sting of the Scorpion

she's not here today. She really picked an opportune time to take off," Alex said, grinning.

"Thanks, Alex. I shouldn't be long...and one of our detectives will be up shortly to collect my statement and probably ask me some questions."

"I'll keep an eye out for him, Stormy."

As Stormy turned to enter the manager's office, Alex followed him, stopping at the door. Stormy took a seat at the desk and switched on the computer, waiting for it to come online.

"Stormy, I just want to say one thing, and then I'll get out of your hair," Alex said, still standing in the open doorway.

"Sure, Alex. What is it?"

"I just want you to know that if you ever tire of police work there is a high level position open for you with Wells Fargo security, probably making triple what you earn here," Alex said.

"I appreciate the offer, Alex. It's tempting, but I still have blue running through my veins," Stormy replied.

"I figured you would say something like that and as a former police officer I understand, but the offer is open indefinitely. Here is my card with my personal cell number in case you ever change your mind," Alex said, extending the business card to Stormy.

"Thanks again. I'll keep the card handy. You never know when circumstances may dictate the need for a change in scenery," Stormy said with a smile, accepting the card.

"I'll leave you to your writing now. Stop by and see me once you're ready to leave. I'm also going to be in town for about a week, so maybe we can do lunch one day."

"I would like that. Maybe we can schedule it one day while I'm out on administrative leave for this shooting...I could even bring my wife along," Stormy said.

"That would be great. Unfortunately my wife is not here this trip, but I would still like to meet your wife," Alex said, gently pushing the door closed and heading down the hallway.

Stormy was still working on the statement when Duncan walked into the office. It was a few minutes earlier than the hour he thought it would take to complete the report, but he was almost finished.

"Hell of a mess, Stormy. But from what I heard downstairs you probably saved a whole bunch of lives taking out that nut job."

"Trust me, Duncan. I didn't want to shoot him, but I also didn't want to get shot. He was turning to mow me down with that AK 47, and my only thought was to stop him any way I could."

"That's not the worst of it, Stormy."

"What do you mean?" Stormy asked, raising his eyebrows.

"The one you left alive began talking like a magpie once we got him to the car. He told us who you killed and proceeded to warn us that there would be severe repercussions from the family and that you would pay dearly."

"The family? What family are we talking about? Who are they, the Mafia?" Stormy asked, sitting back in his chair, clasping his hands behind his head.

"Close, we're talking about the San Peron family,"

Duncan replied grimly.

"You're talking about the same infamous San Peron family that has been so low key for such a long time now? Why would they want to get involved with petty bank robbers?"

"It seems that you have killed his son Eduardo, in fact his only child."

"Who was the accomplice with him?" Stormy asked curiously.

"Alberto Nunez, a childhood friend, also called, 'The Snake'."

"The last I heard they were just a petty little crime team, pulling burglaries, snatch and grabs, you know, all the small stuff street gangs do," Stormy said.

"Well, for some reason they decided to graduate to the big time. They managed to obtain a couple of AK 47's from someone. All I'm saying, Stormy, is watch your back. These people are not only crazy, but very dangerous."

"Alright, Duncan. Thanks for the heads up, and here's your statement," Stormy said, taking the paperwork from the printer tray and handing it to him.

"I suppose we can expect the FBI to take over the investigation now," Stormy said.

"No, not this time. They may commit to a scaled down investigation, but since the robbers didn't get away, especially with any money, they consider the case closed. Of course, they'll leave it up to us to do the full investigation and file the charges," Duncan replied, his distaste for the FBI evident in his tone.

"Well, I'll be on administrative leave, so I won't be

able to help you," Stormy said.

"No problem. We have it covered. If I have any questions, how can I reach you?"

"I'll have my personal cell, so just call. The Captain has the number," Stormy replied, already up and heading for the door.

Chapter 8

Antonio Luis San Peron

ANTONIO LUIS SAN PERON WAS BORN and raised in Bogotá, Colombia, to moderately wealthy parents. As a privileged child he attended private schools and eventually obtained his college degree in Economics. As a young man he attended many social functions with his parents. At one particular event, an anniversary dinner for his father's best friend, he met the love of his life. Isabella Andres, the daughter of the mayor of Villavicencio, Colombia, Alejandro Andres.

After a whirlwind courtship they married less than a year later. In 1994 Isabella gave birth to a baby boy whom they named Eduardo. In the year 2000 business interests brought the family to Hialeah, Florida, in the United States, where they took up residence. Tragedy struck in 2005 when Isabella was diagnosed with advanced breast cancer. She succumbed to the deadly disease in 2006, a devastating blow to both father and son.

Antonio gradually got over her death but Eduardo

never did. His life became one of self-pity, defiance and petty crime, despite his father's efforts to change the perilous path he had taken. Antonio blamed himself for the activities his son had begun to engage in. After all, he was the head of a large crime syndicate in South Florida.

When he and Isabella had moved to South Florida, he was strictly legitimate in his businesses, importing and exporting. It wasn't long before he recognized the possibilities of making millions of dollars using his business for more nefarious purposes. Before long he had a thriving smuggling business and a small army of criminals at his disposal. He had taken his time and began selecting individuals from all over Dade County to form his syndicate. He had a second in command that was in charge of the dirty work, eliminating threats and rebellious competition. He could honestly say he had never killed anyone, but he couldn't say that he hadn't ordered the hits.

Eduardo wasn't a dummy. He had kept his mouth shut as he watched the clandestine meetings his father held late at night, the swarthy armed men attending. He never knew if his mother was aware of the obvious criminal things his father was doing so he kept quiet, never saying anything to her about what he knew. When his mother passed away he sank deeper into a funk until one night he met Alberto. They hit it off from the very start, and before long he was away from his father's house more than he was there. He and Alberto began pulling off small burglaries, not because he needed the money, which he had access to plenty, but for the thrill and the chance to showcase his independence.

Antonio San Peron was sitting alone in his study, Eduardo not at home as usual. Just as he reached to pick up the phone to contact his accountant, whom he had been attempting to reach for over an hour, the phone rang shrilly, startling him.

Finally, it's about time you returned my call, he thought.

"Hello, Franklin. I've been calling you for over an hour," Antonio spat angrily.

"Mr. San Peron, this is the Hialeah Police Department," the voice on the other end said.

Antonio listened in silence as the caller, a Detective Duncan, asked if he would be able to come to the Hialeah Detective Bureau. When he asked why, although he suspected that Eduardo had gotten into more trouble, he was told that it would be preferable that he come there. He asked if he needed to bring an attorney and was told that it wouldn't be necessary. He advised the detective that he would be there within the hour.

Almost to the minute an hour later he was seated in the detective's office.

"Mister San Peron, I'm afraid I have some bad news for you. Would you like something to drink first?"

"What kind of trouble has my son gotten into now?" Antonio asked, thinking it was a minor matter.

"Today at noon, the Wells Fargo Bank branch by Westland Mall was held up. One of the robbers was apprehended, but unfortunately the other was shot and killed during the robbery," Detective Duncan began.

Antonio sat still, fear gripping his heart, hoping that Eduardo was the survivor. He braced himself as the detective continued, "I'm afraid that your son was the one killed."

Antonio sat rigid as a statue, not believing what he had just heard. He was a hard man and had seen his share of death, but he wasn't prepared to hear that his own son was dead. With watery eyes he asked, "Did he suffer?"

"No sir, he did not. He died instantly on the scene," Detective Duncan replied, hating to be the bearer of this type of news to anyone, even a notorious crime lord.

"Where can I see the body?" Antonio asked somberly.

"He's at the medical examiner's office where they're performing an autopsy. We will advise you later today when you can view the body. Sir, I'm very sorry for your loss."

"Were you the one that shot him?" Antonio asked, staring into Duncan's eyes.

"No, sir, another detective was in the bank when the robbery went down. He had little choice. Your son pointed an AK 47 at him from only feet away while he was holding a female hostage."

"Who was this detective that killed my son?" Antonio asked, not really expecting an answer.

"Sir, I can't disclose that information at this time. He's on administrative leave while the FDLE conducts an investigation to determine if the shooting was justified," Duncan answered.

"Just how long will this… so called investigation take?"

"It could take up to two weeks, sir, but usually less than that."

"I'll be at home awaiting your call. You have the number," Antonio said as he stood and began walking to

Sting of the Scorpion

the door. As he opened it he paused and turned to Detective Duncan, "I don't suppose you can give me the name of the other person who was with my son, could you?

"I don't see why not. It'll be released to the media soon anyway. He was Alberto Nunez. Do you know him?"

Without answering San Peron turned and walked briskly from the room, not looking back. He had heard the name as a person his son was running with, but that was not what was on his mind right now. He wanted to find out the name of the detective who killed his son and he wanted to know *now*. He had some contacts in the Hialeah Police Department, and he would find out from them later.

After San Peron returned home, he paced the floor for almost hour, trying to contain his grief, but unable to do so. He loved his son, his only child, even with all of his imperfections and misguided ways. He blamed himself for the path his son had chosen, but now he would never be able to turn him around. It didn't matter to him that his son was committing a crime, only that he was killed by an obviously gun crazy cop. He wouldn't rest until that cop was punished, and by punished he meant an eye for an eye. He was hoping the cop had a family so when he died they could feel what he was feeling now. Finally he sat down on the sofa, taking a rest from the pacing.

The ringing of the phone broke him away from his vengeful thoughts. Collecting himself and reaching over the arm of the sofa, he lifted the receiver from its cradle and listened without saying anything. When he hung up the phone he rose and using his cell he rang for his bodyguard and right hand man, Humberto. He had just been told that he was free to go to the morgue and identify his son.

"Do you know where the county morgue is?" he asked Humberto.

"Yes, sir, it's down on Northwest Tenth Avenue, just off of Eighteenth Street at the Medical Examiner's office. I've been there before," the bodyguard said without elaborating further.

San Peron went to the guest bathroom and splashed water on his face, dried off with a plush towel and collecting his sun glasses to cover his reddened eyes, walked outside to his car.

"To the morgue, sir?" his bodyguard and driver asked softly and respectfully.

"That's where we're going, so let's get started," Antonio said, settling in the back seat of his car.

When they reached the Medical Examiner's office he told his bodyguard to stay with the car. He exited the back seat, smoothed the wrinkles in his linen trousers, straightened his tie and walked purposely with as much dignity as he could muster to the front door. After he entered the office, keeping his sun glasses on, he softly told the receptionist his name and that he was expected. The woman scanned a short list and finding it, crossed off his name. She told him to follow her as she moved from behind her desk and began walking down a fairly long hallway, her heels echoing with each step on the hard tile floor. Antonio began to smell a chemical odor and the further down the hall he walked, the stronger it became.

Stopping at a closed door, devoid of any lettering, she

Sting of the Scorpion

motioned him to go in and then turning away, walked back up the hallway. Antonio watched her as she walked away, listening to the sharp crack of her heels once again until she was back at her desk and the creaking of a chair told him she was seated.

When Antonio entered the large sterile room, the smell was even more pungent, instantly assailing his nostrils and somehow permeating his taste buds. He quickly took out his handkerchief and pressed it softly to his nose, breathing shallowly through his mouth. The smell diminished considerably, although a faint odor still persisted. Looking around the fairly large room, he observed several stainless steel tables in the center, two walls lined with metal doors almost up to the ceiling, and trays of surgical tools, all sparkling clean laid out on a long table. He noticed a huge drain in the center of the tiled floor which sloped slightly from all angles of the room to that particular spot. He couldn't help but stare at the spotless floor. Evidently they cleaned the floor often and the size of drain indicated that they used a lot of water, or at least he hoped it was for water. He wasn't dumb – all of the blood and bodily fluids had to go somewhere.

He was jolted from his visual examination of the room when a man spoke quietly to him, the deep voice coming from his right side. He had been so preoccupied with the room he hadn't noticed the man in a white jacket standing there.

"You must be Mr. San Peron. I'm Doctor Davis, and I'm so very sorry for your loss. Detective Duncan filled me in and advised me you would be coming to identify the remains."

"Yes, I spoke with the detective earlier, and he told me that you would be expecting me," Antonio replied, taking his handkerchief away from his face and putting it in his pocket, then shaking the doctor's hand.

"I'm sorry about the odor, but it's a necessary evil for this kind of work. Mostly it's only chemicals and nothing to worry about," the doctor said, noticing the handkerchief.

"I would like to see my son's body now if you don't mind," Antonio replied, cutting short any further conversation.

"Yes, sir, if you'll just follow me."

Doctor Davis walked to the far wall and opened a metal door about waist high up the wall. Then he gently reached in the cavity and slid out a long stainless steel tray with a covered body lying on it. When the doctor carefully peeled back the covering, exposing the face only, he motioned for Antonio to approach. Antonio correctly deduced that only the face was shown to keep family from seeing the graphic results of an autopsy.

Steeling himself, he drew a deep breath and approached the body on the tray. When he stood over it, he instantly recognized his son Eduardo, looking pale and now resting peacefully, even though his death had been a violent one. The tightness in Antonio's chest began to grow, his breathing became labored and he forced himself to not cry out in grief.

The one thing he noticed immediately was the poorly cosmetically covered bullet hole in Eduardo's forehead. It was something the makeup didn't completely mask, but at least the doctor had tried. Rage mingled with grief began

Sting of the Scorpion

building up inside him, and he had to use all of his self control to keep it reigned in. The doctor was only doing his job and had nothing to do with Eduardo's death. *No, he didn't, but I'm going to find out soon who did shoot my son and there will be hell to pay*, he thought to himself, his rage still fighting the invisible chains in an attempt to be set free.

With watery eyes he turned to the doctor and nodded his head, indicating it was his son. Thanking the doctor he signed a form which he hardly looked at and swiftly left the room, retracing his steps back down the long hallway and exiting the building, not even acknowledging the receptionist.

Taking a deep breath of fresh air once he was outside, he was thankful to be away from that horrible smell, but the image of his son and the bullet hole in his forehead lingered. He felt that as long as he lived he would never be able to rid himself of that image. No man should have to see their child in that condition and then again no man should ever have to outlive their children.

His bodyguard opened the car door and Antonio, with slumped shoulders, slowly climbed into the back seat. The bodyguard thought to himself that the boss had aged ten years since entering the building. He softly closed the door, correctly assuming his boss wouldn't want him to say anything at this time, so he kept quiet during the drive back.

When he arrived home, Antonio exited the car without waiting for his bodyguard to open the door. He entered the house, closed the door and went directly to his study. He sat down on the plush leather couch, buried his head in his hands and began sobbing uncontrollably. After crying for several minutes he finally sat up and dried his eyes with a tissue he plucked from a box on the end table. His body surrendered a small shudder, and he leaned back on the couch.

He allowed his eyes to look up at the photograph hanging on the near wall and choked up once again. It was a picture taken of his beautiful smiling wife, hugging Eduardo, so happy and content. It was taken the year before she passed. They were so happy then, and now they were both gone. The realization suddenly hit him, he was totally alone now. His family was gone, and they were not coming back.

Turning away from the photo his thoughts now took a dark path, one of revenge and retaliation. He thought of how he would severely punish the man responsible for killing his son. He *could* have one of his men take care of the problem once he found out who was responsible, but that would be too risky. An astute detective would soon be able to track his man back to him if he was caught, and he didn't need nor did he want that problem. He could do it himself and if he were caught, it was all on him.

Then it came to him; an out of town professional hit man. He didn't trust any of the local contractors he knew, but he knew someone who could find one for him. Preferably he could find someone from out of town or even out of the state. As soon as he had the name and pertinent information on the detective he would begin by calling his friend for some contacts.

Reaching for the phone he dialed the cell phone number of a contact he had cultivated within the Hialeah Police Department many years ago. When the call was answered he asked the question without preamble, "*Who killed my son?*" He listened for a minute and when he received the answer he allowed himself to smile for the first time today.

"Thanks, detective. There'll be a little extra something coming to you," Antonio said, breaking the connection.

What a corrupt piece of scum, he thought. Although a valuable resource and one he needed in his line of work, he still detested people that could be bought, especially people sworn to a higher standard, such as cops and judges. *Whatever happened to morals, scruples and dignity?* He was not unaware of the type of business he was in, but he did have *some* standards and hopefully some shred of dignity.

Antonio mulled over the name for a minute before remembering where he had heard it before. It was the same detective who several months ago had been involved in a shootout with another cop on some freighter in the Miami River, a serial killer or something.

Jack Storm!

Chapter 9

Administrative leave

STORMY DROVE SLOWLY back to the station. During the drive he called Shaunie to pick him up. She didn't ask many questions knowing that Stormy would fill her in once she arrived. Stormy was deep in thought as he drove, thinking about the situation at the bank and how he could have handled it differently. He ran the scenario through his mind over and over, but each time he replayed it, he arrived at the same conclusion. He couldn't have handled it any differently than he did if he had wanted to save lives. He felt terrible about the security guard's death, but it happened so fast there was nothing he could have done to stop it. Everyone there today was extremely fortunate that no one else had been hurt or killed.

He could tell that the robbers were amateurs, one of the most dangerous breed of criminals to deal with. Nerves played a big part in something as ambitious as a bank robbery and even more so for amateurs. Now that he had been told the name of the robber he had shot, he was

Sting of the Scorpion

slightly surprised. It was a known fact that his father, Antonio San Peron, was a local crime boss and worth a ton of money. Why his son would want to attempt a bank robbery, especially in such a crowded corridor of the city, was puzzling to him.

When he pulled into the parking lot at the station, he spotted Shaunie's gold BMW parked out front. He was slightly puzzled as to how she had gotten there so fast. She must have been in Hialeah already for some reason, a client maybe. He didn't see her sitting in her car so she must have gone inside to wait for him. He pulled into a spot at the rear of the station and parked his car. When he entered the Detective Bureau he could see Shaunie laughing and talking with Captain Paradis through his open office door.

"Come in, Stormy," Captain Paradis said as Stormy approached the open door.

"Hey, hon. The Captain and I were just catching up," Shaunie said to Stormy as she gave him a peck on the cheek.

"Well, I haven't seen Shaunie since the wedding, so I was asking if she now thought she had made the right decision in marrying you," Captain Paradis said with a mischievous laugh.

"Thanks, boss. I love you too," Stormy shot back with a grin.

"No, actually I was just telling her what a great wedding it was and my thanks for inviting me and my wife."

"So, why am I picking you up here?" Shaunie asked.

"The boss laid me off for a week or two," he replied with a stone face while glancing at the Captain.

"Oh, you mean you're on administrative leave," Shaunie replied.

"Girl, you're just too darn smart for me. I'll explain on the way home," Stormy replied with a laugh.

Shaunie gave Captain Paradis a quick peck on the cheek, promising to have them over for dinner one night and then, taking Stormy's arm, walked out of the building.

When they were in her car waiting for the LeJuene Road traffic light to change, breaking news came over the radio. The robbery at the Wells Fargo Bank was the lead story. Stormy reached to turn off the radio, but Shaunie told him to leave it, she wanted to hear about the robbery.

Since her ordeal several months ago she had begun paying closer attention to the news of the day. Stormy had intended to tell her about the robbery himself, but it now appeared she was about to hear it on the radio first. The news announcer finished up the story with how a yet unnamed plain clothes detective was in the bank during the robbery. He went on to say that because of the unknown detective's quick action, he possibly saved the lives of over a dozen people after killing one suspect and capturing another.

Stormy reached over and turned off the radio. After a few moments of silence he turned to Shaunie and explained everything as it happened.

"So you were there on police business when the robbery went down?" she said.

"Yes, I was sitting in for McLean at a meeting since he was out today. It was with the security team and the head of security from Iowa, Alex Krane."

Sting of the Scorpion

"There wasn't any other way to resolve the situation without killing the man?" she asked softly, without condemnation.

"Trust me, honey, I would have utilized any other option if one had been available. I'm not prone to shooting blindly and without justification," Stormy replied. "If the meeting had ended five minutes earlier I wouldn't have been there, but as luck would have it...well, it happened and I *was* there and obligated to take action before someone was hurt."

Stormy didn't say it aloud, but every person he had ever shot or killed in the line of duty had been ruled justifiable. Still, justified or not, it was an up close and personal thing, something you had to live with forever. It doesn't matter how deeply you try to bury the memories, they never leave you and eventually will resurface. Some men are weaker than others, and the weight of those actions become too much to live with. Unfortunately some can't and don't.

"I'm sorry if I seem to be questioning your judgment honey, I didn't mean it that way at all," Shaunie said. "I was not there, and therefore I can't put myself in your place. I'm sure you considered all options before taking any action. Forgive me if I upset you. It was not my intention. I just worry about you. I couldn't handle it if you were to get shot, or even worse."

"I couldn't leave that poor woman in jeopardy when I had the chance to save her, so I took action when the opportunity to do so opened up," Stormy said, somewhat mollified by her apology.

"So, you were put on administrative leave for?"

"It's standard procedure when a shooting, especially involving a death, occurs at the hands of an officer. Either the agency he works for or FDLE investigates the incident to determine if the officer acted properly and within the guidelines of departmental policy. The officer is put on administrative leave, usually with pay, until he is cleared by the investigating agency," he said.

"Why would they need to investigate when there were all of those witnesses in the bank to back up your story?" Shaunie asked, not really understanding some police procedures.

"Because of the knee jerk reactions from the public and that one small segment which thinks the police just shoot at will as in the old wild west days. Because of the media who always seem to pick apart actions such as this and try to piece together the parts that make a more compelling story for their viewers, and because the department does not want to seem biased as to what its officers do," Stormy rambled on.

"I understand, so how long will you be off?"

"Usually it only takes about a week, but sometimes it takes longer, maybe two weeks. There is no set time."

"How about I take off a couple of weeks and we can take a short cruise or maybe spend a few days in the Keys relaxing," Shaunie said.

"That sounds great, hon. It may be just what we both need."

"Which would you rather we do, the cruise or the Keys?" she asked.

"I think I should stay shoreside, just in case I'm needed... you know, for any questions they may have, or whatever. I'm totally up for a drive to the Keys if you like. Maybe we can get in some scuba diving on the reefs in Islamorada. Later we can continue the drive to Key West, grab a brew or two and get in some more diving. Who knows, we may find a shipwreck laden with gold and jewels." Stormy laughed, his mood lighter now.

Stormy left Shaunie to her driving while he called his captain. After letting him know they would be going to the Keys for a week, he gave Captain Paradis Shaunie's cell number also and told him to call if he was needed. He asked that Dakota be filled in on what had happened.

"What did John have to say about going to the Keys?" she asked.

"He told us to have a good time, not to worry and that he was jealous."

"Maybe some weekend we should have John and his lovely wife, join us on a diving trip."

"You want to see John Paradis scuba diving? Now that would be something to watch," Stormy replied with a hearty laugh.

"How do you know he doesn't dive?" Shaunie asked.

"Actually he may, but I've never heard him speak of it and for some reason I can't picture it."

"Well, it really wouldn't hurt to ask. It would be nice to spend some time with them."

"When we get back and this mess is cleared up, I'll ask him, okay?" Stormy said.

"Okay, make sure you do, buck-o," Shaunie replied, playfully sticking her tongue out at Stormy.

"Changing the subject, I was offered a job today," Stormy said.

Earl Underwood

"I didn't know you were looking for another job," Shaunie replied, a frown on her face.

"I wasn't. When I was at the bank, the head of security, Alex Krane, offered me one."

"Out of the blue, he offered you a job. Why?"

"It was after the...incident at the bank. He just came to me and offered the job. Maybe for saving them the money the robbers would have gotten away with. Anyway, I haven't given him an answer yet," Stormy said.

"What do you mean *yet*? Are you considering it?"

"I don't know. Sometimes I wonder if a job change would be good for me. Maybe a job a little less dangerous, and I wouldn't have to constantly worry about shooting anyone again. I'm just thinking of you, honey," Stormy replied. "Besides, the salary would be obscene."

"Jack Storm, have you lost your mind. You would never be happy doing anything other than police work. And as for the obscene money, since when did you care about a lot of money? I married a cop, a damn good one. If protecting the public is at the expense of some creep dirt bag, so be it. I knew you had shot several people in your career, and I also knew you never had a choice. That's the difference between you and some other cops. You have never crossed the line, using your authority as an excuse to harm someone. I know the integrity of the man I married, and I will defend you to the end for any of your actions. You would be so miserable if you were behind a desk, so to speak."

"Wow, honey, you don't pull any punches, do you?" Stormy said, amazed to hear Shaunie speak so passionately.

Sting of the Scorpion

"I mean every word. Maybe when you retire, and I believe they will have to force you out, you can get that desk job. But why would you want to do that? With my company worth millions why would you want to keep working after you retire? We could travel extensively, see the world and enjoy ourselves," Shaunie said.

"What about when we have children. We do plan to have some kids, don't we?" Stormy asked.

Shaunie didn't answer for a minute or so, thinking of what Stormy had just said. She hadn't really thought about having children as part of the equation. She definitely would worry more about Stormy in his line of work if they had kids, now that he had brought it up. But would she worry enough to want him to quit?

"Yes, we are definitely going to have kids, Stormy… definitely."

"Don't you agree having children could possibly affect the way you would feel about the dangerous profession I'm in? I just think I need to keep my options open, just in case."

"I love you and I trust you to make the right decisions and whatever those decisions turn out to be, I'll stand behind you one hundred percent. Now, let's wait until we have those dozen kids before we make any changes, okay?" Shaunie put the discussion at rest, at least for now.

Chapter 10

The Contract

ANTONIO NOW POSSESSED the name he wanted, the man who had murdered his son, and he was determined to make him pay. That man, a detective named Jack Storm, was a walking dead man as far as he was concerned. He sat in his study with his address book open to the page of a friend he hadn't called in many years.

He needed to hire the best assassin he could find. He would spare no expense to that end because he wanted the job carried out to perfection. He picked up his phone and dialed the number from the book. The call was a swirl of beeps and clicks as it was routed through several towers around the country. His friend was a very careful man – he made sure his calls couldn't be traced back to him. Within ten seconds a man's voice answered the call.

"Antonio, how have you been? I haven't heard from you in such a long time," the voice said.

"Hans, it's great to hear your voice. I assume you're doing well," Antonio answered.

Antonio had met Hans Becker through an acquaintance during a vacation to Germany. They had hit it off quickly and became good friends, keeping touch periodically. He knew Hans was a German National, but rumors had it that he had moved his operations to the States. He had no idea where and wouldn't infringe on their friendship by asking. If Hans wanted him to know, he would tell him in his own good time.

"All is well and good here. I know you didn't call to check on my health, so we'll get down to the real reason you called."

"First I need to tell you that my son Eduardo is dead," Antonio began.

"My God, what happened? He was so young."

"He was shot and killed by a detective from the Hialeah Police Department yesterday," Antonio said, a crack in his voice coming through.

"I'm so sorry, Antonio, go on please," Hans said as softly as his deep voice would allow, expressing his concern.

"He and a friend of his were trying to…to rob a bank. I just can't understand why he would do such a thing. If he needed money, he knew he only had to ask. I would have given him anything he asked for."

"Why would a detective be in a position to shoot him? Was there a standoff of some kind?" Hans asked.

"Evidently the detective was in the bank on business at the time, and he murdered my son in cold blood, shot him in the head like an animal. I want him dead – an eye for an eye and the sooner the better," Antonio replied, spewing venom as he spoke.

"Antonio, my friend, are you sure you want to go down this road? Killing a cop is risky, and they won't ever stop looking for whoever did it."

"I don't care if it was the President of the United States who killed him. I want him dead, Hans. You have to understand, after my sweet wife Isabella died, Eduardo was the only thing I had left to love, and love him I did. I know he was into a lot of petty stuff, but I never knew he would try something like robbing a bank. I think he was simply trying to prove something either to himself or to me – I just don't know. His attitude towards life changed drastically when his mother died. It was as if he didn't care what happened to him anymore. Regardless, I loved him, and now, I have no one. My family is gone," Antonio said with passion.

"Because it will be a cop as the target it's going to be very expensive to get someone to do the job. Trust me, you will not want to use any local talent or anyone without a good deal of experience. A botched job will only come back to haunt you. Your best bet is someone from out of the country, someone unknown here and I happen to know just the right man. He doesn't come cheap so be prepared," Hans said.

"I'll pay him five hundred thousand up front if he will take the job."

"Antonio, this man wouldn't even get out of bed for that amount. He will cost you at least a million if not more," Hans said laughing.

"Is he that good?" Antonio asked.

"He's the best money can buy, at least in my opinion."

"What's his name? Have I ever heard of him?" Antonio asked.

"They call him *El Scorpion*," Hans replied, a little reverence in his voice.

"I've never heard of him. He must do most of his jobs out of the country," Antonio said.

"True, he doesn't take many contracts here. He is very organized and cautious. If he thinks there is any chance he can't carry out the hit successfully, he will decline it. The man covers his tracks very well and therefore, the high price tag," Hans replied.

"Very well, make contact with him and tender an offer of one million dollars," Antonio said.

"I'll make the call today, and in the meantime you need to get me a photo of the target and any personal information on him you can dig up. I'll call you in an hour or two, or when I hear from him."

"I'll get the information and a photo for you and I'll be here all day," Antonio replied, hanging up the phone.

Antonio went to the kitchen and prepared himself a tuna sandwich on toast, pulled a beer from the fridge and returned to the study. He turned on the television and flipped the channel to seven. When he was halfway through his sandwich the noon news came on and he turned up the volume.

The lead story was on the bank robbery and shooting, so he put down his sandwich, picked up his beer and leaned back in the chair, preparing to relive the death of his son all over again. Nothing much had changed since the last report except that now they were saying the detective involved, still unnamed, was being placed on administrative leave. This was standard procedure while an investigation into the shooting death of Eduardo San Peron was being conducted, the news anchor said. They also reported that the Hialeah Police Department would be releasing a brief statement along with the name of the detective involved very soon. Antonio took a long pull from the bottle of cold beer, muted the volume and smiled wanly, knowing he already possessed the name of the detective.

Within an hour the call he was expecting came. With anticipation he answered the phone on the second ring and waited once again for the chirps and beeps to end.

"It's me," the familiar deep voice said.

"Do you have good news for me?" Antonio asked.

"The offer of one million was declined."

"Why? What was his reason? That's a hell of a lot of money to turn down," Antonio asked, slightly perplexed.

"It's because of what I told you earlier. It's about killing a cop, and there isn't enough time for him to do a proper in-depth recon, establish an escape route and a myriad other things," Hans replied.

"I want that detective dead. So offer him another million. In fact, offer him a million now and the other million when the job is finished."

"I'll call you back," Hans said, disconnecting the call.

Antonio hung up the phone and took his unfinished sandwich along with the empty beer bottle to the kitchen. He made a few business calls and puttered around the house, trying to stay busy until he received the call. One of the calls he made was to the private cell of his contact at the Hialeah Detective Bureau.

"It's me. I need a few things and I need them fast," He

said to the detective who answered.

He explained about needing the photo and personal information on Jack Storm. He also stressed how quickly he needed it. He was assured it would be emailed to him within the hour. Once he was sure the detective understood exactly what it was he needed, he terminated the call, without preamble.

It was almost two hours later before the next call came in. He had received the photo and information only thirty minutes earlier. Antonio answered and went through the same ten or so seconds while the call rerouted.

"The offer was declined again, but a counter-offer was made, which is unusual for the Scorpion," Hans began.

"What? He declined TWO MILLION DOLLARS!" Antonio shouted into the phone. "Is he that good or just plain stupid?"

"Yes, he *is* that good, and he cited various reasons for declining. He was adamant about it, and no, you can trust me when I say this, he is anything but stupid."

"What was the counter offer?" Antonio asked, his voice lower now.

"He wants one million upfront, whether the job succeeds or not, and another two million upon completion of the contract." Hans said.

"That's insane, just for killing one man?"

"Antonio, my friend, it is what it is. That's his terms and you don't have to accept them. I can try and get someone else much cheaper, but I can't guarantee *their* integrity and professionalism. The reason I suggested the Scorpion is that he has never had a client compromised due to his actions, at least that I'm aware of. What do you want me to do?" Hans asked.

"Let me think a minute," Antonio said, obviously conflicted. Three million dollars was a lot of money, but he was worth twenty times that, at least. He decided that if the Scorpion was that good then he would have to pay the price if he wanted him to do the job.

"Give me the account number he wants it transferred to, and I'll send it after we hang up. The other two million will be sent to the same account when Jack Storm is dead and I can confirm it. I'm sending you the photo and information you requested now," Antonio said. "I also just saw on the news that Storm is on administrative leave pending an FDLE investigation of the shooting. Your man may need to take that into consideration while he's planning."

"I'll give him the okay and send the photo and information as well," Hans said. "Antonio, please be careful and watch yourself. I worry about you, my friend."

"I'll be fine, Hans, especially once my son's death has been avenged."

After Hans hung up the phone, Antonio sat in deep thought for a few minutes. He was satisfied that he had done the right thing – he was obligated to uphold the family honor. At any rate, it was done now, and he would have to await the outcome. Taking one of his coveted Cuban cigars from the humidor he carefully and lovingly clipped the end. He thought about the deal he had just consummated as he gently rolled the cigar under his nose, enjoying the aroma. He went to the kitchen and procured a beer, returned to his study and plopped down in his favorite easy chair. He sipped his beer as he took long satisfying pulls from the cigar. If not for the death of his son, which still weighed heavily on his mind, he would be most content.

Chapter 11

Key Largo

THE LAST NOTES OF "OUR WINTER LOVE" by Bill Pursell were playing on the car radio. Stormy had heard the song many years ago and loved it so much he bought the album. The music had touched many people's hearts for its haunting, lilting and ethereal piano rendition. For years Stormy had played it until compact discs came onto the scene. He had all intentions of buying the CD but had never gotten around to it, yet. Shaunie had never heard the song before now and was almost moved to tears as she enjoyed it so much.

"Stormy, that was so beautiful. Why haven't I heard it before?"

"Well honey, first of all, it came out in 1963, and you weren't even born then," Stormy laughed.

"But *you* have heard it before so where did you hear it?"

"My dad always played fifties and sixties music in the car when we traveled. One night it came on the radio

Sting of the Scorpion

while we were going somewhere, it escapes me now where we were going, and I became transfixed with it. I begged my dad to get me the record and he did. That was in the mid-nineties I think, even though the song was released in 1963. I still have the 45 *and* the album at home, packed away somewhere but no record player to spin them on," Stormy said.

"Well, I want you to buy me that song or better yet, the CD. It was so evocative, wistful, romantic and slightly melancholy, all at the same time."

"I will, hon, as soon as we return home. I'll have to order it. I doubt we can find it in a music store now."

They had risen early and after packing the car had headed south to Key Largo. They had opted to drive the Lexus SUV because of all the diving equipment they were taking. It was normally only about an hour and a half drive but today the drive had taken nearly two hours. They were in no big hurry so they had taken their time, talking, laughing and just listening to the radio, totally relaxed.

Key Largo was the first of the Florida Keys and the location of John Pennekamp Coral Reef State park. One of Shaunie's clients owned a condo there and had months before offered it for her to use whenever she wanted. He said that he seldom used it now since he traveled so much and only kept it because he intended to retire there. It was located at the Ocean Pointe Condos in Tavernier, on Key Largo. The area consisted of sixty acres of protected mangrove forest and was within walking distance to the park. The client also had a boat docked there, and it was also at their disposal if they wanted to use it.

They were excited at the prospect of spending a week alone, just sunning and diving. John Pennekamp Park, a prime destination for scuba divers and snorkelers around the world, was famous for its beautiful and vibrant coral reefs. The reefs were twenty-five miles in length and stretched over three miles out into the Atlantic Ocean.

Packed in the rear of the SUV were their wetsuits, BCD's (buoyancy compensators), regulators, dive watches, scuba masks and luggage. The tanks would be rented dockside at the condo. Shaunie had insisted on strictly the best of diving equipment. She had heard a few stories of inferior regulators and equipment that had either caused disaster or come close to it. She was not one to take chances on safety for the sake of saving a few dollars. The pair of diving watches were Breitling's and incomparable to anything else. The watches were water resistant up to 660 feet. However, they wouldn't be going that deep on this trip. The rest of the gear was either at or near the top of the line in quality.

Exactly two hours and twenty minutes after leaving home they pulled into the parking lot of Ocean Pointe Condos. A valet brought out a cart and helped unload the car, then pushed it inside the lobby. While Shaunie procured the keys to the condo, Stormy tipped the valet, giving him the keys to the car to park. Another valet pushed the cart into the elevator, and they all rode up to the fifth floor, where the apartment was located.

When they entered they both were excited to see that the view was on the ocean side. The balcony was slightly larger than the ones at a hotel and allowed plenty of room for lounge chairs. Stormy could see that he would be spending a lot of time watching the ocean and putting away a few beers while doing so. The condo itself was extremely tasteful in its furnishings, the most modern of appliances and the living room boasting a sixty-five-inch flat-screen television, sound bar and stereo system. The room was spacious but with the open dining area it looked even larger. Shaunie was enthralled with the master bedroom, the king-sized bed and the décor in general. The master bath was a work of perfection with a large marble shower and an oversized tub. His and hers vanities accentuated the room perfectly. Y*es*, she thought. *"This is going to be a week to talk about for awhile."*

They unpacked their luggage and used an empty closet by the front door for their dive gear. When they had finished stowing away everything Stormy realized that they hadn't stopped to eat and he was becoming famished.

"It's almost noon, hon, I need something to eat," Stormy said to Shaunie.

"I could use something also, any suggestions?" She asked.

"Well, I have a strange craving for seafood," he replied innocently.

"Silly, you're in the Keys now. Seafood is everywhere you look," Shaunie laughed.

"Well that explains my strange craving. We'll ask someone downstairs where the best place to go is," Stormy replied with a mischievous grin on his face.

Shaunie playfully punched him on the arm and they left the apartment and headed for the elevator. Once downstairs they asked the same valet that carried the luggage upstairs where to get some good seafood for lunch.

He advised them to definitely go to Snappers on Seaside Avenue – it was one of the best on Key Largo.

When they arrived at Snappers, the parking lot was full. Luckily for them there was a car leaving as they pulled up, and they were able to get a decent shady spot under a palm tree. The outside deck was crowded, the voluminous buzz from dozens of conversations filling the air and live music almost drowning out the chatter. It sure looked as if everyone was having a blast, and it was only lunch time. Stormy walked around and opened Shaunie's door and then locked the car. They opted to eat outside on the deck when they saw there was an available table.

"What will you folks have to drink?" the server asked, approaching almost before they were seated.

"What is a good tropical drink that you could recommend?" Stormy asked.

"The *pain killer* is a very popular drink," The server replied.

"We'll take a chance and try it," he said. "Bring us two please."

The server placed two menus on the table and left to get the drinks. Stormy sniffed the air and laughed.

"Someone is partaking of a little square grouper around here," he said.

"What is a square grouper?" Shaunie asked in puzzlement.

"Years ago when a boat running marijuana saw that the Coast Guard was closing in on them, they would dump the bales overboard. They would eventually wash ashore and the locals would call them square grouper."

"Oh, you think someone is smoking grass out here?"

she asked.

"You can bet on it. I recognized the odor immediately."

"You're off duty and out of your jurisdiction, Stormy."

"I know. I don't have a problem with it, just funny how open it is here," he replied.

"Well, I don't smell anything."

At that moment the server returned with the drinks. When she set them down, she asked if they were ready to order and Shaunie asked for a suggestion.

"For lunch you can't beat the blackened Mahi fish sandwich. As the server was explaining what came with the sandwich, Shaunie took a sip of the drink and her face lit up.

"Stormy, you have to taste this drink. It's wonderful!" She exclaimed.

Stormy took a big sip of the drink and readily agreed with her. He asked the server what was in the drink that gave it such a distinctive flavor.

"It's rum with orange juice, nutmeg and some pineapple juice. I take it you like it," she said.

"It's really good, and we'll go with one of the blackened Mahi fish sandwiches with extra tartar sauce for me and the yellow tail tacos for the lady," Stormy replied, taking another big sip of his drink. "And please, bring us two more of these *pain killers* when you return", He added, lifting his drink up.

They sat listening to the live music as they waited for their lunch to arrive. There was a great view of the ocean with the gentle swells slowly rising and falling on the water. Although there were multiple ceiling fans slowly turning, and one directly above their heads, the steady salty breeze from the ocean gave them better relief from the heat. The ambiance couldn't have been more perfect for the Keys. Soon their lunch arrived and they dug in with relish, their hunger heightened by the wonderful aroma which wafted up from the hot food.

When their lunch was finished, and a great tasting lunch it was, they settled the bill and left a sizable tip for the server before heading for the car. They drove back to the condo at a leisurely pace while deciding if they wanted to begin their diving today. The decision was made that they would relax today by taking a walk on the beach and a little night life later. Then they would prepare for a diving trip the next morning.

After a long and leisurely walk on the beach, most of it spent wading along the water's edge, they began looking for the dockmaster at the condo's pier. Finding him, they advised him they needed the boat prepared for use the next morning, gassed up, ice chests and several tanks of air onboard. He assured them everything would be ready when they arrived in the morning. It was late afternoon, so they began heading back to the condo to shower and change for dinner. Of course the shower soon led to more than just washing themselves as they both showered together.

Stormy and Shaunie lay on the bed, spent and totally relaxed, half watching the news on television and half struggling to keep their eyes open.

"I suppose we should get dressed and go out to dinner before the restaurants close," Shaunie said.

Sting of the Scorpion

"Do we really have to? I'm too comfortable to even try to get up," Stormy replied.

"Yep, get your tail up, buck-o. I'm starved, so let's go eat," Shaunie said, playfully slapping Stormy on the arm.

Thirty minutes later they were on the road, headed for the Old Tavernier Restaurant and Lounge which came highly recommended. Although they were in the Keys where seafood was the choice for most, they realized they were going to be there for a week and didn't want to overdose on seafood. When they arrived at the restaurant the parking lot was almost full, an indication of good food, most of the time. After they were seated, a server quickly took their orders for cocktails.

Once the cocktails were brought to the table another server promptly arrived to take their order for dinner. They declined appetizers. Both ordered the filet mignon with baked potatoes and extra sour cream for Stormy.

The noise level was not overly loud but still a little noisy for Shaunie. They watched others in their animated conversations, chatted a little and before they knew it, the meal arrived. The filet mignon was cooked perfectly and was so tender it could have been cut with a fork. They didn't talk much until the meal was almost finished. After paying the bill and tipping both servers, they left for the condo. They wanted to get a decent nights rest since they would be out on the water most of the following day.

* * * * * * * * *

The boat, a fairly new twenty-two foot Sundeck Searay 220, boasting a 300-hp stern-drive Mercruiser engine, was more than enough for Stormy and Shaunie. Thankfully it came with a bimini top that could be raised to ward off the direct heat of the blazing sun if they so desired. It was a pleasant morning, around eighty-five degrees with a nice breeze blowing in off the open ocean, so they decided to leave the top down, for now.

Just as Stormy had requested the dockmaster had topped off the fuel tanks, filled the built-in ice chests with ice and when they arrived, loaded their dive equipment. Stormy checked to make sure the red and white dive flags were onboard. At the Park anyone scuba diving or snorkeling were required to put out the flags. Shaunie wasn't ready to dive yet, so she decided to simply ride the boat for awhile and enjoy the wind in her face and blowing through her hair. She wanted to feel the salty spray gently blowing on her face, the warmth of the morning sun enveloping her like a blanket on a chilly winter's night. She wore a small bikini to get a complete tan before returning home.

After about an hour or so of cruising aimlessly on the waters of the area, they made the turn and headed for one of the buoys where they would need to anchor before diving. After tying up to the buoy, Stormy put out the dive flags and checked the tanks and regulators. Everything was in order, so they strapped on their tanks, slipped on the flippers and sitting on the dive platform, they spat on the inside of their masks to keep them from fogging up. The water was warm to their feet and after thumbs up from Stormy they flipped over backwards and began to sink into the clear waters.

Neither of them had ever been diving at Pennekamp,

and at the top of their list to see was the Christ of the Abyss. They also wanted to dive the Molasses Reef, French Reef and the Benwood Wreck if time permitted. The water was crystal clear and warm, and immediately they became enchanted with their surroundings.

They soon saw the Christ statue which loomed some thirty feet in height. Swimming around the area there were an abundance of tropical fish, the kaleidoscope of flashing colors all around them. All too soon Stormy, who had been keeping an eye on the air tank gauges got Shaunie's attention and pointed up. They began their ascension and bobbed up in the water five feet from the boat. After climbing onto the dive platform, they shed their tanks.

"It's almost noon. Did you remember to bring anything to eat?" Shaunie asked.

"I had the harbor master make sure we had drinks and sandwiches before we left. Let's check the ice chest and see what we have."

Opening the ice chests they found plastic containers with several sandwiches and chips inside. There was plenty of water, now ice cold, and a few cans of Coke and root beer. They ate with relish and drank the water instead of soda. The rest of the day was spent diving and lying on the front deck of the boat, soaking up the sun's rays.

The following several days were a repeat of each other, their time spent diving, swimming and sunning. All worries and stress had been pushed to the furthermost back edge of their minds. The nights were spent at various local bars listening to the bands, dancing and purely enjoying themselves.

They took a drive to Key West and spent the night at a local motel. The following day they toured the island by trolley, bought some gaudy souvenirs that would probably never see the light of day after the novelty wore off, and pigged out on more fantastic seafood. The most memorable sight was watching the sunset – the dazzling rays of the sinking sun splayed across the Gulf waters as if someone had taken a can of paint and tossed it into the air, allowing the ocean winds to paint a watery canvas. On the drive back they stopped on Grassy Key and toured the Dolphin Research Center.

Day eight was the day that Stormy's phone rang – he had a feeling the vacation was probably over. He was tempted to not answer. He didn't want this vacation to ever end. They were enjoying it almost as much as their honeymoon, and he didn't want it to end this soon. He couldn't remember the last time he was this relaxed. He vowed to do it more often.

"Hello," He answered.

"Stormy, John Paradis here. Are you ready to return to work?"

"Hi, Captain. No, I'm not," Stormy answered, slightly annoyed.

"Well, FDLE has cleared you. Said all of the witness's verified your actions and more than one said they probably owed their lives to you because of what you did to stop the robbers. Our own IA investigation concluded several days ago, arriving at the same conclusion. Dakota is driving us nuts having no partner to work with, but if you want a few more days off I can arrange it for you."

"Give me two more days, and I'll head back," Stormy

Sting of the Scorpion

said.

"Okay, you can take more if you like. Not much pressing here at the time," Captain Paradis replied.

"No, I'll just take the two days. See you Monday morning Captain," Stormy replied, ending the call.

"I take it we are done with the vacation," Shaunie said.

"I'm afraid so, hon. Dakota misses me, so I have to get back," Stormy replied with a grin.

"Oh, is that so? I'll Dakota you, buster," She said, laughing.

"John said the FDLE and IA had finished their investigation and everything is justified."

"So, when are we heading back?" Shaunie asked.

"I managed to get us two more days, unless you want to go now," Stormy said playfully.

"Oh, I think I can find something to do for two more days." She answered back.

They pulled into the slip, and after tying off the boat, jumped onto the dock. As they were walking to the condo, Stormy's cell rang again.

"My, aren't we the popular one today," Shaunie said.

"This better be important," Stormy said, answering the phone gruffly.

"Stormy, *mi amigo*, how are you doing?"

"Pablo, it's been awhile since we talked, my friend. To what do I owe the pleasure of this call?" Stormy replied, his gruffness instantly dissipating.

"I just received some information through my connections that you need to be aware of," he replied.

"I'm on vacation, Pablo. Can it wait until I return to

work?"

"Oh, I'm sorry Stormy. I didn't know you were on vacation, but this won't take long and there is nothing you need to do for now," Pablo replied.,

"What's the info you have?"

"I've been advised that *El Scorpion* is here, in Hialeah to be exact," Pablo said.

"Who the hell is *El Scorpion*?" Stormy asked, slightly puzzled but intrigued also. Shaunie noticed the change in the timbre of Stormy's voice and began watching him for signs of a problem.

"The Scorpion is a highly paid professional assassin from Colombia. He hardly ever comes to the States but wherever he travels it usually means someone is going to die." Pablo spoke with a soft tone of reverence.

"I've never heard of him, and besides, what does that have to do with me, Pablo?"

"I don't know what it has to do with anyone at this point. I just wanted to let you know in case something big happens in Hialeah, or anywhere else near here. It may be nothing, but my gut and my sources believe that he is here on an assignment. As I said, he is very highly paid. It will have to be someone very important. I just wanted you to be aware, that's all," Pablo replied.

"I do appreciate it, Pablo. If you hear anything more definitive, please, give me a call," Stormy said, pushing the information to the back of his mind.

"Take care, Stormy, and enjoy your vacation, my friend, and please say hi to Shaunie for me," Pablo said, ending the call.

"What was that about?" Shaunie asked, her curiosity

aroused.

"That was Pablo. He had some info he wanted to give me on someone. He didn't know we were on vacation."

"What kind of information? And who is this Scorpion?" she asked inquisitively.

"My my, what big ears you have, grandma," Stormy said jokingly.

"I couldn't help *but* overhear. We're only standing two feet apart," Shaunie said testily.

"Hey, I'm joking. He's some big criminal from Colombia. Pablo doesn't know why he's here, and he hasn't done anything yet so there is nothing to think about at this point. Anyhow, it doesn't affect me since I don't even know who he is. Mr. Scorpion is probably on vacation also, so let's not think about him, just concentrate on us," Stormy replied apologetically.

"Okay, let's just enjoy the rest of our time and not think about work," Shaunie answered, mollified somewhat.

Chapter 12

Reluctant hero

STORMY WALKED INTO THE DETECTIVE BUREAU the same as he had every other morning, hearing the sounds of keyboards clicking away, the familiar smell of freshly brewed coffee faintly assaulting his nostrils and the low murmur of voices from around the room. Stormy was a well liked and respected man in the bureau with no enemies that he knew of. He had one of the Bureau's highest clearance rates on his cases. Sure, he had been involved in several shootings, some resulting in death, but they had all been deemed justified. He never participated in office gossip and almost always had a kind word for everyone. He minded his own business but readily provided assistance to anyone that asked. He wasn't a saint by any stretch of the word and would express his own opinions when asked for or the need arose.

As he walked to his desk, after nodding to several other detectives, a small smattering of applause broke out. It was his fellow detectives showing their appreciation

Sting of the Scorpion

and relief that he had been cleared of any wrongdoing. Smiling and giving a definitive wave to the guys, he sat down at his desk. Dakota was sitting across from him, sipping her ever-present cup of coffee.

"Hey, partner, did you miss me?" he asked, presenting a smile.

"Oh, did you go somewhere?" she asked, flashing a smile of her own.

"I wish you could have gone with us. Diving in the crystal clear waters of Pennekamp Park, sunning most of the days, boat cruising, partying at night…you know, all the fun stuff," Stormy replied grinning.

"I hate you, Jack Storm. You really know how to hurt a gal," She said, sticking her tongue out jokingly.

"I'm glad you were at City Hall when that shoot went down. At least you didn't have to go through it again," Stormy said in seriousness, referring to a gunshot to the leg she received from Rolando a few months earlier.

"Yeah, but I missed all the fun," she replied.

"How fresh is that coffee?" Stormy asked, steering the conversation away from the bank shooting.

"I just made it myself. You want a cup?" she asked.

"That would be great, partner."

"Then you wouldn't mind refilling mine when you get yours?" Dakota said, laughing.

"Boy, I fell into that one." Stormy replied with a mock frown on his face as he reached for her cup.

Stormy walked around the desk and headed to the rear of the room where the coffee urn was located. Just as he was passing the Captain's office he suddenly remembered he had to retrieve his badge and gun. Tapping lightly on

Earl Underwood

the closed door he was told to come in.

"Welcome back, Stormy. Hope your vacation was pleasant," Captain Paradis said, gesturing to a seat.

"It was fantastic, Captain, although it would have been nice if we could have had another week. A revelation came to Shaunie while we were diving one day and you had better be forewarned," Stormy replied.

"Forewarned about what?"

"It seems that she thinks you and your wife should take a weekend down to the Keys with us to go diving," Stormy said, grinning at the Captain's look of dismay.

"Stormy, you tell Shaunie there are things in the water that I don't like. Then there's the hot sun, seasickness, and God knows what else. But on the other hand, tell her we would be delighted to go for the boat rides as long as the water is calm. Just let us know when, and we'll try and make the time. I've never been much for the diving scene, but who knows, I just may want to try it," Captain Paradis said, looking a little green around the gills.

"I'll let her know." Stormy said with an understanding smile.

"I guess you'll need these," the Captain said, taking a gun and badge from his desk drawer and laying them on top of the desk.

"I received an interesting phone call while down in the Keys," Stormy said, holstering his weapon and hanging his badge on his belt.

"And who was that from and interesting how?"

"Pablo called me to give us a heads up on someone called *El Scorpion.* He said that the Scorpion was in Hialeah and that we should be on the alert."

Sting of the Scorpion

"Who the hell is this *El Scorpion*?" Captain Paradis asked, his eyebrows raised, puzzlement written on his face.

"Pablo said he was some very high paid assassin, hit man, something of that sort. He said that if the Scorpion was in town, he evidently was here for no good, probably to take out someone," Stormy responded.

"Isn't it just possible he's here on vacation, or some other legitimate business? Besides, I've never even heard of him," The Captain said, not holding back his skepticism.

"Neither have I, but he's highly respected in his line of work and very deadly, according to Pablo. I told him we would keep our eyes and ears open just in case."

"Let's move on to another matter now," Captain Paradis said, changing subjects. "The Mayor has decided to award you the city's Medal of Valor for your rescue of the hostages."

"Captain, you know how much I hate going to those things. Can't you just get it for me and say a few nice words?" Stormy said, feeling blindsided. He had always disliked going to award presentations because he felt he was only doing his job, a job he was paid to do. The public expected to be protected, and although the awards were nice, the politicians always seemed to use these events to further their own popularity.

"Well, you can't get out of this one, Stormy. The Mayor is presenting it personally and expects you to be there. Your reluctance for attending these functions has been brought to his attention, but he insists, in fact he sort of made it an order," the Captain said with finality.

Earl Underwood

"I won't be able to bring Shaunie. She'll be out of town giving a class to some big business outfit."

"Too bad, she could have stood on the stage with you, holding your hand to calm your little baby nerves," John said with a laugh.

"When and where is this presentation happening?" Stormy asked resignedly.

"Tomorrow morning, the Milander-Soto Convention Center at eleven o'clock sharp, so wear clean underwear and your best suit."

"That's very funny, Captain, very funny," Stormy said smiling, rising to leave the office.

"So where is my coffee partner?" Dakota asked as Stormy returned to his desk.

"Oh crap, I left it sitting on the Captains desk. Be right back."

"Here you go my lady, still nice and hot." Stormy said as he returned, sitting the cup of coffee on her desk.

"Thanks, I really should stop drinking so much coffee, but mornings are the only time I really enjoy it," Dakota said as she gingerly picked the cup up, softly blowing on the steaming beverage.

"So what are we doing today? I don't really have anything pressing going on," Stormy asked.

"I heard you have something pressing going on tomorrow," Dakota said with a knowing grin.

"Does everyone know but me? I hate those things."

"I'll go with you and we can make an excuse to leave early, if you want," Dakota replied.

"That might not be a bad idea…you coming with me, but we'll have to stay for the full agenda according to the

Sting of the Scorpion

Captain. It's the Mayor's big deal for the month I guess. Anyhow, we get a free meal out of it."

"Well so much for making an excuse and leaving," Dakota replied. "I suppose it'll be the standard baked chicken and undercooked veggies."

"Don't forget the cold rolls and soggy salad," Stormy said laughing.

The day passed slowly as they caught up on paperwork. They had lunch at Chico's, a favorite spot for the Cubans and locals to eat. After lunch they followed up on some minor cases and soon the work day was over. Stormy drove Dakota back to the station to pick up her car. She had declined a take-home unit since she was now partnered with Stormy, not to mention the limited parking at her apartment.

"I'll pick you up in the morning, and we can have a little breakfast and follow up on a couple of cases before heading to the Convention Center," Stormy said, as she exited the car.

"Great, I'll see you in the morning partner. It seems as if all we do besides fight crime is eat and sleep. I don't know why I don't weigh a lot more than I do," she said, closing the car door and walking over to hers.

Chapter 13

The Medal of Valor

STORMY PICKED DAKOTA UP the following morning at eight o'clock sharp. She was just walking out of her ground floor apartment when he pulled up. She knew how punctual he was and especially how much he hated anyone being late, for most anything. Usually he was fashionably early for everything, and if ever late, there was almost always a very good excuse. Stormy had on a navy blue blazer, khaki pants and a white shirt with a coordinated tie. Dakota was wearing a very stylish pair of white linen slacks, a pastel peach colored blouse and a pair of black low heeled shoes that complimented the blouse. She looked very attractive, and they both were probably overdressed for the occasion, but, hey, the Captain said to dress nice.

"My, my, you sure clean up nice, Jack," Dakota said as she entered the car.

"Quit flirting with me or I'll tell my wife," Stormy responded with a heartfelt laugh.

"In all seriousness she *is* one lucky lady," Dakota said.

"Well, I do have to say, you sure look *marvelous,* darling." Stormy said, slowly dragging out the word.

"Okay, now that we know how great we look, what's the chance of getting that quick breakfast you mentioned yesterday?"

"I thought you were tired of eating. Something about how all we seem to do *is eat and sleep.*"

"If we have three hours until the ceremony, I'm going to need at least a Danish and some coffee," Dakota responded.

"I'm heading there now. By the way, where do you have your weapon and badge?"

"They're in my purse. I don't think I should hang a gun and badge on my waist dressed like this, do you? It would take away from these expensive slacks and blouse I bought just for your ceremony," Dakota bantered.

"I hope you don't need it before noon," he said with a smile.

Stormy pulled out from the parking lot and onto west Sixteenth Avenue and then headed south. Dakota lived in an upscale apartment building in Miami Lakes, not too far north of where Stormy used to live before marrying Shaunie. From there it was only a few minutes' drive to the restaurant just south of Forty Ninth Street.

Lucy's Café was a small but crowded place tucked away in the corner of a small strip mall. The locals knew how to find it and greatly enjoyed the excellent sumptuous breakfasts. Stormy didn't plan to eat a big breakfast since he would be eating lunch at the awards ceremony in about three hours. But like Dakota, he would need a little something, especially some Cuban coffee to begin his morning.

After downing the coffee and a small portion of eggs and toast they left Lucy's and drove to an apartment complex just south of Forty Ninth Street on West Sixteenth Avenue. Stormy needed to follow up on an assault between two neighbors involving loud music. One of the neighbors had refused to lower the volume when asked to do so by his next door neighbor. An argument ensued and punches were thrown. The police were called, but no arrests were made since neither one wanted to file charges. Stormy had made phone contact to confirm their decision, and the older neighbor advised he had changed his mind. He now wanted to file charges of battery on the younger neighbor. As they approached the apartment where the complainant lived, the sound of loud music could be heard down the hallway, well before they arrived at the apartment.

"If this is what your victim heard that night, I don't blame him for complaining" Dakota said.

"Let's talk with Mr. Acosta first and then we'll pay a visit to the noisemaker," Stormy responded with an evil looking grin.

"Yes, I help you?" The man who opened the door said in slightly broken English.

"I'm Detective Jack Storm and this is Detective Dakota Summers. We're following up on your decision to file charges against your neighbor in reference to the altercation the other night."

"*Sí*, yes, please come in," Mr. Acosta said as he

stepped inside, holding the door for them.

"I kept wishing him to turn down the loud music. He keeps laughing at me and poked me in the chest. When I push his hand away he punches me in face. I defend myself and hit him back," Mr. Acosta stated in slightly broken English.

"Why didn't you press charges when the police officers were here?" Stormy asked.

"I live here long time, long before he moved in. I press charges he still lives here. You see the problem I face?"

"Yes sir, I do. But I'm somewhat curious. What has changed for you to decide to press charges now?"

"My wife, she makes me do this. She says he has no right to fight with me. I try to explain how it only brings trouble to us, but she insists," Mr. Acosta responded, resignation written on his face.

"Were you injured when he struck you?" Stormy asked.

"Only a little, I think I hurt him more even though he is much younger," Mr. Acosta said proudly.

"If you really feel that you need to press charges, I will give you the report case number and you can go to the States Attorney's office and present the case to them. If they feel that charges are warranted, they'll guide you from there," Stormy told Mr. Acosta.

After giving the case number to Mr. Acosta, Stormy and Dakota walked down to the next apartment where the loud music was still blaring. After knocking on the door several times, Stormy suddenly balled his fist and pounded hard on the door, rattling the entire wall. Immediately the volume of the music was substantially lowered.

"Yeah, dude, whadda you want?" The man who appeared to be in his mid-twenties asked, as he jerked open the door.

"I want you to turn down the music to a more respectable level, that's what I want," Stormy said in calm and measured voice.

"And just who the hell do you think you are?" The young man asked belligerently, his hands on his hips defiantly, openly staring at the way the two people were dressed.

"I'm the man holding this badge," Stormy said, yanking it from his belt and pushing it so close to the man's face that he had to back up a step.

"Hey, you can't talk to me that way. I got rights."

"Look into my eyes, pal, take a real close look. You don't have the right to play your music so loud that it disturbs your neighbors. You do have rights, but not that one according to the law. Turn it down or I will personally take you in, and I mean right now, for refusing a lawful order. *Do my eyes tell you I'm joking?*" Stormy said, accentuating each word.

"No sir, I don't want any trouble with the law. I'll turn it down, okay?" the man said a little subdued.

"You do that, pal. If we receive another noise complaint from here, I'll make sure that *I* take the call personally, and I don't think you want to see me again. I won't be in this nice of a mood the next time, you get my drift?" Stormy said his voice deadly calm.

"Yes, sir, I'll keep it down."

"Wow, you don't pull any punches do you?" Dakota

laughed as they walked down the hallway. "You even had me scared."

"I have never been able to tolerate arrogance and stupidity, especially when they come in the same package," Stormy responded.

"You don't worry that he'll call in a harassment complaint on you?"

"I didn't touch him. I just quoted the letter of the law. I may have caressed the borders of a threat just a little. Anyway, maybe he'll keep the noise level down, and we won't have to come back," Stormy said.

"If we do have to come back, it may be interesting to watch you in action," Dakota said, smiling mischievously.

"You've seen me in action. What you see is usually what you get."

"Oh really, you said usually? You mean there may be even more lying underneath that calm exterior?" She responded with an even bigger laugh.

Stormy looked at her with a big grin and said nothing. As they walked out of the building, the smell of rain was in the air. Some people ask how you can smell rain since it's only water. Most of the time it's a waste of effort attempting to explain it. Heavy dark clouds were rushing in, the top edges rolled back with a wisp of white gracing the tops, a sure sign of some possibly heavy wind. Not wanting to get caught in a downpour with their fancy duds on, they dashed to the car and barely made it inside before the bottom fell out. With almost forty-five minutes before they needed to be at the Convention Center, they decided to wait it out. As with a lot of Florida thunderstorms, if not most of the storms, they would dump an inch or two of rain and then move on.

For about fifteen minutes it came down in buckets, the wind swaying the trees precariously as they waited it out. As expected, the sun suddenly poked through the diminishing cloud cover and you could see the steam beginning to rise in wavering wisps from the hot pavement. Several small tree branches and lots of leaves littered the parking lot but nothing overly large. Just another day in paradise! Stormy started the car, and they began the drive to Palm Avenue where the Convention Center awaited them.

The Milander-Soto Convention Center on Palm Avenue had only been completed about three months, the doors opening to the public barely two months ago. It was a multi-faceted complex, consisting of food courts, meeting rooms and of course, the ability to host a small convention which could accommodate several thousand people. If it were compared in size to the centers in Miami or other large cities, it would be considered small and inadequate. It wasn't built to be in direct competition with Miami, but it was a start.

* * * * * * * * *

The now second term Mayor, Miguel Soto, had been elected to his first term on the promise of rebuilding Hialeah's reputation, cleaning up the city and making it less a concrete jungle and more a city beautiful. He had his work cut out for him, and in the first term made tremendous visual progress. The results were now beginning to stand out, and the completion of the Convention Center was a major step. With his expertise in grants and budget

Sting of the Scorpion

management he had begun to upgrade the fire stations. The police department was not far down the list. Two major corporations were now in negotiations to move their headquarters to Hialeah. It seemed that the Mayor could do nothing wrong and his own personal reputation remained spotless.

When he ran for his second term, he won by a landslide, his opponents never really standing a snowball's chance. Mayor Soto was very popular and was greatly revered by the citizens of Hialeah. He refused requests to name the Convention Center after himself but agreed to share the name with another popular mayor of days gone by, Henry Milander. The old Milander Auditorium was left standing for historical value, smaller events, and to keep costs down. The new Convention Center was a showcase for the city and only endeared the citizenry more to Mayor Soto.

* * * * * * * * * *

Stormy and Dakota pulled into the parking area designated for police and emergency personnel, on the south side of the building. They could have chosen the parking garage because of the possibility of more rain, which looked likely based on the dark ominous clouds beginning to appear in the east. Stormy chose to park outside, for no particular reason other than convenience.

They were about fifteen minutes early, but by the time they got inside and located where they were to be seated it would be close to eleven o'clock. To their delight they saw Captain Paradis, the Chief and several others they knew at the table to which they were assigned. At least they would be seated with people of similar interests who should keep the conversations from being banal.

Glancing around the room, Stormy was surprised to see his old neighbor Stan, who was at the bank during the robbery, sitting at a table near the rear of the room. Giving a smile, he acknowledged Stan and his wife with a slight wave of the hand. Seated at a special table near the stage were the Mayor and his staff, along with several City Council members. Off to one side of the stage, in a designated area for the media was the only television station that had arrived to cover the awards, Channel Seven. There were several reporters from local newspapers in the same area.

"Good to see you, Jack," the Chief said as he stood with his hand out.

"You too, Chief, been awhile."

"Well, some say that *not* seeing me is usually a good thing," the Chief said laughing.

Others at the table stood and spoke a few words to Stormy and Dakota, then they all took their seats. Promptly at eleven, the servers began bringing out the meals, which to Dakota's surprise was not chicken. The prime rib looked delicious and to Stormy's delight had a side of creamy horseradish. When everyone at their table had been served, they began eating, making small talk between bites. Although the prime rib wasn't up to the standard of some of the better steak houses, it was still exceptional for a venue of this type.

The low murmur of various conversations could be heard throughout the room, not loud and obnoxious but tolerable. When they were finished with their meal, the servers immediately removed the dishes, and other servers began bringing out the coffee and dessert-laden trays held aloft above their heads. As Stormy savored the first bite of his coconut crème pie he watched the Mayor and several others begin to take to the stage. It was apparent that the ceremonies were about to begin, so he reluctantly put down his fork, wiped his mouth and gently swished a swallow of water around. It wouldn't do for him to be called up to the stage and have food in his mouth and teeth.

"Ladies and gentlemen, could I have your attention please," Councilman Diaz said as he rapped a gavel on the podium. He stood with the gavel poised, ready to rap it again if necessary. Slowly the volume of conversations diminished and there was silence.

"I would like to welcome you to this awards ceremony, the first of many in our new convention center. In a few minutes we will be calling personnel from various departments around the city as well as some civilians. Those selected for an award today were done so by a committee put together by the City Council. The criteria ranged from years of service to the city, to acts of heroism and honors to bestow on some of our citizens. I trust you all enjoyed the sumptuous meal provided today. We would like to thank the members of the press and Channel Seven for their coverage of this event. Now, please put your hands together for Mayor Soto," Councilman Diaz said, backing away from the podium and clapping.

Mayor Soto stepped up to the podium greeted by a rousing round of applause, a testament to his popularity.

He smiled and enjoyed the moment for a minute before holding up his hand. Everyone who had stood now took their seats and waited for him to begin.

"Today I welcome all of you, and I appreciate your applause. But we aren't here today to honor me, nor am I giving any speeches. We are here to pay homage to several of our city workers, the ones who have gone above and beyond. You also may have noticed there are several attendees who are not city workers or government officials, but they are here as our guests to honor one man in particular. I will get to him later, but first we need to move along. I have long said that if an employee is happy in his or her job, they will give it their all. The employees I call up here today *have* given their all and much more. As I call your name please come to the stage."

Mayor Soto began calling names, and the first dozen were from different departments in the city. The awards were for twenty-five and thirty years of service. One was for forty years, having started with the city as a teen. There were other awards for cost cutting and saving untold amounts of money for the City of Hialeah. The last two, before Stormy was to be called up, were firemen who pulled three children from a house fire, putting their own lives at risk in the process. Finally Stormy was called to the stage. Many in the room had watched the drama played out on television when he had rescued Shaunie from the freighter on the Miami River, so they all felt they knew him. As he walked onto the stage the applause was as thunderous as a rock star could expect. Everyone was on their feet in a show of respect. Those who really, really knew Stormy would know that he was very uncomfortable with this exorbitant amount of attention. When he reached the podium the Mayor turned and held his hand out, almost a pose for the media, but the Mayor was a very unassuming man so it was unlikely he was posing.

"Jack Storm, the City of Hialeah and its citizens owe you a debt of gratitude. Not only did you foil a bank robbery in broad daylight, but you possibly saved the lives of many innocent citizens. You exhibited true professionalism in your actions and used not only your training, but also your vast experience in thwarting a possible disaster. Jack, I've personally known you for a few years, and I understand that you are uncomfortable accepting accolades, but believe me, this is long overdue. Before I present the award would you care to say a few words?" Mayor Soto said.

Stormy put on a strained smile but turned and approached the podium. He was far from shy and crowds didn't intimidate him in the least. It was being the focus of attention that bothered him.

"I don't really know where to begin," Stormy said, looking out at the crowd.

Another vigorous round of applause began but subsided quickly when he held up his hand.

"The first thing I want to say is that there is another hero here today. He was not recognized, but he is a hero to me. He was in the bank that day and astutely refrained from indicating I was a police officer. Through those actions he possibly saved my life. That allowed me some time to formulate a plan which I was able to follow through with. Please stand up Stan Kowalski. I thank you for helping me carry out my job."

Stan slowly stood as the crowd began applauding him. He also looked uncomfortable, but had a smile on his face that stretched from ear to ear.

"Your wife Linda should be very proud of you, I know I am," Stormy said, suddenly remembering her name.

Once the applause died down and Stan had taken his seat, Stormy cleared his throat and addressed those assembled there.

"I'm not one for making speeches, but I will say a few words and I promise to make it short," Stormy said, receiving a polite trickle of laughter.

"Police officers in today's society have their work cut out for them. Almost everyone today has a phone with a camera. An officer is under scrutiny with every move he makes, good or bad. Ninety-nine percent of officers today follow the law, the rules and try their best to carry out their job without conflict. All they want to do is make sure they are home at night, having dinner with their loved ones, tucking in their children. Naturally self-survival is always in their thoughts, but the protection of the public is their first and foremost concern. It's their job, the one they chose as a career, and even being under the microscope, a burden which you can't imagine, they continue to carry on. I won't address the one percent that seems to make the news in a negative way, that's not why you are here. I just want to impart to all you how sometimes an officer has to make split-second decisions that may or may not change his life. Not everyone is cut out for this type of work, and those who aren't usually don't last.

Sting of the Scorpion

I just happened to be in the bank conducting some business the day the robbery went down. I guess you could say, after the fact of course, that I was in the right place at the right time. No sane person wants to hurt anyone, much less take their life. Most officers will spend their whole career without ever firing their weapon. Unfortunately, I have had to make that choice more than a few times, and most of the time it resulted in saving an innocent person's life. I always look back to see if I could have handled the situation any differently, and not once have I found a better course of action than the one I used. This may not be a proper phrase to use today, but it needs to be said.

In the heat of battle an officer usually has mere seconds to make a decision. That's not a lot of time to make life or death decisions. Sometimes there is no time for making an informed choice, so instinct takes over.

I would like to also mention that prayers for the family of the slain bank guard would be appreciated. He was another man just doing his job, anticipating going home after work. Unfortunately he will *not* be going home. He died a senseless death, and his family will grieve for a long time.

I will end this speech now imparting this to you. The next time you encounter an officer doing his job, just remember, he wants to end his shift without strife and go home to his family, just like you. Thank you and God bless all of you."

Stormy, slightly embarrassed, stood silently as thunderous applause shook the room, everyone rising to their feet. He felt a hand on his elbow and turned to see the

Earl Underwood

Mayor reaching out to grasp his hand. He shook the Mayor's hand and couldn't help but notice his eyes were a little watery.

"Now if you will take your seats, I will award the highest medal the city has to offer to Detective Jack Storm."

Mayor Soto walked to a table set up behind the podium and retrieved a ribbon for Stormy's uniform shirt, a medal attached to a multi-colored lanyard and a plaque. He walked over and placed the medal around Stormy's neck, handed him the ribbon and turned to the audience.

"This plaque pretty much says it all Jack," The Mayor began. "Detective Jack Storm, in appreciation for placing other lives above your own, you have earned the eternal gratitude of the City of Hialeah and its citizens. You personify the definition of a dedicated police officer." Applause began once more.

Another member of the City Council came to the microphone and said, "This concludes the awards ceremony, and I want to thank each and every one of you for attending."

Almost everyone began leaving the room. A few stood around, talking to others. But soon the room was almost empty. Dakota came up on the stage and stood near Stormy, proud of her partner. Stan and his wife Linda walked to the front of the stage and reached up to shake Stormy's hand. Stan was beside himself with pride because Stormy had mentioned him during the ceremony. His wife Linda couldn't stop smiling, and Stormy was happy for them.

At last the only ones left were several Councilmen

Sting of the Scorpion

and the Mayor and of course the Convention Center staff cleaning up the room. As a group, with Dakota walking by Stormy's side, they crossed the room and headed out the door.

Once they were outside on the porch, the Mayor stopped and once again gave Stormy his congratulations. Several of the Councilmen paused to shake his hand, and they soon began descending the steps, heading for their cars. As Stormy turned to tell Dakota it was time to leave, the Mayor suddenly reached over in front of Stormy to shake her hand. At that very moment the Mayor's head seemed to explode, the blood splatter creating a red mist that seemed to fill the air like a dense fog. His limp body quickly lost the battle with gravity and dropped to the cold marble floor. As he lay there deathly still, a pool of dark blood began to spread outwards, creating a macabre ring of blood around the Mayor's upper torso.

Chapter 14

The escape

WHEN THE SCORPION LEFT THE CONDO he walked casually but briskly. He clutched the gun case in his left hand like a piece of luggage. He carried it in his left hand by design in order to keep his gun hand free, in case the need to use it arose. As a precaution he had sequestered a small Glock 9 mm in the small of his back in the waistband. His shirt was pulled out of his pants to cover it. He was hoping he wouldn't have to use it since it would be a complication he didn't need.

He walked north for a block until he reached Forty Ninth Street, where he then headed west for a couple of blocks to the bank on the North East corner of Palm Avenue and Forty Ninth. He had parked his car in the fairly large bank parking lot as far from the building as he could.

When he reached his rental car, he quickly scanned the area, looking for anyone paying undue attention to the car. Not seeing anything out of the ordinary, he opened

Sting of the Scorpion

the trunk, placed the leather gun case inside and without looking around closed it. He started the car and sat there for about a minute. If anyone had been staking out the car they would surely have made a move by now.

Taking his time, he exited the parking lot, still watching for any threats. He turned south onto Palm Avenue. The traffic light was red, and he was several vehicles back in a line of cars waiting to turn East onto Forty Ninth Street. He hoped the light would change soon – he needed to make haste for the airport, and he knew that within minutes the street would be flooded with patrol cars.

After the light changed, he made the turn as it was changing to yellow. But another car behind him also made the turn, so it put him at ease. After driving several blocks, Victor, aka the Scorpion, eased into the right lane in order to make the turn onto LeJuene Road, which was coming up soon. He made sure he was going with the flow of traffic as far as speed was concerned. He was intent on blending in with the other motorists to avoid attracting attention.

Suddenly all traffic came to a stop, tail lights popping on all down the street. There was a police car in the intersection with the overheads flashing, an officer standing in the street. Victor almost panicked, thinking that he had been followed after all and that a road block was being set up to trap him. Slowly he leaned forward and carefully retrieved his weapon from his waistband. He placed it on his lap and waited for what he thought was going to be his last stand.

Then the marked units, sirens blaring and blue lights flashing, began turning west onto Forty Ninth Street, coming from North LeJuene road. One after another they were flying in his direction, some unmarked units in the mix also. He maintained his composure and sat rock still, watching the patrol cars through his tinted sunglasses, his hand covering the weapon resting on his lap. Then just as quickly they sped past him, at least a dozen of them. The officer in the intersection quickly jumped into his unit and fell in behind the others. When they had all passed, he let his breath out in a gush. He hadn't realized he had been holding it until they had passed him.

Traffic resumed and he soon made the turn south on LeJuene Road. He had a couple of miles before he would reach the Airport Expressway. For several tense minutes he drove with white knuckles on the steering wheel, watching other patrol cars heading in his direction, and then continuing on. They were probably zone cars called to the scene, he surmised. Victor knew that it wouldn't be long before roadblocks could be set up so he sped up, now aware that there probably weren't any patrol cars left ahead of him. He had to take the chance and get to the airport before that happened. Breathing a sigh of relief he merged with the moderately heavy traffic onto the Airport Expressway and headed for Miami International, leaving Hialeah behind.

After he exited to the airport, he drove directly to the long-term parking ramp and didn't stop until he was buried among the empty parked cars. After opening the trunk and again wiping down the gun case he took the car keys and headed for the entrance to the terminal, leaving the gun case in the trunk, the car locked up tight. His plan was to leave the car parked long term and hope it wouldn't be discovered for at least a week or maybe even longer. He would be back in Colombia long before then. He would be impossible to find if somehow they ever did identify him as the one that took the shot. The gun in the trunk was not much of a concern for him since the numbers were eradicated, and it couldn't be traced back to anyone. Also he had worn latex gloves when he handled the weapon so there wouldn't be any prints at all to be lifted.

As Victor entered the terminal he immediately spotted several Metro-Dade officers walking among the crowd, looking carefully at everyone. Then he saw several others coming from the opposite direction, all performing the same procedure. Stemming the panic he felt rising inside, he tried to act normal and casually turned and walked back out the door he had just entered, returning to the parking garage.

He had left the 9mm in the trunk with the gun case after wiping it down since he could never have boarded a plane with it on his person. Now he wished he had it on him as he didn't plan to go down without a fight. If he were arrested his prints would be run and he would surely be identified and subsequently returned to Cuba, a fate worse than dying here. Even with all the years he had been a defector to Colombia, Cuba would not be forgiving in the least.

Victor sat low in the seat in his car in the parking garage for fifteen minutes, wondering how they could have reacted so quickly. He had made it to the airport in what he thought was record time and yet they had made it ahead of him. Was he missing something? Did someone at the bank put them onto him? Impossible, he was too careful, and he hadn't noticed anyone acting suspicious towards him. It must have been some sort of a built in safeguard between all the police agencies in Dade County, shutting down public transportation in an attempt to apprehend a subject.

Finally, realizing he had no other choices available he made a decision. He couldn't leave for home via the airport at this time. He couldn't stay in the parking garage. So the only choice he had was returning to the motel in Hialeah and coming up with an alternate plan of escape. He had left his clothing in the room because of the urgency to get out of town. He had rented the room for a week, so there would be no reason for the room to be cleaned out. As far as the people at the motel were concerned, they had no reason to expect him to not return.

Unfortunately for Victor, he couldn't have known that the extra police presence inside the airport was in response to a suspicious package left at a booking desk. He just assumed the worst. The officers he had seen were converging to formulate a plan for clearing out the area while they checked out the suspicious package. If he *had* known he would have been on his plane by now and well on his way.

Chapter 15

Pandemonium

THE MAYOR'S BODY had barely hit the floor when Stormy and Dakota reacted. Crouching quickly, they drew their weapons instinctively and began scanning the immediate area for the threat. Stormy turned and after taking one look, knew that the Mayor was dead, half of his head missing. Still, following protocol, he called dispatch on his hand-held, advised that there had been a shooting and that so far one victim was down. He also requested EMS and all available police units to respond.

He looked around and saw that the Chief and his staff, along with Captain Paradis were still near the porch and had their weapons out also. They began forming a human barricade around the Mayor, Stormy and Dakota, their eyes searching the area for the shooter. The officers on the scene were mature and experienced – their quick and precise reactions reflecting their years of training.

Without a second thought, Dakota quickly ripped off her blood-splattered blouse, buttons flying everywhere.

Kneeling down she wrapped the Mayor's head in the blouse, aware it was all in vain once she got a close look at the carnage on the floor. Although she was clad only in her flesh-colored bra now, no one on the porch paid any undue attention to her, their professionalism keeping them focused on the threat at hand. In the distance, the sounds of many sirens could be heard. The cordon of police would maintain their stance until back up arrived.

The media had left the porch after taking photos and filming the awards. Most had just been standing around the news van conversing when Mayor Soto was shot. At first they had ducked for cover, but then their roles as reporters took over, their courage emerging and the news story quickly took precedence. They immediately began filming the chaotic scene before them, starting a running commentary into the camera mikes, all the while casting a wary eye over their shoulders. The film crew tastefully tried to avoid filming Dakota cradling the Mayor while clad in her bra. It was impossible to get a decent shot of the scene without her in it, but the reporters had confidence the editors would make the decision to blur Dakota on film before it was shown, so they continued with their coverage. Channel Seven was live now, and the broadcast was a coup for them since no other television coverage was on the scene.

The first of the police units arrived at the Convention Center, the officers exiting their cars with weapons drawn almost before their car had come to a complete stop. Captain Paradis ran down the steps towards the officer, ordering him to begin cordoning off the area as quickly as possible. At that moment several other units arrived, and the

Sting of the Scorpion

officer relayed the order given to him. Within several minutes the area surrounding the Convention Center was cordoned off. The Lieutenant in charge of patrol had now arrived and took command of the scene. He directed several officers to keep curious onlookers, who had now started to approach the scene, well behind the crime scene tape.

Stormy holstered his weapon and was relieved to see EMS pulling up to the porch area. The EMT's quickly jumped from the vehicle, opened the side door and after retrieving their emergency equipment, sprinted up onto the porch. One of the EMT's was a familiar face to Stormy from past calls. Josh was a fairly young EMT but very competent, obviously taking his job very seriously. He gave a grim smile and nod to Stormy as he dropped to his knees and began examining the Mayor. Although it was apparent the Mayor was deceased, Josh still attached an IV needle, pressure sleeve and with the help of his coworker, loaded the Mayor onto a gurney. They quickly wheeled him to the EMS vehicle, loaded him and with sirens blaring, left for the hospital which was only a few minutes away. The task that awaited CSI was not going to be a pleasant one.

Stormy suddenly thought of Dakota and jerked off his navy blazer. He saw her standing by the wall, shivering a little, probably from the shock of how close she had been to getting shot. She had her arms clutched to her chest, covering her bare upper body, a few splotches of blood from the Mayor present on her neck, face and bra. Stormy carefully placed his blazer around her shoulders and pulled it together in the front. He took her chin in his hand

and gently tilted her face up so she was looking at him.

"Are you okay, Dakota?" he asked.

"I'm fine, Stormy, just shocked and sad at what happened to Mayor Soto. Do we know where the shot came from?" she asked.

"We haven't gotten that far yet. They just took the Mayor to the hospital. I'm no doctor, but it didn't look very good to me," Stormy said.

"But why, Stormy? Who would want to kill Mayor Soto? He was a good man and not your typical politician. He really cared about this city and its people," Dakota said, her eyes beginning to water.

"I don't know, Dakota. I just don't know. I *do* know we are going to find who did this and make them pay. Right now you need to take my car and go home, change clothes, clean up some and then come back and get me. We have some foot work to do, and the longer we wait the more likely this cowardly piece of scum will get away," Stormy replied.

Taking the car keys from Stormy, Dakota said, "I'll be back in twenty minutes."

Stormy watched her leave, concern for her written on his face. He shook it off, knowing she was a strong woman and would have complete control of her emotions when she returned. Stormy knew that when you're that close to death, knowing it could have been you, it affects you, but everyone differently. Some can handle it, some can't and need professional help dealing with it.

As he walked over to Captain Paradis, he suddenly noticed his plaque lying on the floor where he had dropped it when the shooting started. He stooped and picked it up, absently noticing the chip on one corner, clutching it as he continued on.

"Captain, Dakota went home to change her clothes and clean up a little. She'll be back in about fifteen or twenty. I'm going to begin canvassing the area and see if I can find where the shot came from," Stormy said.

"Wait for CSI first and see if they can triangulate the shot. By that time Dakota will be back and you can begin the investigation. I want you two to find the person who did this despicable thing. Mayor Soto didn't deserve to die this way." It was one of the rare times Stormy had heard him get this upset.

"Is it official? He's gone?"

"I just received confirmation from the hospital, sadly he was DOA," Captain Paradis said. "The damage to the head was too traumatic for anyone to have survived."

"Why do you think he was targeted?" Stormy asked.

"That's what you and your partner are going to find out, and I want some answers soon, Stormy!"

"I intend to get them, Captain. I just hope we can find him soon before the trail gets cold."

"Stormy, how is Dakota? Is she going to be okay to work? She was within inches of the shot and that has to get to her," Captain Paradis asked. He had the responsibility for determining whether Dakota was mentally fit to return to work. He had known her a long time, as well as her parents. He was fond of her and had promised her now deceased father that he would watch out for her as well as he could. He also knew that she would *have* to undergo a counseling session, but it was his call as to when she would have to go. He figured he would make

145

that call when she returned and he could see how she acted.

"She's fine, Captain, just sad that the Mayor was killed," Stormy replied.

"You sure that's all she feels now?"

"Look, Captain, all I know is that she is a strong woman and I feel that she will be up to the task once she gets back. If I thought for one minute she wasn't fit for duty, I would be the first to say so. I don't want this investigation soured because of unchecked emotions," Stormy said.

"Alright then, I'll make the determination when she returns. Until then you can canvas those gawkers behind the line, see if someone observed anything, anything at all," Captain Paradis said. He then turned and responded to a question directed at him from the Chief who was standing nearby.

Stormy walked down the steps and headed to the north side of the Convention Center. Palm Avenue was blocked by a patrol car on both sides of the center and traffic was rerouted. Other television stations were now arriving on the scene, but they were being stationed behind the barricades. Channel Seven had drawn the short straw by being the only television station covering the awards ceremony and therefore was sequestered *inside* the crime scene, much to the envy of the other stations.

When he reached the boundaries of the crime scene tape, everyone began yelling questions at him, wanting to know what had happened. Stormy just stood and stared at the curious crowd yelling the questions. Soon they realized that he wasn't going to say anything until they calmed down. When the shouted questions ceased and the noise of the crowd was lowered to a tolerable level, he spoke.

"I cannot and will not comment on what happened at this time. This is an ongoing investigation into a shooting, and that's all I can say at this time. If anyone here saw or heard anything, now is the time to speak up. Any information you may have, no matter whether you consider it important or not, will be appreciated. Now, did anyone see or hear anything unusual. Like someone running away from here or maybe a gunshot? Have you heard anything at all? Come on people, speak up."

After waiting for a minute or so and no one stepping forward, Stormy turned on his heel and strode back towards the Convention Center. He could hear the bevy of questions shouted out again but he ignored them, just as they had him.

He was so intent trying to piece the scene together he didn't hear the vehicle pull up next to him. A voice coming from inside broke his concentration, and he turned to see the CSI van beside him.

"Hey, Linda, you have your work cut out for you today. It's a mess up there," Stormy said, motioning towards the Convention Center.

Linda Ward had been with Hialeah P.D. a few years longer than Stormy. They had hit it off on the first crime scene he had been involved in and been friends ever since. He placed a lot of value in her opinions, and more times than not they were instrumental in solving a case for him. He never failed to give her and her team, the credit they deserved but usually didn't get.

147

"I heard. Any ideas why the Mayor was targeted? He was so darn popular I can't imagine anyone having a grudge with him, at least enough to kill him," Linda responded.

"No, but then again we are just starting the investigation. If you come up with something, please let me know. It'll be more than I have now."

"Where's Dakota? I thought she would be here with you."

"She was, but a change of clothing was in order. She was standing next to Mayor Soto when he was shot. Needless to say she and her clothes got a little messy," Stormy answered.

"Okay, we need to get over there and do some work. Talk with you later, Stormy."

The CSI van pulled up to the front of the Convention Center and before Stormy reached them they were out, their bags in hand and walking up the steps. While Stormy waited for Dakota to return, he leaned against a police unit and watched Linda Ward do her work. They began by ushering everyone off the porch and securing it with crime scene tape. One of her techs began taking pictures of the scene, first from an angle looking down then from the door looking out.

They were very meticulous and dozens of photos were taken of the blood splatter, on the floor and the walls. The splatter was crucial in determining the direction a shot came from. Out came the triangulation lasers and tripods in an attempt to determine the origin of the fatal shot. One of the techs left for the hospital to use probing rods on the Mayor to determine the angle of the wound to his head. It was a measurement that would be used in the calculations from the lasers and could pinpoint the general location the shot came from using the Mayor's height.

Stormy heard the distinctive sound of his Dodge Charger as it pulled up. He straightened up and began walking over to the car, noticing that Dakota had completely changed her clothing. Her hair was still a little damp, an indication she had taken the time for a quick shower.

She stepped out of the car and smiling asked, "Are you ready to catch this bastard?"

It was at that moment that Stormy remembered the call from Pablo.

Chapter 16

Change of plan

VICTOR SAT ON THE EDGE OF HIS BED in the motel room, his mind racing, trying to determine what he would do next. The airport was out of the question for now. He only knew one person in Florida, and he wasn't even sure that person was anywhere near Hialeah. He hadn't been in contact with them for several years now but remembered fondly how well they worked together on a contract he had needed help with. Right now that would be priority one, an attempt to find out if she was anywhere near here and would help him at least find a safe house.

He turned on the television and watched as the news broke about the shooting. It seemed that one of the stations had been on the scene from the start and had first hand coverage. Since it had been only a little over an hour since the shooting occurred, it was possible that the investigation hadn't gained much foothold yet. He continued watching and he was right, they had no suspects at this time. Most of the commentary was about the Mayor and how much he was respected and admired. With some emotion, he felt bad that the Mayor had died, but accidents happened and that was the unfortunate part.

All of a sudden there he was, big as life on the screen, Detective Jack Storm. He studied him for a moment without any animosity. It wasn't personal, and it was just a job.

He muted the television and took out his laptop. He would have to check his email sooner or later, he was sure his broker had seen the news by now. His signal bounced around several towers before he made a secure connection to his email. Sure enough, his broker had left a short but demanding message, "*Call me.*" After retrieving a burner phone from his luggage he sat back down and made the call, mentally preparing to receive some flak.

"What the hell happened?" the broker asked when the connection was made.

"The Mayor stepped in front of the target at the last second, and it was too late, I had taken the shot," Victor replied curtly.

"Our client is not going to be a very happy man. I expect a call at any time now. What do I tell him? Are you going to take the non-refundable million and just return home?"

"Normally I would, but there is something about this contract that intrigues me, so I *may* decide to finish it."

"Are you sure? Do you need anything?" the broker asked.

"No, I have what I need in the trunk of the car. I may need to change motels though, since this one is in Hialeah and once the detectives began investigating, they may start canvassing all of the motels and hotels in the city," Victor said.

"Where are you staying?"

There was a deafening silence on Victor's end of the line. The broker had just violated protocol by asking a taboo question.

In a low, almost menacing voice Victor said, "I don't think you need to know. Why do you ask?"

Quickly the broker responded, "I apologize, the question just popped out of my mouth. I really don't need to know, so forget I asked." He had made a huge mistake by overstepping the boundaries honored in his profession and he knew it.

Victor wasn't at all convinced by the broker's attempt at sincerity, but he didn't push it any further, for now. The broker had never in all the years he had dealt with him asked a question like that, and it bothered him. He didn't think for a second it was a spontaneous utterance and that raised a red flag. He would have to be careful now, and in the near future he would find another broker to deal with. On second thought, he wouldn't need a new broker, he was going to retire. If he finished this job he was definitely retiring, his mind made up.

He could take the million and walk away, but something nagged at him, a gut feeling warning him to finish the job. Victor never ignored his gut feelings. Usually they were spot on and had saved his life more times than not. Maybe the client was pissed about his missed shot of the target, or regretted agreeing to the non-refundable million and now wanted to get to Victor. He would finish the job since he didn't want any other reasons to keep looking over his shoulder when he retired.

Now he had to find the most opportune time and place to finish the job. Jack Storm had to die – it was now a matter of professionalism and pride in his craft.

It was now well into the afternoon, and Victor was getting hungry, the rumbling in his stomach continuous. He hadn't eaten since early this morning, and the adrenalin rush earlier had sapped what nourishment he had left in his system. He decided to take a chance and drive west on Okeechobee Road and find somewhere to grab a quick bite.

He soon found a small Cuban café in a strip mall and quickly whipped into the parking lot. Coming directly towards him was a Hialeah patrol car. If not for his training and quick reasoning he would have been tempted to make a rash decision. Instead he continued on and casually averted his face from the patrol car as it passed. He watched in the rearview mirror as the police unit continued on, turning out onto Okeechobee Road and merging with the traffic. This was a good indication that they didn't have a car description, so he relaxed some, parked the car and went into the café. He decided that he would eat a hearty meal, go back to the motel and take a long nap. He was tired and men in his profession didn't last long when they were overtired and refused to grab a nap when the chance arose. Sleep deprivation dulled the senses and caused many to make bad decisions. However, he had a small mission to carry out before he could safely take a nap.

Chapter 17

The wrath of a client

SAN PERON HAD JUST FINISHED WATCHING the latest news on the shooting death of Mayor Soto. He paid special attention to the reporter's interviews with the Public Information Officer on the scene. He could see Jack Storm in the background, talking with other plainclothes detectives and the CSI personnel processing the scene. From what he was hearing the Mayor had been shot from an unknown location by an unknown person. There were the usual discussions between the news anchors and their guesses as to why the Mayor had been targeted, but nothing concrete came from those discussions. They didn't know any more than anyone else. One thing for sure was that the police had no motive, no suspect and didn't have a clue that the Mayor was not the intended target.

Frustration couldn't begin to describe the feelings San Peron was experiencing at this moment. He was furious that a professional hit man, a man that came with high recommendations for marksmanship, could have missed

Sting of the Scorpion

his target so blindly. He could not have cared less about the death of the Mayor – he didn't vote for the man anyhow. His only concern was that the death of his son had not been avenged. The killer cop was still walking around and his son was dead.

He muted the television and began dialing the number for the contact who had arranged the hit. The call was answered after several rings, just when he was on the verge of hanging up.

"I was expecting your call, San Peron."

San Peron began with a calm voice, but it began to rise in timbre as he spoke. "What the hell happened? I thought you said this guy was the best in the business. He sure didn't show it today, and I'm out a million bucks, and for what, a dead politician?"

The broker began talking softly, trying to maintain a civil discussion. "I know that mistakes happen, not often in this field, and rarely with him, but they do happen."

San Peron began to raise his voice again, interrupting Hans, "I just lost a million dollars, a million dollars and nothing in return. I know the deal, but I want answers. In fact, I want to know his name and where he is at right now. I'll deal directly with him."

The broker said, "That's not going to happen. You agreed to the terms of the contract and if he decides to walk, that's the cost of doing business. I can't tell you where he is because I don't know. As for his name, I'll tell you what he goes by and you can snoop around for yourself, but you'll never find him, unless he wants to be found. He goes by the name of *El Scorpion*."

"The Scorpion, what kind of bogus name is that? I

want his real name and I want it now."

Still trying to maintain his cool the broker said, "I won't give you his real name. I have no intentions of becoming his next target for doing something stupid, such as divulging his name. If you continue this line of questioning, I will have to hang up and you'll never hear from me again. Do you understand, Antonio?"

"Yes, Hans, I truly apologize. I'm not in a good frame of mind now, so please, forgive me."

"I understand, my friend, but you do need to calm down. The Scorpion has told me that he plans to finish the job. It will just take a little while longer."

"Why didn't you just tell me that before I went off on you?" San Peron asked.

"I was getting to it, but you didn't give me a chance. Give him a few days and see what happens," Hans said.

"Alright, Hans, but I expect results and I expect them soon, or I'll to find a way to finish the job myself," Antonio replied, severing the connection.

Antonio San Peron was not a man to take defeat gracefully. He had just lost a million dollars for nothing. He understood that sometimes things didn't go as planned but for a million dollars he damn well expected, no, he demanded things go as planned.

He had no intentions of waiting for Mr. Scorpion or whoever he was, to fix his own mistakes. He had more than enough connections in Hialeah and South Florida to find out exactly where the Scorpion was staying. Once he found out, he would take care of him first and then he would take care of Detective Storm himself.

He smiled to himself knowing he would feel much

better and more vindicated if he personally handled Storm's demise. He even envisioned pulling the trigger himself. The thought gave him immense pleasure.

He summoned his bodyguard and gave him explicit instructions. Find out where the Scorpion was staying!

Chapter 18

The shooter's roost

STORMY AND DAKOTA PULLED AWAY from the crime scene at the Convention Center and headed for the Detective Bureau. They needed to sit down and piece together what they had, determining where they needed to start first. The Mayor was dead and no suspect was in custody. It was obvious that the shot came from quite a distance away. Hopefully Linda Ward and her team would be able to point them in the right direction.

Stormy glanced over at Dakota and asked, "Are you okay?"

Dakota waited almost fifteen seconds before answering. "I'm okay physically, but mentally I can still see the surprised look on the Mayor's face. I hope the poor man didn't suffer."

Stormy waited a respectable minute before answering.

"Dakota, you've seen people who were shot before. I know you were so close this time, but it's the nature of the job. I'm just happy you weren't injured, which you could have been. In answer to your concern about him suffering, I don't think he ever knew what happened – the lights just went out for him. I don't mean to sound calloused, but we have to focus now and find who did this terrible thing. If you need some time off, let me know now. It'll be no problem."

Dakota quickly answered, "No, I'm fine. I don't need any time off. Don't you dare suggest such a thing to the Captain. You hear me, Jack Storm?"

"Okay, but you'll most likely have to convince the Captain. He'll probably order you to make a trip to lie on the couch just to cover his butt, and if he does, you *will* have to go."

They rode in silence the rest of the way to the station, each lost in their own thoughts about the shooting. When they arrived Stormy let Dakota out and continued on to the pumps in the rear where he gassed up the tank in the Charger. When he finished, he parked near the back of the station and entered the Detective Bureau. A couple of the guys were attempting to get Dakota to tell them about the shooting, but when they saw Stormy and the look he gave them, they turned and wandered back to their respective desks.

"Thanks, Stormy. They couldn't seem to take the hint that I didn't want to talk about it."

"No problem. You want a cup of coffee, water, anything before we start?" Stormy asked.

Dakota took a seat at her desk and shook her head, "I'm fine, let's just figure out where we need to start."

"Well, for starters we know that the shot came from some distance away. That means that someone was a very good shot and that the Mayor was targeted. If we can find out why then maybe we'll be able to narrow it down some. I think we need to interview his inner circle first and see if we can come up with something to go on," Stormy said. "Maybe they will be able to shed some light on who may have had a motive for his death."

Dakota tapped her cheek with a pencil for a minute and then said, "I agree. But more importantly, let's check with Linda Ward first and see if she has anything new for us. Maybe they've come up with a viable location where the shooter could have been."

Using his hand-held Stormy called Linda on the radio and asked her to call his office. Within thirty seconds his phone rang and Stormy snatched it up.

"Detective Bureau, Storm speaking," he answered.

Dakota listened in as he asked Linda if she had any more usable evidence they could start with. She smiled as he silently nodded his head several times, as if the caller could actually see him doing so, and then he hung up the phone with a hasty goodbye.

"Well? Did they have anything for us?"

Stormy smiled and told her, "We have an approximate location where the shot came from, so let's get moving."

As in most investigations, especially homicide and kidnappings, time is of the essence. The more time that passes without a valuable lead or an arrest, the more likely the perpetrator will escape. Maybe they'll be caught later, but with good leg work and not wasting time the case can usually be solved a lot sooner. Stormy had a feeling that with this particular case they had to move fast and utilize every minute they could chasing leads, interviewing witnesses and getting lucky with everything falling into place for a successful arrest.

This wasn't an ordinary drive-by shooting. All signs were pointing to a professional hit. That meant they weren't dealing with local gangbangers or street thugs. This person would have planned the murder ahead of time and would have his escape well planned. He and Dakota would have to move fast to prevent him from getting out of their reach. For now they didn't even have a description of the subject and didn't know if it was a male or female. Therefore, they couldn't alert the airport, bus depots or train stations to be on the lookout for any particular description. They wouldn't know who to be on the lookout for. They had to get to the scene of the shooting, the actual location from where the shot was taken, and hopefully find some evidence. As it stood they had nothing, zero, zilch!

When they pulled up to the crime scene at the Convention Center Linda and her crew were still there, taking measurements, filming and lifting blood samples from the floor. They knew this was going to be a highly scrutinized case and wanted to have all their evidence in order and documented. As Stormy exited the car, he saw Captain Paradis talking with a news crew, one of the late arrivals. He spotted Stormy and excused himself from the reporter, then walked over to him.

"Stormy, Linda may have something for you," he said.

"I spoke with her on the phone and she told me. Captain, I need you to get a couple of officers to interview everybody standing around here, see if any of them saw anything, anything at all. I also need you to send a couple of detectives to me. I have a special detail for them."

"What kind of detail?"

"I have to interview the Mayor's staff and anyone that had direct contact with him, official or otherwise," Stormy said.

"Why would...never mind, I get it. You want to see if someone has information about a grudge or problem with the Mayor," the Captain began.

"Yeah, but I want to make sure they ask the right questions and note any evasiveness from anyone."

The Captain smiled and said, "I'll send McLean and Clark to you. Where do you want to meet up with them?"

"They can meet me right here. If I'm not here when they arrive tell them to wait, I'll be back."

Captain Paradis walked away while pulling his radio from his belt and raising it to his mouth. Stormy turned and with Dakota walked over to the van where Linda was waiting for them, a knowing smile on her face.

Stormy smiled at Linda and asked, "Why the big grin? No, let me guess, you determined where the shot came from."

"Yes sir, I surely did, Mr. Storm, or at least the general vicinity," she said, laughing.

Linda turned and pointed east at several new condos rising above a neighborhood several blocks to the east. Some were almost finished, but a couple were still under heavy construction.

Linda smiled and said, "according to the angle of the entry wound in the Mayor's head, his height and the direction he was facing, the shot came from that general direction. According to the calculations it had to come from near the top floor of one of those condos."

"Linda, you're a sweetheart. Great work!" Stormy said, as he leaned down and gave her a kiss on the forehead.

Stormy and Dakota hurriedly walked back to the car and squealed out of the parking lot. With the blues in the grille flashing, Stormy carefully but swiftly, pulled into traffic onto Palm Avenue and headed to Forty Ninth Street. At the light he turned and drove east for two blocks before seeing the gate to the construction site.

Luck was with them as the gate was opened for a truck to enter the site. They followed, the blues still flashing, and went around the truck as it stopped thinking they were being pulled over. Stormy stopped at the second condo and both of them exited the car. A heavyset man with a hard hat on, obviously a foreman of sorts, walked up to them, asking what was going on. Stormy flashed his badge and told him he needed to enter the condominiums, and asked if workers were present in all of them. He was told the workers were concentrating on finishing up all of the other condos except the first one. It was empty of workers.

Stormy turned to Dakota and said, "I think the first one is where we start."

"What makes you think that?" She asked.

"This guy is a pro, and he wouldn't be one to take a chance on using a building that workers were in. There would be too big of a chance of him being seen, and he would definitely have stood out of place like a sore thumb."

Stormy thought for a minute then said to Dakota, "We'll check the first one out now and if we find nothing we'll talk with some of the workers in the other condos. Maybe they saw something out of the ordinary, something we can use."

Stormy turned to the foreman and asked, "Does the gate stay closed all the time while workers are here?"

The foreman said, "Usually it does. If we receive a call that material deliveries are coming, we open the gate."

"Does anyone stand by the gate until it's closed again?"

"No, we keep everyone working."

"Did you notice a strange car parked in here today?"

"No sir, only the employee vehicles, and they are parked on the other side of the site."

"I'll need to speak with some of your employees after I finish going through this condo."

"No problem. I'll let them know you will be coming."

"No, don't tell them just yet. I'll be over shortly, and I would like for you to keep my visit to yourself for the time being, okay?"

"Yes sir, I have to check out some things in the next condo over. Just let me know when you want to go and have your talk."

"Thanks...I didn't get your name," Stormy said.

"My name is Jose, Jose Luis, sir."

"Jose, you've been a big help, and we really appreciate it. I'll get with you later, and once again, thanks."

Stormy turned to Dakota and motioned towards the first condo. They went inside and didn't have to go far before finding the elevator. It seemed to be the only thing in this building that was completed. Most of the walls needed the sheet rock put up, only the metal studs visible now.

They entered the open door to the elevator, and Dakota appeared leery at first, looking it up and down. Stormy looked at her and smiled, "You afraid it may not make it to the top?"

"Damn right, Stormy. This building isn't even finished yet, and we're going to take it to the top floor?"

Still smiling Stormy said, "Get on the elevator, girl. I'll make sure you get there."

The ride up was smooth and fast, no different than any other elevator. The doors opened and they stepped into what was going to eventually become a hallway. The walls were not in place yet and they could see throughout the entire fifteenth floor. Walking to the west side of the building they looked out the open window and could clearly see the Convention Center. The crime scene was still active, CSI and investigators covering the area. Nothing was in the room except for building materials, dust, lots of dust and a few tools left behind. There were lots of shoe prints, but they could have been from the workers.

The window they stood at was the perfect angle for the assassin to have taken his shot. Looking around the window area they could find no evidence at all of the crime. As they spread out to check the rest of the open space, Stormy's cell rang. Glancing down, he recognized the number.

Answering his phone Stormy said, "Pablo, I expected you might be calling."

"Stormy, amigo, I told you so. When I saw on television that the Mayor had been shot I knew it had to be him. I told you, Stormy, when he is in town someone will die," Pablo began.

"I know, I know. Have you heard anything else that would place *El Scorpion* here at the scene?"

"I just put out feelers, so if and when something comes to me I will let you know," Pablo said.

"I really need a name besides *El Scorpion*. See if you can come up with a name for me, Pablo, okay?"

"I will try, but everyone I talk with does not know his name. It's like he is a ghost or something," Pablo said.

"Okay *amigo*, do the best you can. I'll meet up with you later and we can talk," Stormy said.

While he was talking with Pablo, Stormy was looking around the wide open room, hoping he would find some piece of evidence. His eye caught a fast food bag lying on its side near the north corner of the room, about ten feet from the window. He walked over expecting to find trash. Tipping the bag up, he found his treasure resting on top of a half-eaten hamburger. It was a spent shell casing and was just sitting there as if it had been placed there deliberately. Calling out to Dakota, he pointed to the bag as she approached.

Leaning over she peered into the bag and said, "Is that what I think it is?"

Stormy kneeled down and picked up an unopened drink straw from inside the bag. After stripping the paper off of it, he used one end to insert into the shell and then carefully he lifted it from the bag. He held it to his nose, and as he sniffed, the strong smell of recently fired gunpowder assailed his nostrils.

Sting of the Scorpion

Carefully he placed it back in the bag and on the burger exactly as he found it. He would call Linda Ward and her team to come and process the scene. This find was a good indicator that the shooter had used this room to fire the shot that killed the Mayor.

When he finished his call to Linda telling her what he had found, Dakota called out to him. He walked over to where she was standing, intently gazing out the window.

"What are you looking at?" he asked.

"You see the bank over at the corner of Palm and Forty Ninth Street?"

"Yes, what about it?"

"They'll have video cameras and probably ones for the parking lot," She said.

"Good observation, Dakota. Maybe they caught something we missed. Evidently the shooter has to have transportation and he didn't park here...so maybe he got cocky and parked at the bank."

"I don't know about the cocky part, but he had to park somewhere and the only places between here and there are residential homes. I imagine if he parked at one of those, they would have called and complained."

"Unless he found an empty or foreclosed house on the street and parked there. We'll have to check that out, but if he did, we know he's gone now.," Stormy said.

"We can look around here some more while we wait for CSI, then we can check out the bank," Dakota said.

It was nearly twenty minutes before Linda and one of her techs arrived at the condo. Stormy had sent the elevator down for her, and when she exited on the fifteenth floor he called out to her. He proceeded to show her the shell casing in the fast food bag then explained that he had actually taken it out with the straw and sniffed it. Linda smiled at him and playfully said, "Stormy, how many times do I have to tell you to not tamper with evidence?"

Giving her a grin, Stormy replied, "I didn't want you to waste a trip over here."

"Yeah, Stormy, that's really considerate of you. Don't let it happen again, and now, get out of here so I can work my magic," Linda responded. She had been through this with Stormy for years but never had his mishandling of evidence caused a case to be lost. He was astute enough to hug the line and know just how far to go.

Dakota followed Stormy to the elevator and after assuring Linda they would send it back up, he pushed the down button once the doors closed. When they reached ground level Stormy briefly considered finding Joe Luis, the foreman for the project, and arranging the questioning of the other workers. For now that would have to wait. He would have McLean come over and handle it.

Dakota was right, they needed to check out the houses between here and the bank and then view the camera footage at the bank. Dakota started for the car, but Stormy stopped her saying, "We're going to hoof it from here, there are too many houses to stop at along the way."

Dakota let out an exaggerated sigh and said, "Oh, man, me and my big mouth."

Stormy let out a big laugh and began walking to the front gate, tiny dust devils swirling behind him as he walked through the sandy lot and Dakota rushing to get past the plumes of dust. It had rained a few hours earlier,

Sting of the Scorpion

but now the ground was dry from the overhead sun.

When they walked through the side gate designated for foot traffic, they turned west and split up, one on each side of Forty Ninth Street. Working their way up the street they stopped at each house to question the residents about a strange car that may have been parked in their driveway. At many of the homes, no one answered the door, the occupants probably still at work. The ones who were home stated they hadn't seen anyone or anything unusual. They made good time and soon arrived at the bank, albeit a little hot and thirsty.

When they entered the bank, the first thing Dakota did was go to the restroom. She felt dusty although only her shoes were coated. Stormy found the water cooler in a corner and drank two paper cones almost in two gulps, the cold liquid quenching his thirst. Dakota came out and drank a cup also then tossed the used cup into the nearby trash can.

Stormy walked over to one of the bank officers sitting at a desk and asked if the manager was in. Looking up and giving Stormy one of those forced smiles, she asked, "Is there something *I* can help you with? He's a little busy right now."

Stormy looked at her and smiled, not in a mood for the brush-off game and held his badge up. "Please tell him to get un-busy, I have a murder to solve, and I need to speak with him now," he said calmly, still smiling. "But detective, I can..." The woman began but was quickly interrupted by Dakota. "Lady, just get the manager for us. I doubt you have the authority to give us what we need, and time is of the essence."

169

Earl Underwood

Giving Stormy and Dakota an icy glare the woman stood and stalked off to an office nearby. Without knocking she opened the door and entered. In less than a minute she came out and walking over to Stormy said, "Mr. Bucciante will see you now." Without any further acknowledgement she stiffly strode past them, returning to her desk, her displeasure obvious.

"Daniel Bucciante, how may I be of assistance to you, detectives?" he asked. The office was empty and the desk clear of paperwork. If he were busy, he must have been on a phone call.

"I'm Detective Storm and this is my partner Dakota Summers. We apologize for the interruption, Mr. Bucciante, but we need your assistance as quickly as possible. I don't know if you're aware, but the Mayor was just shot and killed two blocks from here," Stormy said.

"My God, when did this happen? Who did it?" Bucciante said.

"It happened within the last hour, sir. We don't know who did it, yet. That's why we're here asking for your help," Dakota responded.

"How can I be of assistance? I know… I mean I knew Mayor Soto quite well. We went to the same high school and our families have dinner together occasionally. Oh, this is terrible news," The banker rambled on.

"Sir, we would like to go through your security video footage for the outside parking lot. We think the shooter may have possibly parked in your parking lot. We're not sure, but we can't rule it out," Stormy said.

"Yes, by all means. Follow me please. I'll take you to the security room at once," Bucciante said, leading them out the door.

"We really appreciate your cooperation, Mr. Bucciante. We assumed we would have to obtain a warrant to view the tapes and that would have delayed our investigation somewhat," Dakota said as they walked to the rear of the bank.

"Normally you would need a warrant, but I have the authority to override that. I can see the need for speed in this instance."

When they reached the rear of the bank, Mr. Bucciante opened a door using the numeric keypad. When they entered the small room, Stormy noticed several monitors and two employees sitting at a desk watching the lobby and parking lots. After being introduced to the head of security, Gordon Bing, Mr. Bucciante told him to render whatever assistance Stormy and Dakota needed.

Stormy advised Mr. Bing that he wanted to see the video tapes for the front and side parking lots from the time the bank opened this morning. Since the day was barely half over the tapes were still in the machines and readily available. Stormy and Dakota were seated at another desk adjacent to the ones used by the two employees.

Shortly the footage was brought up on screen and after being shown how to scroll through them, fast forward and reverse, they were left to their task. Settling in for a boring chore, they began to watch the footage, watching car after car enter the parking lot, then leave, only to have more arrive. Coffee was brought in for them by another employee, courtesy of Mr. Bucciante. They had at least an hour, or maybe two, of video to look at and time was not on their side. The longer it took, the better the odds of the shooter slipping their grasp.

The process was so boring and repetitious that Dakota was having trouble staying awake. Stormy fared a little better probably because he drank more coffee. Then, there it was, a dark car pulling into the front lot, parking on the east side, almost out of the surveillance cameras view. What caught Stormy's eye was after the car pulled in a male exited the car and popped open the trunk. He watched as the man took a piece of luggage from the trunk, looked around the parking lot and began walking eastward away from the bank, in the direction of the condos. He replayed the video again, making sure of what he was observing. He prodded Dakota who instantly became alert, realizing she had almost dozed off.

Looking at Stormy, she asked, "What is it, did you find something?"

"Yeah, take a look at this," he responded, backing the video up to the timestamp he had written down.

"Oh, man, that has to be him," she said as she watched the scene play out. "Who comes to a bank, takes luggage from their trunk, and then walks away?"

After watching the scene play over several times they concentrated on trying to read the license plate. The footage was a little grainy and the angle was askew from the camera, making it hard to make out the numbers on the plate. Stormy decided he needed to take a copy of the video to his friend at the FBI office in Miami. They possessed the capabilities of blowing up the image and enhancing the plate number. He told Gordon Bing what he needed and within a few minutes a copy was made and in his hands.

On the way out of the bank he stopped in and thanked Mr. Bucciante once again, explaining that he may have found what he was looking for. Stormy was assured that anything else he needed he only had to ask.

Chapter 19

Confrontation

VICTOR FINISHED UP HIS MEAL, paid the check and left the Cuban Cafe. He casually stood on the sidewalk in front of the Cafe for almost a minute, a toothpick between his lips, observing the parking lot and his parked car. He didn't fail to scan the area across the highway and down the block. His eyes darted all around from behind the mirrored sunglasses he wore. No one was able to see that he was scanning the area. With his deeply tanned skin he looked like any other Hispanic in the area. He was an expert at detecting stakeouts. Seeing none of the signs that he was being watched, he began walking to his car.

Halfway across the lot he noticed another patrol car turn off the highway and into the shopping area, cruising slowly towards him. Not prone to panic, he maintained his pace and continued on to his car. Without looking back, he had almost reached his car as the police unit slowly drove past him, the heat of the engine blowing gently against his back. The car passed him by without incident, and he opened the door and climbed into his car. Waiting for the police unit to exit the parking lot, he started the engine and backed out of the space.

When he was back in traffic on Okeechobee Road heading to the motel, he let out his breath. He really hadn't realized he had been holding it. He knew it was possible he could be stopped for a minor traffic infraction, real or made up, so he decided he had to get rid of the car. He had already planned to dump it tonight, but he decided to do it now. He would try to find some area where he could leave it and take a taxi back to the motel. He wasn't concerned about the rental company or the name used to rent it under. He had other identification he would be using now, since he couldn't go to the airport.

After driving for an hour he found an area in Miami that was perfect for dumping the car. It was one of the impoverished areas of town with rundown housing and grass that looked as if it hadn't been cut for a year. There was discarded junk and furniture along with piles of garbage lining the street curbs. Between some of the houses were vacant lots with junk cars abandoned.

He slowly pulled to the curb behind another car and parked. He didn't bother to take the key with him. He just popped the trunk release and retrieved his automatic weapon and spare clips, which he covered from view as he shoved it into the back of his waistband. The sniper rifle and tripod, which he had wiped clean of prints earlier, were left in the bag within the trunk. He couldn't take the chance of getting stopped carrying the bag and besides, he wouldn't need it any longer. He planned to be close enough to his target to use the Glock 9mm.

175

Earl Underwood

Without looking back at the car, he casually walked away, hoping to see a taxi but doubted one would be caught dead in this neighborhood. There were only a few people visible, most sitting on their porches, some standing in small groups talking.

When he neared the end of the block and in sight of a major road, three young black men stepped from the doorway of an empty boarded up store blocking his path. Two of them looked to be in their late teens and the other about the mid-twenties. All had their pants hanging down below their hips exposing their boxer shorts and wearing bandanas on their heads. Their stance and swagger was an indication that they thought they were real "gangstas." The older of the two had the tape wrapped butt of a gun sticking out in front of his pants, his hand casually resting on it. Victor was not intimidated in the least, but he *was* irritated that they were slowing him down. He needed to get back to the motel and make plans to take care of Storm and then get out of Florida.

"Yo, spic, watcha doing in our hood?" one of the teens asked sarcastically.

"I'm not looking for trouble guys, so if you don't mind stepping aside I'll soon be out of your hood."

"Oh, mistah spic wants to leave our hood. What, it's not good nuff for you?" The other teen asked.

"I told you I'm not looking for trouble. Just let me pass please," Victor said, his voice lowering somewhat.

The older of the three hadn't said anything yet, and Victor knew he would be the most dangerous to deal with. He just stood quietly and watched Victor. Victor figured that he was not going to be allowed to get out of here

Sting of the Scorpion

peacefully, so he backed up a step, relaxed and placed his body in a combat stance. His hands were by his side but could move in a blur if needed. He decided that if any of them made a move he would take out the punk with the gun first and then concentrate on the older man. He didn't plan to use his weapon if he could help it. He didn't need to draw any more attention to himself than necessary.

"How about you empty out your pockets, spic?" the teen with the gun said.

"And if I don't empty my pockets, *hijueputa*?" Victor responded through slightly gritted teeth.

"Hajj...what kinda name you calling me, spic?"

"I've told you twice, I don't want any trouble. Just step aside and I won't hurt you," Victor said as the punk tightened his grip on the butt of his gun. He attempted to jerk it free of his pants, but Victor was much too fast, already springing into action. His first move was a swift hard kick to the kid's kneecap, which he heard shatter, and without missing a beat, wrenched the weapon from the teen's hand, tossing it out into the street. Screaming the kid crumpled to the ground, clutching his busted kneecap, writhing in agony.

Now the second teen made his move, swinging his fist in a roundhouse at Victor. He never finished the punch; Victor parried the blow and delivered a devastating punch to his midsection. The second teen fell to his knees, the wind knocked completely out of his lungs, gasping and trying to catch his breath. Victor looked at the last man standing and was amazed to see a slight smile on his face.

"You may have taken care of my boys, and that's exactly what they are, but can you handle a man?" the older one asked.

"It's your turn to find out. Either step aside or make a move," Victor said, carefully watching the man's hands without actually looking at them.

"You made a mistake by tossing Darryl's gun into the street, my friend. You should have kept it."

"First of all, I'm not your friend. I'm a little choosier in who I pick for my friends," Victor said as he slowly edged closer to the man, a slight smile on his face.

Victor never took his eyes off the man in front of him, now only about three feet away, the cocky smile still plastered on his face. Suddenly the man moved his hand towards his back. The smile quickly left his face as he felt the barrel of Victor's gun pressing against his forehead, his hand frozen in place. It happened so fast he barely saw Victor reach behind his back and pull the weapon.

"Unless you want to start breathing through a hole in your forehead you may want to reconsider where you place that hand, *friend*," Victor said.

"It's all cool, man, it's all cool. I don't think you want to shoot me here in front of all these witnesses," he said.

"It's not cool, man. I only wanted to go about my business but you and your punk friends felt otherwise. I would shoot you in front of everyone here without blinking an eye and not lose any sleep over it. Now, we are going to reach an agreement, do you understand?" Victor said.

"What kind of agreement?"

At that moment the teen that had been catching his breath from the blow Victor had delivered, stood up from the sidewalk and began walking towards Victor's back, oblivious of the gun in his friend's face. His friend saw him and without flinching said, "Breadman, back off. We're cool here!"

"I'm not cool here. I'm going to rip off that spic's head," Breadman said with venom dripping from his voice.

"I said back off. You don't want *me* to take your head off, so get back. NOW!" the man said loudly.

Breadman stopped, suddenly seeing the gun pressed against his friend's forehead.

Victor slowly walked around the man, telling him to turn with him. He wanted to be able to watch the other two punks. He didn't have to worry very much about the one with the busted kneecap. He was still in a fetal position on the sidewalk, clutching his knee and moaning. Victor watched as Breadman looked at the gun lying in the street.

"Don't even think about it, get over here and face the wall," Victor said in a menacing voice.

Breadman reluctantly complied, walking over to the storefront and facing the wall. Victor turned his attention to the man he had his gun pressed against.

"You see that car down the street, the dark one nearest to us?" Victor said to him.

"I see it. What about it?"

"The keys are in the ignition. Tell your friend Breadman to go get it and drive back over here. If he so much as tries to do anything funny, or leave, you will definitely not like what happens next. You get my drift, *friend?*" Victor said.

"Breadman, you heard what he said. Go get the car

and bring it back here. Don't do anything but that, and I mean it, Breadman. Do what he said."

"What's your name?" Victor asked the man.

"Cassius. What's yours?" the man replied without as much as the blink of the eye.

"You don't' need to know mine. Your mom was a boxing fan, huh?"

"Yeah, she loved Cassius Clay."

"Well, Cassius made something out of himself…you should consider that path yourself."

About that time the car Victor had parked down the street pulled to the curb and stopped, Breadman behind the wheel.

"We're getting in the car, you'll be in the front, and I'll be in the back. Don't make the mistake of underestimating me, Cassius. Do exactly as I say, and you both will be fine," Victor said as he escorted Cassius to the front passenger seat.

"Hey, man, at least let me drive. Breadman is not a good driver."

"No, I want Breadman to drive. You just sit still with your hands on the dash, okay?"

"It's all cool, man. Where you taking us?"

"Not far…just down the road and out of your hood," Victor replied.

Getting in the car, Victor tapped Cassius on the shoulder, letting him know that he was under the gun so to speak. He told Breadman to drive carefully, not to speed and head to a shopping center he had passed on the way in. Breadman told him he knew where the shopping center was located and began to drive. When they reached the shopping center, Victor told Breadman to pull in and park near the street. Once the car was parked and the motor switched off, Breadman asked, "What now man?"

"I suppose one of you has a cell phone with you. Call me a taxi and then we wait." Victor said, his gun still aimed at the back of Cassius' head. He leaned back in the seat and watched as Breadman made the call.

"They said a taxi will be here in ten minutes, okay?" Breadman said ending the call.

"That's fine. When it arrives I want you two to stay in the car. I'll get out and then you can leave, you can even have the car. Don't even think about trying to follow the taxi because I'll have him stop and you won't get a second chance. You understand?"

"We get the drift, man. Just don't get nervous with that piece, okay?" Cassius said.

The taxi pulled into the parking lot in about eight minutes flat, and Victor exited the car, his gun tucked in his waistband, his loose shirt covering it. He winked at Cassius and turned around, getting into the back seat of the cab. He watched as Breadman started the car and pulled from the parking lot. Victor waited on giving the cab driver directions until he could see that Breadman was driving back the way they had come, only then did he have the cab driver head towards South Hialeah.

"Man, we need to follow that smart-ass dude and show him who da boss in this hood," Breadman said as they drove away.

"Shut the hell up, Breadman. You wouldn't know a pro if one bit you in the ass. We're lucky to be alive, so just shut your mouth and drive," Cassius said.

Chapter 20

FBI assistance

WITH THE COPY OF THE SURVEILLANCE VIDEO from the bank in hand, Stormy and Dakota drove to the FBI office in downtown Miami. At the front desk in the lobby, Stormy asked if Agent Lawrence Foresman was available. The receptionist called an extension number and after hanging up the phone asked for identification from the two of them. After producing their identification they were given visitor passes and allowed to use the elevator. When they reached the fourth floor they were met at the door of the elevator as it opened.

"Stormy, great to see you man. How's Shaunie doing? And by the way, it was a great wedding," Lawrence Foresman said, holding out his hand to Stormy. "And how are you, Dakota?"

"I'm fine, Larry. Good to see you," Dakota responded.

"Doing great, Larry, and how have you been?" Stormy asked.

"Oh, hanging in there. Lots of bank robberies…oh,

Sting of the Scorpion

you would know about that, wouldn't you?" Lawrence said laughing. "I'm sure you weren't just in the neighborhood and dropped in to see your old buddy. I must have something you need from me."

"I'm sure you heard about the Mayor being shot and killed earlier today. We have some video from a bank surveillance camera and I need your assistance in enhancing the tag number. It may have some ties to the shooter. I'm not sure, but it looks like a viable lead," Stormy said.

"I told you he only wanted me for my connections," Lawrence said to Dakota, giving forth a big laugh.

"Yeah, he does that a lot," Dakota said, laughing also.

"Follow me, and we'll see what we can do."

They followed Lawrence as he chatted away while they walked down a long hallway. Lawrence stopped at a closed door, the nameplate on it reading, HTVA, High Tech Video Analysis. After rapping twice on the door they were told to enter.

Stormy was surprised to see the size of the room. There were video monitors covering one complete wall, all at eye level and desks in front. Several of them were occupied, and no one turned from their work when they entered the room, all seemingly concentrating on their work at hand. Lawrence walked to a desk in one corner and spoke to the man sitting there. "George, can you check out a video for me now or should I leave it and come back later?"

"I can get to it now, Larry. Tell me what you have and what exactly are you looking for?" George asked.

"These are friends of mine from Hialeah Homicide, Jack Storm and Dakota Summers. They are working the shooting death of the Mayor of Hialeah earlier today. Jack has a bank surveillance video and it may hold information related to the perpetrator. He needs the tag on the car blown up and cleaned so we can get the plate numbers," Lawrence said.

"No problem at all," George said, rising from his seat and holding out his hand to Stormy.

"George Von Hartman. Pleased to meet you."

After shaking hands Stormy handed over the video copy and followed George to an empty desk. George sat down and inserted the disc into a machine. Stormy looked at the monitor as the video came up.

"It's fairly grainy, but I think we can do something with it. Give me a minute or two and we'll see what we have." George said as he began working the controls on the machine.

Stormy and Dakota watched in fascination as the image on the monitor began clearing up, the grainy image began to sharpen and the tag suddenly filled the screen. The numbers were still at a slant but they were able to make them out now. Writing down the tag number, George stood and handed it to Stormy.

"Thank you very much, George. We apologize for coming in cold but we don't have the capabilities to do what you just did for us."

"It was my pleasure. You ever need anything again just let Larry know and consider it done," George said, shaking Stormy and Dakota's hands again, holding on to Dakota's a little longer.

After promising to have Larry over for dinner one evening soon, Stormy and Dakota left the FBI building and headed back to the Hialeah Detective Bureau.

"I think George was a little infatuated with you," Stormy said to Dakota.

"No way. Why do you say that?"

"Oh, the way he looked at you, all gooey-eyed and the way he held your hand, for starters," Stormy said grinning.

"You're crazy, Jack Storm!" Dakota said, redness starting to rise in her cheeks.

"Nope, I think George will be calling you, soon."

"Well, he was a good looking man," Dakota conceded.

"Maybe I'll invite him to dinner also when Larry comes. You want to come too?" Stormy said playfully.

"Maybe you should check with him first, Stormy," Dakota said, inwardly pleased with the idea.

They soon reached their office, and once inside Dakota immediately went to dispatch and had the tag number run. The lead dispatcher pulled the printout and handed it to Dakota, stating that it came back to a car rental company at Miami International Airport. She returned to the office and told Stormy what she had found, and they checked the date it had been rented. Surprisingly the date it was rented was two weeks before the shooting. That didn't make sense, and they could feel the only lead they had at the moment slipping away.

"I think I'll call the rental company. I have a few more questions that need answering," Stormy said, picking up the phone on his desk and dialing the extension for dispatch. When the dispatcher answered he asked her to find the phone number for him of the rental company at the airport. In fifteen seconds she came back with the number. Stormy thanked her and after breaking the connection, dialed the number she had given him.

Dakota held up her coffee mug but Stormy shook his head, he didn't want coffee just now. Dakota walked to the rear of the squad room to the coffee pot while Stormy began talking with someone at the rental company.

When Dakota returned with her steaming mug of coffee, Stormy had concluded his conversation with the rep at the rental company.

"What did you find out?" She asked as she sat down at her desk, blowing on the hot coffee.

"Well, the car was rented on the date on the printout. If we want the name of the person that rented it, we'll have to obtain a warrant. They stated privacy concerns and protecting themselves from lawsuits," Stormy said.

"That was all you found out? I could have told you that."

"There was something else. I also asked if they had GPS's in their car."

"Oh, why didn't I think of that?" Dakota said.

"Maybe it's because I'm the senior detective here," Stormy said with a grin. "But there's more."

"Oh, and what else is there, oh mighty master?" Dakota asked playing along.

"They have to have a warrant to use that also. I guess we'll need to find a judge to sign one for us. That shouldn't take too long if we can find one in Hialeah."

Dakota sat sipping her coffee while Stormy thumbed through his directory to find a judge in Hialeah to get a warrant signed. He found one he had used several times before. Judge Beverly Wentworth had been on the bench for almost twenty years and had a spotless reputation for fairness and compassion. Her rulings and stiff sentences for criminals were legend among the judges in her circuit. She was a former police officer twenty years earlier and had an affinity towards helping LEO's.

Stormy began writing up the articles for the warrant, making sure the wording was correct and the probable cause aspect perfect. Just as he finished his typing his phone rang.

"Stormy here, how can I help you?" he asked as he answered the phone.

"Actually it's how I can help you Stormy," the voice on the other end responded.

"Linda, how is my favorite CSI girl doing? Did you find something for me?"

"The place was sterilized, at least as much as it could have been in a room under construction. The only thing was the spent cartridge shell you found. I managed to do some research on that for you," Linda responded.

"What did you find that I can use?" Stormy asked his interest piqued now.

"Well, for starters, it's a very nasty round."

"What do you mean by *nasty*?" Stormy asked.

"It was designed by the Russians a long time ago, for accuracy and killing power. The nasty part is that it has a lead knocker in the head which tumbles when it strikes a target, causing massive damage. It's a real killer round," Linda began.

"Man that is nasty," Stormy said.

"Yeah, it's a 7N1, 7.62 round, and the *piece de re-*

sistance, it's mainly used in sniper rifles."

"Any specific brand of sniper rifles it's used in?"

"From what I determined it's used in the Russian Dragunov SDV rifle. I've never heard of that one," Linda said.

"I have. They've been around since the fifties I think. Good work, sweetie. Now we know where the shot was taken from."

"Bye ,Stormy, if you need anything else let me know," Linda said, disconnecting the call.

Stormy spent the next several minutes explaining to Dakota what he had just learned from Linda. He printed out the affidavit for the warrant and stood, waiting for Dakota to drain her last drop of barely warm coffee.

"Before we go to the judge I want to put out a BOLO for Dade County on the car and tag number," Stormy said.

He and Dakota walked over to the dispatch center and wrote out the BOLO for the lead. Once he heard it dispatched, they left and headed for Judge Wentworth's office. When they reached the office they were informed that the Judge was out of town until the following morning.

"I guess we'll have to return tomorrow first thing. It's a little late to find another one now," Stormy said.

At a stalemate now, no warrant and no other leads to pursue, they decided to call it a day. Normally they would stay on a case of this magnitude until all the leads were exhausted. Stormy told Dakota he would pick her up around seven the following morning so they could get a jump on meeting the Judge before her schedule got underway.

Chapter 21

An arrest

CASSIUS AND BREADMAN CRUISED AROUND North Miami in their newly acquired car. They were really enjoying the ride and the looks of envy they received from some of their friends. The radio was blasting loudly through the open windows, even though they didn't have the amp they wished was in the car. To them, louder was better. But, for now, they had to settle with what they had.

Cassius was driving and had his seat lowered as far down and back as it would go. Breadman was in the same position, his arm hanging out the open window, tapping to the rap music playing on the radio. They had just put ten gallons of gas in the tank and planned to return to their hood later in the evening.

The car would then be parked and covered in an abandoned lot next to Cassius's house, mainly so he could keep an eye on it. They would take the plates off of another junk car later and exchange them. He planned to drive the car for another few days before dumping it – he figured the spic may have reported it stolen by then. But for the moment, everything was cool and they were enjoying the ride.

Nothing else was mentioned about the fiasco earlier. Breadman was street-smart but still young and naive, also not so stupid as to push his luck with Cassius. So he kept his mouth shut.

After riding around Liberty City for an hour or so, Cassius pulled into the Shoppes of Liberty City, a small shopping center a few blocks northeast of Charles Hadley Park, and parked the car. They sat there watching the street, listening to more loud music, just killing time. They had no particular place to be, so whatever they decided to do they would do, simple as that.

A few friends pulled in and chatted with them over the course of time, asking about the car and just hanging out. Cassius was vague about the car, and soon the conversations would turn to other mundane topics. Around midnight traffic began tapering off and most of their friends were either home or in other areas hanging out. Cassius decided to head home and get the car under wraps for the night.

They hadn't gone but three blocks when suddenly the blues from a Miami police unit lit up the rear view mirror. Cassius felt his heart begin thumping harder in his chest, but he forced himself to calm down. Maybe the cops were on another call and would pass them by. Maybe they would be stopped for the loud music, although that usually didn't happen in this part of town. A short chirp of the siren was all it took to realize that they were the ones being pulled over.

Sting of the Scorpion

"What we gonna do, Cassius?" Breadman asked, attempting to mask the fear in his voice, but not succeeding.

"Just be cool Breadman, be cool," Cassius said, pulling over to the curb.

"What if the spic reported the car stolen? He probably did, you know."

"I said to be cool. It hasn't even been a day, so it's not likely been entered in their puters yet," Cassius said, pulling his driver's license from his pants pocket.

He waited for the cop to come up to the window and ask for his license. But no one was getting out of the patrol car yet, so he sat and waited patiently.

"Driver, place both of your hands out of the window," The speaker of the patrol car suddenly blared.

"What the hell, Cassius. I told you they found out it was stolen. We going to jail bro. My momma gonna kill me," Breadman said in a panic.

"Shut up, Breadman or *I'll* kill you. Just do what they ask and leave the talking to me."

Cassius held both of his hands out of the lowered window like the officer requested. He didn't want to give them any reason to shoot. Many times friends of his failed to comply with directions by the police and ended up either getting tasered or shot. Neither one appealed to Cassius, so he complied fully.

"Passenger, place your hands out of the window also. Do it now!" The speaker blared again.

"Do it, Breadman. Don't get crazy on me," Cassius said.

Breadman placed his hands out of the open window, his legs involuntarily jumping nervously.

"I think I'm going to make a run for it, Cassius," Breadman said.

"You try that and when I find you, your legs won't be able to let you run again by the time I finish with them. Stay calm man, don't be an idiot. I can handle this," Cassius said, the threat in his voice credible.

Cassius with his hands outside the window took a quick peek into the side view mirror. What he saw caused a shiver to run down his spine. Evidently this wasn't just about a possible stolen car. There were two other police units behind him and several officers standing in front of them with their guns drawn, aimed directly at him and the car.

"Driver, use your right hand and turn off the engine. Do it slowly and do it now!" The voice blared from the speaker.

Cassius complied and slowly moved his right hand inside the car, careful to not move his left. He switched off the engine and waited.

"Now driver, toss the keys out of the window."

Breadman was near the breaking point. He had never been stopped by the police before for anything this serious, and all of his punkish bravado was now gone. He fought back the tears he felt welling up because he didn't want Cassius to see him cry. It would have been a sign of weakness, and Cassius didn't tolerate weak people hanging out with him. He wanted nothing more now than to be home with his momma where he would be safe and sound. He had seen the news lately where cops were shooting black men for apparently no good reason. He viewed it with a blind eye, mostly slanted by some of the media but he knew deep inside that there was usually a valid reason for shootouts with the cops. Deep down he was a good kid and had only wanted to fit in with the gang in the hood. He realized now that taking that road wasn't going to be all it was cracked up to be. He silently promised God as he sat in the car with his hands out the window, *"Don't let me get shot and I'll go to Church with momma like she asks me to do."*

Cassius pitched the keys out of the window, hearing them land on the street with a clink. He placed his right hand back out the window and waited for further instructions, although he had watched the news and movies and knew what was coming.

"Passenger, use your left hand and please open the door slowly and then get out of the car. Stand with your back to me and with your hands clasped behind your head. Do it now and do it slowly."

Breadman was about to wet his pants, but he managed to do as instructed and soon was standing with his back to the police, his hands behind his head.

"Passenger, slowly walk backwards towards me and keep your hands where they are," the disembodied voice said.

Breadman walked backwards slowly and before he knew it a strong hand was gripping his wrists and quickly he was in handcuffs. The officer walked him over to a patrol car and made him lean over onto the trunk. The same process was relayed to Cassius, and before long the both of them were side by side, cuffed and leaning onto the trunk of a police car, legs kicked wide apart. Cassius wasn't nearly as intimidated as Breadman and said, "Officer, my driver's license is on the front seat. We haven't done anything wrong. Why are we being treated this way?"

"Son, I would advise you to keep quiet until you get to the station. This car was reported stolen and was used in a murder, so you have a serious problem," the officer said calmly.

"What murder? Stolen car? We ain't killed anyone, officer. We were given this car and were just driving around town," Cassius said earnestly.

"Son, do you realize how stupid that sounds? Someone just gave you a nice new car, for no reason at all?" the officer said laughing.

"It's the truth, officer. You've got to believe me."

"It's not my job to believe you. Like I said, wait until we get to the station and you can tell your story to the investigators," the officer said.

"Well, looky here," another officer said, standing behind the stolen car, the trunk open.

Cassius and Breadman looked up and saw the officer had taken a broken down rifle from a bag in the trunk and was holding it up for the others to see. A sergeant walked over to the rookie and admonished him for handling the weapon without rubber gloves.

"Let's hope you didn't mess up any prints on that weapon, officer. You should know better. Put it back into the bag and close the trunk. Make sure you tell the investigators you handled it, so they can eliminate your prints," the sergeant said his voice low so as to not embarrass the rookie any further. The slightly chagrined officer turned and placed the weapon back into the bag and carefully

Sting of the Scorpion

closed the trunk.

"Hey, we didn't know that was in there. Honest man, it's not ours," Cassius burst out.

The Sergeant walked over to the officer guarding the two men and said, "Take them to the station. I'll have dispatch notify Hialeah we found the car."

By now Breadman wasn't holding back the tears. Even in his limited knowledge of the law he knew they were in really big trouble. Cassius was concerned also, but he maintained a calm attitude on the outside. Inside, he was a twisted bundle of nerves. From what he heard and saw, they were facing some serious problems.

Chapter 22

Deadly confrontation

THE PHONE RANG SHRILLY, jerking San Peron awake from his horrible nightmare. He had been dreaming of his son who was holding out his hands to him, begging him to save him. About the time the phone rang his son's head suddenly exploded, drenching him in blood. He couldn't stop shaking, but in his grogginess, managed to grab the phone from its cradle.

"Who is this? It had better be important to be calling this late."

"Mister San Peron, this is Emilio Sanchez. You told me to call you when we found the man you call El Scorpion. You said no matter what time to call…"

"Yes, yes, I know what I said. Have you found him?" San Peron said suddenly sitting straight up in bed, cutting him off mid-sentence.

"No sir, well, maybe sir…" Emilio began.

"Well did you or didn't you?"

"We think we may have sir, but we can't be sure

Sting of the Scorpion

without a good description. Our sources led us to a motel in South Hialeah. The man we think is him was seen driving a rental car earlier, but it's not at the motel now. There was a light on in the room but it went out a couple of hours ago. Someone is in there, but since the car is not in the parking lot we're not sure," Emilio said.

"Is your source reliable and do you think he is there?" San Peron asked.

"The source is very reliable and I do think he is there. We questioned the manager and he said that no one else had rented the room."

"How did your source figure out who he is and where he was? The police don't even have a clue as to *who* his is," San Peron asked patiently. He didn't want innocent people killed because of a mistaken identity, but if there was any chance at all it was El Scorpion, he was going to have him taken out.

"Our source called in some favors, and he's sure that our target is at the motel."

"How many men do you have with you?" San Peron asked.

"Including me there is four of us."

"Are you armed and ready to take him out?"

"Yes sir. We will deliver his head to you if you want," Emilio said confidently.

"Then do it and do it as quietly as you can. Make sure you use silencers and bring me proof of his death. Take a camera phone with you for photos which will be enough proof for the time being."

"Yes sir. We will not fail you."

"And there's one other thing, Emilio."

"Yes sir?"

"Don't call me back with any excuse why he isn't dead. I picked you and your crew for your expertise and four of you should be able to get the job done. Just don't underestimate this man. He is a professional killer and won't go easy. Do you understand what I'm saying?" San Peron said.

"Yes sir, I understand. He is as good as dead, and you can expect photos soon."

San Peron cut the connection, climbed out of bed and walked to the kitchen. He took a bottle of water and carried it into the living room. There was no way he could go back to sleep now. He would stay awake until he heard from Emilio. Once El Scorpion was out of the way he would concentrate on how he was going to arrange for Jack Storm's death. San Peron took a sip of the cold water, a deadly smile of revenge on his face. Yes, everything was going to work out even though he would still be out one million dollars, and that truly galled him to no end.

* * * * * * * * *

The black GMC Denali slowly pulled into the parking lot of the motel, parking in a space several doors down from the room the target supposedly was in. They had cut the headlights as they pulled in to avoid any chance of alerting the Scorpion that someone was arriving this time of the morning. The angle they had to enter the parking lot from the street would have allowed the headlights to splay over the windows of the motel rooms.

These men were highly skilled, deadly and without

being overconfident, sure of the outcome of what they were being paid to do. They planned to deliver photos of the dead target to Mister San Peron, collect their sizable compensation for the job and go their separate ways until another job came up. They were dressed in all dark clothing, their faces smudged with black make-up and weapons affixed with silencers.

Inside the dark motel room, Victor had pulled up a chair to the window. He was having trouble sleeping, which wasn't unusual for him after a hit. He usually needed at least a full day for the adrenalin rush to subside. At this moment he regretted having given up smoking two years ago. These were the times he really missed it and if a pack had been available he would probably have relapsed this time. He had been staring out the slightly parted curtains for an hour when he saw the black Denali pull into the parking lot, the headlights turned off. Alarms immediately went off in his head. It wasn't a police vehicle, of that he was sure. But who was it? He instinctively knew they were there for him and not just coming for a friendly visit to someone else.

He only had to wait about thirty seconds before he saw the doors open and four men in black clothing exit the vehicle, all holding something in their hands. The dim glow from the street light on the corner caused a brief glint on one of the objects in one man's hand, evidently a weapon with a nickel finish. It was an amateurish mistake for any gunman to make when operating in the dark.

Victor sprang into action. He already had his pants on so within seconds he put his shoes and shirt on and had his Beretta out with a round chambered. He grabbed the extra magazine from the nightstand and stuck it in his rear pocket. He ran to the bathroom to see if by any remote chance there was a window and wasn't overly surprised to see none available.

Realizing he would have to make his stand here he quickly pulled the covers back on the bed, placed several pillows lengthwise in the center and pulled the covers up over them. In the dark they should pass for someone sleeping in the bed, or at least he hoped so.

His main advantage was that he had been fortunate enough to have seen them pull into the lot, giving him extra precious minutes to prepare for their arrival. The deadbolt was on and the flimsy chain was attached to the door jamb. These men looked like pros and he knew that the door would be breeched very quickly. They had no idea he would be waiting for them and he wanted to stall their entry for as long as possible, allowing him time to prepare for their arrival. The optimum advantage would be if they were all inside the room at once, but he knew that possibly wouldn't happen since they looked as if they knew what they were doing.

The men spread out in pairs and began walking stealthily from both directions, the plan being to reach the door to the room at the same time. A door at the end of the motel suddenly opened and a couple stepped out, laughing and obviously drinking. All four of the men stopped and watched intently, waiting to see if they would have to take action. Mister San Peron had insisted that no innocents be harmed, so every effort to abide his wishes was made. The couple totally ignored them, even after seeing one of the men from three feet away. They contin-

Sting of the Scorpion

ued on to a car near the door, got in and drove away. The man known as Emilio looked at the others and nodded, everyone continuing on to the room where the man they were hunting should be located and sound asleep.

Victor was running out of time and he knew it. He quickly took the desk, brushed everything off of it and turned it up on its end near the bathroom. It wouldn't afford very much protection from the bullets he knew could be coming, but it was all he had to use for cover now. His eyes were adjusted to the darkness of the room and he knew that the men outside would be at a slight disadvantage when they entered the dark room, even though they were in the dark outside. He took up station behind the upended desk with his 9mm leveled over the top of it, his aim at the center of the door. He knew it would only be a matter of seconds now before they tried to enter the room.

Emilio and the rest of the men reached the door at the same time, a well practiced move they had used many times before. Emilio took out the pass key he had convinced the clerk to give him an hour earlier. He was a master at veiled threats, but it hardly took any convincing at all. Two men leaned against the wall and one stood behind Emilio as he inserted the key card. There was a very soft click as the lock disengaged and Emilio slowly turned the door handle. The door inched open then suddenly stopped when the chain latch caught. Emilio had expected that would probably happen and immediately shoved his shoulder into the door, wrenching the chain off the door jamb.

All four men rushed into the room. Seeing the figure

on the bed, they opened fire, the silenced guns making muffled burping noises and the figure on the bed jumping with every hit. They emptied their guns and then began walking towards the bed. That's when all hell broke loose.

Victor's eyes were slightly more adjusted to the darkness of the room so he could distinguish all four of the men, two of them silhouetted against the open door. He stood and in rapid succession fired four rounds, the noise deafening in the small room. He didn't have the luxury of a silencer as they did but he wasn't concerned about the noise. He didn't plan to hang around when this threat was eliminated.

Three of the rounds were well placed head shots, the men dead before they hit the floor, their weapons falling from lifeless hands onto the carpeted floor. The fourth shot was deliberately placed in the upper leg of the last man. He wanted to question him before leaving the motel. He was fairly sure he knew who put the hit out on him but needed to be certain. He walked from behind the upturned desk and swiftly strode to the man on the floor that was clutching his leg and trying to reload his weapon with one hand. Victor stepped on the wounded leg, causing the man to drop the gun and clip, screaming in pain.

"You made a fatal mistake, my friend," Victor said, looking down at the man.

"Screw you. Your life won't be worth a plugged nickel now," the man said through gritted teeth.

"I'm a man of my word. Tell me what I want to know and I'll walk out of this room, and you'll still be alive. Who sent you?" Victor asked, his 9mm unwavering in his hand as it pointed at the man's head.

"If I tell you that you may as well shoot me now because I'll be a dead man anyway," the man said.

"What's your name, I like to know who I'm dealing with and may have to kill."

"Emilio, my name's Emilio," the man reluctantly spat out.

"Emilio, as I said before, I'm a man of my word. I have nothing to lose by shooting you in the head right now, but if you give me the name, I promise you I will let you live. Otherwise you should start praying to God if you need to. How you avoid getting killed by your boss or anyone else is your problem, not mine. This is the last time I'll ask since I need to get out of here. What is the name?"

Emilio was in severe pain and took several precious seconds to think before divulging the name. He knew that San Peron wasn't a man to cross, but he could come up with a story to protect himself. After all, his men were dead and couldn't contradict anything he said.

"San Perón, Antonio San Perón," Emilio said in almost a whisper.

"A little louder, Emilio. I didn't catch that."

"Antonio San Peron is his name," Emilio said a little louder. "Are you going to shoot me now?"

"Nope, I told you, I'm a man of my word. You just need to figure out what you're going to tell the police when they get here. Who has the keys to your car?" Victor said, pressing the gun to Emilio's forehead for emphasis.

Turning his head slowly and carefully Emilio pointed

to the body nearest him. Victor stepped over to the dead man and rifled his front pockets, finding the GMC key ring. Without looking back at Emilio, Victor stood and walked out of the room, leaving the carnage behind. He could hear sirens wailing in the distance so he sprinted to the GMC. Once he was inside he started the engine and drove away in the opposite direction the sirens were coming from.

Emilio painfully crawled from the room as quickly as he could, managing to lift himself upright by holding onto the outside wall. He could hear the sirens getting closer and made his way to the end of the motel as fast as he could hobble. Before the first police unit arrived he was almost a half a block away. He hoped that none of those units were K9.

Chapter 23

The interview

THE PHONE RANG LOUDLY SEVERAL TIMES before Stormy was awake enough to answer it. Fumbling with the receiver and looking at his watch, he said in a gruff voice, "It's two in the morning, so this had better be good."

"Alright, Stormy, rise and shine. We have some work to do," Dakota said, her voice cheerier than it should have been at this time of the morning.

"Dakota, don't you ever go to bed?" Stormy said, pushing the covers back as Shaunie turned a sleepy eye to him with a questioning look. He motioned for her to go back to sleep as he swung his legs around and sat up on the side of the bed. He had fallen asleep with his arm curled under his head and now he tried to shake out the stiffness. Running his fingers through his hair, he asked, "What's going on?"

"A couple of Miami officers stopped the car we ran the BOLO on and made an arrest," she responded.

"Why didn't you say so? I'll pick you up in thirty minutes. Are we going to Miami P.D. or to the Dade County jail?"

"They're holding them at the Miami Detective Bureau and waiting for us."

"They're holding 'them'? What do you mean them…oh, never mind, I'll be there shortly. Be ready," Stormy said.

"Be ready?" Stormy, I am ready. They called twenty minutes ago," Dakota said with a laugh.

"Alright, give me a few…on my way."

Stormy hung up the phone and headed for the bathroom. He took a quick shower, snatched a shirt and some pants off the rack in the closet and dressed quickly. Shaunie sat up and asked him what was going on. He told her that they had a break in the case and to go back to sleep, that he would call her later in the morning. Used to his being called out in the middle of the night, she lay back down, and within fifteen seconds was softly snoring.

It took forty-five minutes before Stormy pulled up in front of Dakota's house and tapped the horn. She walked out the door and as she entered the car looked at her watch with a grin.

"Thirty minutes, huh?"

"It took me a little longer to wake up. So they arrested two in the car?"

"Yep, and that's not all. They found a sniper rifle, scope and all, in the trunk," Dakota said.

"Something's not kosher here. What would they be doing out riding around and not hiding if they had just killed a public figure," Stormy said, the gears turning in his head.

"I was thinking the same thing. We'll see when we get there and start questioning them," she said.

* * * * * * * * *

After parking in the rear parking lot at Miami P.D., they were granted entry through the back door after Stormy presented his I.D. to the camera. A police officer with his hand lightly resting on the butt of his weapon stood just inside the door. He double-checked the I.D. of both before allowing them to proceed further. Stormy had never seen this officer before but couldn't fault the security at this time of the morning.

"You know the way to the Bureau?" he asked.

"Yep, we've been here a few times. I believe they're waiting for us upstairs," Stormy said politely.

"Yeah, they've been here for a couple of hours now. It seems as if they've made a big arrest, some sniper or something. Hang on and I'll walk you to the elevator," The officer said, turning and walking away. Stormy knew the way by heart but said nothing, just smiled and followed the officer.

When Stormy and Dakota stepped off the elevator, they noticed a beehive of activity, probably unusual for this time of the morning.

"Stormy, Dakota, over here," a familiar voice called out.

"Hey Leo. They got you up too, huh?" Stormy said, smiling at his friend.

Leo Sharp had been wounded on an anchored freighter when they had cornered Rolando several months earlier. The ensuing shootout had left Leo severely wounded. Rolando fell off the freighter into the Miami River after being shot by Stormy. His body wasn't found, but a few months later he was found dead in a room in the French Quarter in New Orleans. It was ruled a heart attack but even though Stormy knew better, he had never said anything.

"Haven't seen you since the wedding, pal. Whatcha been up to?" Leo asked.

"I guess you don't follow the news too much Leo," Stormy said grinning.

"Oh, you mean that little bank robbery thing." Leo said, teasing Stormy.

"Oh, you do follow the news. Did you read about that million dollar reward I received from the bank?"

"Give me a break, Stormy. I definitely would have heard about that," Leo said laughing.

"What do we have here, Leo?" Stormy asked, turning the conversation serious now.

"A couple of our uniforms found the car you put the BOLO out on and made an arrest. In fact there were two arrests."

"Where did this take place?" Dakota asked.

"Over in Liberty City. They were just driving down the street, music blaring, you know, cruising."

"What's this I hear about the gun in the trunk?" Stormy interjected.

"There was a bag, like a piece of luggage, and inside was a sniper rifle and tripod," Leo said as they walked to the rear of the office.

Sting of the Scorpion

"Can we see the weapon, Leo?" Dakota asked.

"Sure thing, Dakota, It's in my office. They called me in once they connected everything with the shooting of the Mayor. I met him a couple of times before and he was a genuinely nice person," Leo said as he entered his office.

"Was the weapon dusted for prints yet?" Stormy asked before he lifted the weapon from the bag.

"Yeah, but nothing was found. Both the rifle and tripod was evidently wiped clean before being placed in the bag."

"How about the bag, did they try for prints on it? I know it's hard to print some materials, but this seems like a vinyl of some type," Dakota asked.

"I don't think they attempted to dust it. As you said, usually they consider it a waste of time."

"Maybe you can get them to try the old 'super glue' trick…you never know!" Stormy said.

"I'll have them try. But don't forget, the officers brought it in carrying it in by hand."

"If you do find anything, we'll just eliminate the officer's prints," Stormy said, a little disturbed that the officers had picked up the bag, possibly contaminating it with their prints.

Stormy asked for some rubber gloves and when they were brought in, he slipped them on before hefting the rifle from the bag. He was somewhat surprised at how much it weighed. Guessing correctly, it wasn't one of the new models with the hard plastic stock. As he carefully looked over the weapon, an idea clicked in his head.

"Leo, I would like for your tech to do a scrape on the

209

lens of the scope. If the shooter didn't think about wiping it clean, we may be able to get some DNA."

"I'll take care of it. Now I see why you're the hot shot investigator," Leo said in jest.

"Are you holding the arrestees here or at the DCJ?

"I knew you'd be coming, so I kept them here in interrogation. They've been kept separated since transport and they haven't been processed yet," Leo said. "You want to talk with them now?"

"Yeah, I'm ready. You want to sit in with us?"

"I think I'll pass this time. It's a Hialeah case, and I don't need to be subpoenaed on this one," Leo said.

He led them to one of the interrogation rooms and after letting them in, he closed the door and left. They observed a kid sitting at the interview table when they entered and noticed he was dressed like a gang-banger. Stormy and Dakota took a seat on the opposite side of the table and took out their recorders and legal pads before looking at the kid. His ankles were cuffed, and he looked as if he had been crying, his eyes puffy and bloodshot.

After advising him of their names Dakota asked, "What's your name, son?"

"They call me Breadman, but my real name is Wesley, Wesley S. Johnson, mam."

"Wesley, what does the S. stand for?" Stormy asked.

"It's Shirley, sir, but I don't use it. My friends would make fun of me if they knew," Wesley said in a lowered voice, slightly embarrassed.

"There's nothing wrong with the name Shirley. I had a good friend in the Army whose name was Shirley, and he wore it proudly. You want to know why?" Stormy said, making an attempt to put the kid at ease and temper his embarrassment some.

"No sir, why was he proud of his name?"

"Because it was the name his parents gave him, a name they took from the bible. He never tried to hide his name even though he could have."

"I didn't know it was a biblical name, sir. My mother liked that name, but she never told me why she named me that."

"Do yourself a favor Wesley and wear your name with pride. Honor your mother by doing so since she saw fit to bestow you with that name," Stormy said compassionately.

"Yes sir. I believe I will, yes, I believe I will," Wesley said, sounding sincere.

"Now Wesley, I have to read your Miranda rights before I can talk with you. Do you understand what those rights are?"

"Yes sir, I do. I have had them read to me before."

Without asking why he had been arrested before, something he would find out when he went over the rap sheet, Stormy read him his rights and then had him sign the paper copy.

"Before we start can I get you something to drink, a soda, or maybe some water?" Dakota asked.

"No, mam, I'm fine. Thank you though," Wesley said.

Stormy was baffled by the politeness exhibited by this young man. His appearance didn't fit what he was hearing. It seemed as if Wesley was an imposter, playing at being a gang-banger. His diction wasn't perfect but better than most he heard in that area.

"Wesley, why did you and your friend shoot that man in Hialeah?" Stormy suddenly asked, going for the shock value intentionally.

"We didn't shoot anyone. Honest. We didn't shoot a soul," Wesley exclaimed.

"Where did you get the gun we found in the trunk?"

"That's not ours. We never even looked in the trunk. The car isn't even ours, detective," Wesley said.

"Then whose car is it?" Dakota asked.

"There was a man, a Latino, I think, over in the hood. He parked the car and then started a fight with me and Cassius," Wesley said. "He gave us the car...said we could have it."

"What do you mean he started a fight? And why would he just give you his car?"

"We asked him for some cash and he started fighting us. Honest, then he told us we could have the car," Wesley said, leaving out some of the details of the fight.

"You think you can describe that man for us, Wesley?" Dakota asked.

"Yes mam, I can."

"Your cooperation is really appreciated and won't go unnoticed," Dakota responded.

"We are going to send in a sketch artist and he will lead you through the process. Just do everything he asks and hopefully we will be able to get a decent rendering. It will go a long way in validating your story, Wesley," Stormy said.

"Yes sir, I will do all I can to help. I ain't killed anyone, never have and never will."

Stormy and Dakota left the room and advised Leo that

they needed a sketch artist. He told them he would make the arrangements.

"Do you want to talk with the other subject now?" Leo asked.

"Yeah, we need to see how his story stacks up with the one Wesley just gave us. Give me his rap sheet and show us the way."

Leo made the call to have an artist come to the Detective Bureau and then he handed Stormy the records printout on the other prisoner. Stormy and Dakota sat at a desk for several minutes as they perused the rap sheet, taking note of the arrests and charges. Cassius Jermaine Croaker was a black male, twenty-four years of age and strangely enough, had only two arrests. One was for shoplifting when he was seventeen and the other for vandalism and criminal mischief around the same time. He was placed on probation for both offenses and had been a model citizen every since, or smart enough to not get caught again.

"Mr. Croaker, I'm Detective Jack Storm and this is my partner, Detective Dakota Summers. We have a few questions to ask but first we need to advise you of your Miranda rights."

After reciting the Miranda rights verbatim and having Cassius sign the form acknowledging he understood, Dakota took the paperwork and placed it into a folder. Stormy stared Cassius in the eyes until Cassius finally averted his gaze. Stormy realized that this guy was going to be difficult to get anything out of and once he asked for an attorney, the questioning was over, just like that. He had to be careful in his line of questioning and try to not

Earl Underwood

push Cassius to the point he would clam up and ask for counsel.

"Is there anything I can get for you, Mr. Croaker? Maybe something to drink, we can probably drum up a cold soda for you," Stormy started.

"No, I'm fine. Ask your questions."

Stormy laughed and said, "Right to the point. I like that."

"We would just like to know where you got the gun we found in your trunk."

"It's not my gun and once you print it you'll know I haven't touched it," Cassius replied, a knowing smile on his face.

"If it's not your gun, how did it get in the trunk of your car?" Dakota asked.

"If you detectives have done your homework, and I suspect you have, you know it's not my car," Cassius said with a smirk.

"You care to tell us who the car belongs to if it isn't yours?"

"If I told you, I don't think you would believe me," Cassius said.

"Try us!" Dakota said.

"Would you believe that someone just gave it to me?"

"Could you be a little more specific? Who gave it to you, and why?" Stormy asked.

"We had this little misunderstanding with a white guy, Latin I think, and he told us we could have the car."

"Misunderstanding, huh? What kind of misunderstanding?" Dakota asked.

"We asked him what he was doing in our hood, and he

started fighting us. When we got the best of him, he told us to take the car, that we could have it."

"Just like that he gave you his car. Really, Cassius, come on. You can do better than that," Stormy said with a chuckle.

"I told you that you wouldn't believe me, but it's the truth."

"One last thing, Cassius. Were you ever in the Service – Army, Navy, Marines?" Dakota asked.

"You're kidding, right? No way I would up and join the military. Not my game, man," Cassius said with disdain.

"Can you describe this man for us? If I sent in a sketch artist, would you be willing to give a description of him. It would go a long way in convincing us that he gave you the car."

"Sure, send the artist in. I can give a good description of him," Cassius said, leaning back in his chair.

As Stormy and Dakota walked out of the room, Leo walked up to them and asked, "Can you nail it on them?"

"Leo, do you really think those two amateurs could pull off something as complicated as an assassination on a public figure? Plus, there's no way they are competent or skilled enough to use a sniper rifle, in my opinion. The older one has never even been in the Service, so he hasn't had any extensive firearm training."

"I had my doubts when I saw who they arrested. How do you suppose they got the gun?" Leo asked.

"The car is a rental and hasn't been reported stolen yet. But that said, it's possible they stole the car and didn't know the weapon was in the trunk. Once we get the forensic artist in and he is finished, the only thing you have to hold them on is possession of a deadly weapon. Maybe unauthorized use of a vehicle, but I don't think any of that will hold up in court, if it gets that far. The younger kid is scared to death, and he seems like a decent kid. We can tack on the charges and at least hold them for awhile so we can do some more investigating. I'm anxious to see the sketch, and we will need to get it out as quickly as possible to all units in Dade County, maybe even the state," Stormy said.

Stormy and Dakota sat and chatted with Leo for almost an hour before the forensic sketch artist came into the squad room. He took a seat at an adjacent desk and spread out the two sketches. Leo, Stormy and Dakota stood and looked down at the renderings.

"He appears to be of Latin descent based on his features. That sizable scar above his eye will be a big help also," Dakota said.

"I'm looking at the remarkable resemblance between the two of them. Both subjects gave almost the same description, down to the scar, which is highly unusual," Stormy said, still comparing the pictures. "Leo, if you will have copies made for me, I would appreciate it."

Leo called over a young detective and handing him the sketches ask him to make laser copies for Stormy. He took the sketches and headed for the laser copy machine. He quickly returned and handed the copies to Stormy, who nodded his thanks.

"Kudos to the artist, it's a great lifelike sketch," Dakota said, nodding to the artist. The artist smiled and nodded back, appreciating the compliment.

"It's almost six a.m., so we'll take the copies back to Hialeah and get them out on a BOLO for all of Dade and South Florida before shift change. I really appreciate the help Leo. We should get together for drinks one night soon," Stormy said, shaking Leo's hand. Leo agreed and promised to set up a date soon. He gave Dakota a hug as she and Stormy left the squad room heading for the parking lot.

On the way down the elevator Stormy looked at the sketches intensely, committing the images to memory.

Chapter 24

Chance meeting

VICTOR DROVE AIMLESSLY ALL AROUND the south Miami area in the newly acquired GMC Denali, glad the gas tank was almost full. He wasn't too worried about the car being reported stolen, not yet at least. Three of the occupants were dead and the other wounded and either arrested or on the run. After the shootout in his motel room, he had to leave in hurry to avoid the police who were coming fast. He did manage to grab his small tote bag of clothing on the way out. Since he had nowhere he could go, he just drove around while he considered what he would do next.

He now knew the name of the client, and also knew he would have to take care of him eventually. He had no doubt another hit team would be coming in search of him. He could actually understand why the client was upset. After all, he had missed the target, and the client was out one million dollars. What the client didn't know was that Victor intended to finish the job, but he had no way of telling him.

Therefore, the only way he could take the heat off and track down the target was to find the client first. It would be difficult enough without having to continuously look over his shoulder for San Peron's men. Even with San Peron out of the way he still intended to finish the job of killing the target, Jack Storm. It was a matter of professional pride!

Victor finally made a decision. He would return to Hialeah and find out about this San Peron and where he lived. He still had a substantial amount of cash in his money belt, so he would find a decent motel and use the phone book first. It would be a start but he doubted he would find San Peron in the phone book. If not he would hit the public library later in the morning. Daylight was just breaking as he used the on ramp from Northwest 54th Street to get onto I-95 northbound. His GPS told him he could exit onto Northwest 103rd Street and shoot straight into Hialeah. He merged onto I-95 heading northbound and paced his speed with the flow of traffic which was fairly light this time of the morning.

* * * * * * * * * *

While Victor was merging with traffic, Stormy and Dakota, already on I-95, slowed for him, allowing the Denali to merge into traffic. They had decided to use this route and exit onto Northwest 103rd Street also, heading back to the Hialeah Detective Bureau. Dakota was still looking at the sketch when Stormy pulled around and alongside the black GMC. Traffic was already beginning to back up somewhat as commuters began their daily trek to work.

She looked up from the sketch for a minute and glanced over at the car next to them. At first she thought she was seeing things, but a second glance stunned her. She saw the driver of the GMC casually look her way, and she knew he had seen her reaction. Turning her head forward she slowly reached over and tapped Stormy on the leg. When he didn't immediately respond, she tapped a little harder.

"What is it, Dakota?" he asked without turning his head.

"You're not going to believe this. The guy in the car next to us looks like the sketch, exactly like it," she said with her lips hardly moving.

Stormy was astute enough to not lean over and stare at the driver next to him. He slowed the car until he had dropped back several feet, allowing him the opportunity to see the driver. He was at an angle that didn't afford him a full facial view, but it was enough for him to see a resemblance. He inched the car forward until he was able to get a better view. The man looked over again and from the look on his face Stormy could tell that he was about to flee. Dakota was right – the man was a dead ringer for the sketch.

Victor recognized the woman in the car next to him. She had been the one he saw through the scope just before he took the shot that killed the wrong man. He immediately knew from the look on her face that she had somehow recognized him. His mind was racing as he tried to figure out how she had recognized him.

Sting of the Scorpion

He knew he had to get ahead of them in the traffic and make a quick exit. The car ahead of him had moved forward enough to allow him to surge forward and jump into an open space in front of the car ahead. He floored the accelerator and swiftly moved into the open space, putting a car between him and the other one. Traffic was beginning to move faster now, reaching speeds of about fifty miles an hour.

Out of the passenger side view mirror he watched as the gray Charger suddenly swung into the lane he had just vacated. He knew he had to take action quickly if he stood any chance at all of getting away. He pulled the 9mm from his waist band and placed it on the passenger's seat for quick access. He maintained the fifty plus miles per hour speed as he watched the charger pick up speed, closing in on him fast.

When the car was parallel to his, he glanced over and saw that the driver, his original target of all people, was staring hard at him. He reached over and quickly raising the 9mm aimed it at the driver, Jack Storm. Stormy had reacted to the arm rising and slacked off the gas instantly, his car dropping back out of the line of fire.

* * * * * * * * * *

Stormy watched as the suspect sped up and put another car between them. Seeing an opening in the right lane he quickly pulled over into it and sped up in an attempt to catch the GMC. As he pulled even with the car he looked over and saw the driver turn to him and raise his arm once again, a weapon in his hand now. Quickly lifting his foot from the accelerator pedal once again, his car dropped back but not before several bullets struck the drivers windshield and the hood of the Charger.

Pulling his own weapon and yelling for Dakota to call for back up, he sped up again. As he pulled up alongside the back door of the GMC it happened. The car veered sharply, crashing into him, effectively forcing him off the road. Dakota screamed as the Charger went over and down the embankment, causing it to roll several times. It finally came to a rest upside down at the foot of the embankment, half on the side road below.

Stormy was stunned from his head slamming into the door jamb as it rolled. He looked over to see if Dakota was okay and through blurry vision saw that she was bleeding profusely from her head, her eyes closed and her body hanging limp from the seat belt. Stormy could feel himself drifting towards unconsciousness while hearing the dispatcher persistently calling his unit number in the background...then, blackness.

* * * * * * * * * *

Victor could see the car rolling down the embankment, dirt and dust swirling in the air, cars already slamming on their brakes and stopping. He couldn't tell if any of his rounds had hit Storm or not. Although the drop down the embankment was substantial, maybe twenty or thirty feet, he doubted it would cause much more than minor injuries or possibly some broken bones. He couldn't take the time to worry about that now. Too many people had witnessed what happened and someone was bound to give a description of the GMC, if not the tag number.

His exit onto 103rd Street was coming up soon, and he figured he would be in Hialeah before any witnesses could be interviewed. He would ditch the car there and find another one somehow.

In the past he had found that attempting to lose a car in a shopping center did not usually work. It was the first place patrol units now looked after getting a BOLO. What he had discovered that *did* work, and this was from past experience, was dumping a car in a public parking garage, preferably a multi-storied one.

A day before he had taken that fateful shot he had driven around Hialeah to get his bearings, preparing a route to Miami International airport. He had driven past a casino in the center of Hialeah, so he knew where he needed to go. Before long he was westbound on Northwest 103rd Street, wending his way through the morning traffic, careful to not speed. He kept an eye peeled for any undue interest in him or the GMC. He crossed the city limits of Hialeah and upon reaching Palm Avenue, headed south to the Hialeah Race Track and Casino he had seen only a few days earlier.

Soon he arrived and turned into the casino, quickly spotting the parking garage. Driving almost to the top floor, he found a space between two cars near the center of the crowded garage and deftly backed the Denali in. After thoroughly wiping the car down to erase his prints, he walked to the elevator, his footfall echoing in the vast garage.

He avoided looking directly at the security cameras

that were prominent on every row by keeping his head lowered. He discreetly shielded his face without appearing to do so deliberately by cupping his hand to his ear as if he were talking on a cell phone.

Victor went down to the ground floor using the stairway at the end of the garage. The security cameras in the elevators were highly sophisticated, so he wasn't going to take any chances that he would be filmed and leave video evidence that he had been there. He began walking back the direction he had just come from, north on Palm Avenue.

He hailed a taxi that was stopped at a traffic light further up Palm Avenue and climbed into the back seat, telling the driver to take him to the Hialeah Inn. He had a feeling that the local police would now believe he had fled the city, or at least he hoped so. He didn't think they would consider there was any possibility that he would return so close to the scene of the crime.

Then it struck him! He had forgotten to retrieve the spent shell casings from the car. In his haste to dump the car he had failed to remember firing the gun, leaving the casings to fly about the car. It would be too much of a risk to go back for them now. He was aware he was making many mistakes on this mission, and it was beginning to worry him somewhat.

Victor registered at the Hialeah Inn using his false identification. He took his key card and went around to the rear of the building to his room. He had insisted on a ground floor room even though the clerk, a young girl in her late teens, had attempted to give him a room on the second floor. It was a moment she would probably remember if ever questioned, but he had a policy of taking ground floors for good reason. If he had to suddenly flee he didn't want to have to worry about jumping from an upper floor. His ability to flee unhindered by limitations was worth taking the chance of standing out to the clerk.

Victor checked the room over and after closing the door, he walked across the street to the mall, hoping to find a drug store available. He needed toiletries and a new shirt. He wanted to change his appearance. He also decided to dye his hair a little lighter. He couldn't make the change too drastic since his passport would reflect the difference in his appearance.

Once he made his purchases he grabbed some fast food and returned to his room to begin the preparations of changing his hair color. Once he was finished he would start thumbing through the massive phone book lying on the desk. He needed to find San Peron soon, but if he couldn't, he would just have to keep an eye out while he tracked down Storm, if he hadn't died in the car crash. He would check the nightly local news later.

Chapter 25

Unsettling news

STORMY REGAINED CONSCIOUSNESS in the emergency room at Miami General Hospital. He and Dakota had been taken there by ambulance after their car had gone over the embankment on I-95. Slowly everything began to come back to him. He and Dakota had been heading back to Hialeah and had spotted *El Scorpion* in a car next to his on the interstate. He remembered the Scorpion firing a weapon at him and then ramming his car, causing him to lose control and go over the embankment. Suddenly he remembered seeing Dakota, hanging upside down, bleeding profusely from her head, her eyes closed. With a feeling of dread he yelled at a nurse walking past.

"Yes, Mr. Storm, do you need the doctor?"

"No, I want to know how my partner is. Is she okay?" Stormy asked the concern evident in his voice.

"You just lay back and rest, Mr. Storm. The doctor will be in shortly," The nurse replied.

"Lady, if you don't answer my question right now, I'll

get off this bed and go look for her myself. Do you understand?" Stormy said, his concern for Dakota outweighing his common sense at the moment.

"I'll go get the doctor for you," the nurse replied brusquely.

As she turned and walked from the room, Stormy sat up, wondering why he had an IV in his arm. Just as he attempted to swing his legs off the bed, Captain Paradis walked into the room.

"Stormy, don't even think about it. The doctor told me you had a mild concussion and that he would be in soon."

Stormy reluctantly pulled his legs back onto the bed and looked at the Captain.

"What about Dakota? They won't tell me anything. Have you heard anything at all about her condition, Captain?" Stormy asked quietly, preparing for the worst.

"The doctor said they were monitoring her carefully. She also suffered a possible concussion, plus a deep laceration on her head causing some blood loss. She'll be fine Stormy. Now, relax and tell me what happened," Captain Paradis said, taking a seat next to the bed.

Stormy spent the next several minutes going over everything that had happened since he and Dakota had received the call from the Miami Police Department Detective Bureau. He began to wrap up by explaining how Dakota had spotted the Scorpion in traffic next to them at the same time she was looking at the sketches. That's when the Scorpion fired shots at them and then forced their car off the road. Before Stormy could say any more, the doctor walked into the room with Stormy's nurse in tow.

"Detective Storm, I hear you've been giving my nurse

a hard time," he said half jokingly with a smile on his face.

"I would like to apologize to her for my behavior, doc. I was totally out of hand, but I was also really concerned for my partner. I know it's no excuse, but please accept my apology," Stormy said, extending an olive branch to the nurse. She smiled at Stormy and told him she understood and that she accepted the apology.

"Well, I have some good news, Detective Storm. If you will rest here for a few hours I can release you, barring any unexpected developments. The concussion is mild enough that you may only experience a headache. We just want to monitor you for a few hours to make sure. You have no broken bones, although I'm somewhat surprised from what I heard happened. You will have some contusions, but they aren't severe. Just rest and don't give the staff a hard time," the doctor said laughing.

"No problem, doc. What about my partner? Is she going to be alright?"

"She didn't fare as well as you, Detective. Her concussion is a little more severe than yours and the laceration required about a dozen stitches. She put up quite a fuss when we attempted to shave her hair from around the cut. Also, she has two cracked ribs, probably from the seatbelt. Luckily, both of you were wearing them or it could have been a lot worse than it was," the doctor said.

"When can she be released?" Stormy asked.

"Not for at least a day. She needs plenty of bed rest and twenty-four hour monitoring for the concussion. I have instructed my nurse to keep you updated while you are here in case something changes," the doctor replied.

Sting of the Scorpion

"If there are no further questions I need to make my rounds."

"No, and thanks, doctor. I really appreciate it," Stormy said.

As the doctor left the room, his nurse tagging behind, Stormy's cell phone began chirping from his pants on the chair next to the wall. He asked the Captain to hand it to him, thinking it was Shaunie calling.

"Hello, this is Detective Storm," he answered.

Stormy listened quietly to the caller for a minute before thanking him and hanging up the phone.

"That was Pablo, Captain. He did some more digging and came up with some pertinent information on *El Scorpion*. It seems we have a little twist in the Mayor's assassination. He was not the intended target!" Stormy said.

"Then who *was* the target?" The Captain asked.

"It seems as if it was *me*. *El Scorpion* missed me and hit the Mayor by accident."

"*You* were the intended target?" The Captain asked in bewilderment.

"Yes, and I think I know why. This has just become personal, very personal," Stormy replied.

"You want me to call Shaunie?" Captain Paradis asked.

"If you don't mind, I would appreciate it. Tell her about the accident if she hasn't already seen it on the news, but let's not mention me being the Scorpion's target, not just yet."

Armed with the news that Stormy was a target for assassination, Captain Paradis made arrangements for the Miami Police Department to place two guards at the door.

229

As a precaution he also had an officer standing at the door of Dakota's room. Stormy protested, but it was in vain as Captain Paradis was determined to protect his people at all costs.

Shaunie called Stormy's cell within minutes of talking with Captain Paradis and was assured by Stormy that he was okay, just a little bruised. He talked her out of coming to the hospital explaining to her that he would be released in an hour or two. True to his word, the doctor returned to Stormy's room an hour after he had left.

"I'm releasing you, Detective Storm, but I would prefer that you go home and rest for the remainder of the day. I know you're not going to do that but I have to say it anyhow," the doctor said.

"I'll be fine, doctor, but I would like to see my partner, if it's okay with you," Stormy replied.

"She's awake, although a little groggy, so I guess it will be okay if you only stay for a few minutes."

"I just want to speak with her a few minutes, and then I'll leave her to rest. Thanks doctor, I appreciate all you've done for us," Stormy said.

After the doctor left the room, Stormy climbed off the bed and dressed. Looking in the mirror over the sink, the image looking back at him was one of a bruised and banged up man. He had been lucky and although banged up, he felt fine. He walked gingerly, with Captain Paradis down to Dakota's room. When they entered the room she was sitting up in bed, propped by several pillows behind her back. She didn't look happy at all with the situation and said so when they walked into the room.

"Hey, Stormy, you look a little rough. Hello, Captain

Paradis. Can we get out of this place? I'm tired of getting poked, prodded and stuck with needles," Dakota said, swinging her legs off the bed.

"Whoa, hold on there a minute, Dakota," Captain Paradis said holding up his hand. "The good news is you're gonna live. The bad news is that you will have to stay overnight. No objections, that's the way it's going to be."

"But I feel fine, Captain. I really want to get out of here."

"Sorry, Dakota. The doctor said you really have to stay for observation overnight."

"Man that really sucks! Why is there a Miami police officer at my door? Am I under arrest or is there something I don't know about?" Dakota said, pointing at the officer standing outside the door.

Captain Paradis looked over at Stormy, allowing him to explain the situation to Dakota. After explaining everything he ended by telling her that he had been the Scorpion's target, not the Mayor. That was the reason they were forced off the road. *El Scorpion* had recognized Stormy about the same time Dakota recognized him.

"Wow, Stormy, what are you going to do?" Dakota said in disbelief.

"First we have to find out where he is and then we're going to take him down," Stormy replied with a slight smile. "I have a feeling he's not through with me yet if he thinks I'm still alive and kicking. That means he'll come looking for me, but I'll be expecting him this time."

"I'm coming with you," Dakota said, swinging her legs over the side of her bed.

"Whoa! Hold on Dakota, hold on a minute," Captain

Paradis said, "You're not going anywhere and that's an order. The doctor said you were to stay here, and that's exactly what you're going to do."

"But Captain...," she started.

"No *buts* this time, Dakota. Stormy can pick you up tomorrow once the doctor releases you."

Dakota looked from the Captain to Stormy, frustration causing her to tremble. Slowly she put her legs back on the bed, crossed her arms and looked away with an exaggerated pout.

"Dakota, relax. I'll be here in the morning for you. Nothing's going to happen before then, so get some rest and I'll be back," Stormy said.

"You had better, Jack Storm. I owe that low life a little something too."

Stormy and the Captain left Dakota stewing a little. After collecting Stormy's personal property, they left the hospital for Hialeah. Stormy was in need of a new ride.

Chapter 26

Lies can kill you

"**WHAT THE HELL DO YOU MEAN HE GOT AWAY?**" San Peron shouted at Emilio. "There were four of you, FOUR, and only one of him, and yet he got away? You had better have one good explanation, mister."

Emilio stood silently as San Peron yelled and ranted. He had made good use of his time on the way to San Peron's house to come up with a plausible story. He had briefly considered not returning at all, but instead leaving town for good. He wisely reconsidered knowing the long reach of San Peron's organization. It would find him sooner or later, and the outcome could only result in his death.

"Somehow he was waiting for us, Mr. San Peron. We were ambushed as soon as we entered the room. He killed all three of my men, and I was lucky to have only been shot in the leg. I was in the doorway when I was shot, and the noise of his weapon was attracting a lot of attention. I fired several shots at him even though I was wounded. I think I may have hit him at least once but I left quickly, knowing that you wouldn't want me to have to explain to the police what happened, sir."

Emilio gestured to his wounded leg. He prayed the story he had concocted would be believable to San Peron.

San Peron took a deep breath, glared at Emilio and said, "How is it possible he knew you were coming?"

"I don't know, sir, but he was waiting for us when we entered the room. My guys didn't have time to react. That guy you call *El Scorpion* is one good shot. I was lucky to get out alive."

"You managed to get away before the police arrived. Did anyone see you in your car?" San Peron asked.

"Uh, that's the other thing, sir, I…I… well, he took the car, sir," Emilio said falteringly, realizing he hadn't thought his story out enough.

San Peron stood open-mouthed and stared at Emilio for a minute, Emilio wilting under his intense gaze. San Peron suddenly turned and walked over to the couch, brushed a cushion off onto the floor and sat down. He didn't say anything for several minutes, obviously in deep thought. Emilio stood silently, hoping he had weathered the worst of the onslaught from San Peron.

Finally San Peron looked up and said calmly, "I'm not going to ask how he managed to get your car. All I know is that something's not making sense right now. Go to the kitchen and get something to eat while I think some more. I'll have to straighten up your mess, and I hope that the car thing doesn't lead the police here to me. At least you had better hope not.

Emilio breathed a sigh of relief as he walked to the

kitchen. In fact he felt he had dodged a bullet since Mr. San Peron hadn't questioned him further about how he had lost the car to *El Scorpion*. Emilio opened the fridge, took out some cold cuts, and looked around for the bread. He was hungry since he hadn't eaten for several hours now. After he made a huge sandwich he took a *Cerveza* from the fridge and sat down at the small kitchen table. He didn't dare go back out into the living room until he was summoned.

San Peron picked up his cell from the coffee table and pressed one number, the one used to summon his loyal bodyguard, Humberto. When Humberto entered the room he walked over to San Peron and waited. In a few seconds San Peron looked up and in a soft voice said, "I have a mess in the kitchen. I need you to clean it up."

Without a word Humberto turned and strode to the kitchen, his feet barely making a sound on the Italian marble floor. He softly entered the kitchen and within three steps was standing behind Emilio. He snaked one of his massive arms around Emilio's neck so fast that the food he was chewing virtually spewed from his mouth. With the crook of his arm under Emilio's chin he grasped his wrist with his free hand and began squeezing, shutting off the air supply. Emilio, not a small man himself, began violently struggling, kicking the table and scattering food and dishes onto the floor. Trying as hard as he could to break the iron clad grip of Humberto, but to no avail, He half stood before being slammed back into the chair. Within a few seconds Emilio began losing the life-saving oxygen that fed his brain, blackness beginning to close in on him like a velvet curtain. He knew he was going to die now, and there was nothing he could do about it. He had once heard that your life flashed before your eyes just before death. That wasn't true – his only thoughts were to get loose, right to the end. His struggling soon ceased, and his body went limp. But Humberto still held on until he was sure Emilio was dead.

Walking over to the rear door of the kitchen he opened it. He then went back and picked up the dead body of Emilio and carried him out the back door.

San Peron had turned on the television to catch the news, raising the volume to drown out the ruckus in the kitchen. Emilio had failed to carry out the hit on *El Scorpion* and that could have been forgiven, but he knew he had been lied to about how it went down and that couldn't and wouldn't be forgiven. San Peron had zero tolerance for lying and disloyalty.

Now, without dwelling on what had just happened, he began watching the news to determine what the police knew and just how much. The news only referred to the debacle at the motel as a drug deal gone sour with three dead and no suspects yet. San Peron laughed at the drug deal angle, pleased that they had nothing further to go on at this time. There was no mention of the GMC Denali that Emilio was driving, so he breathed a little easier.

The news story of a Hialeah police detective and his partner being run off I-95 by an unknown vehicle was next. The unmarked police unit had rolled down a steep embankment, and the condition of the detectives was unknown at air time. Several witnesses driving on I-95 saw the incident happen but no one had obtained a license number, or at least no one had come forward yet. The de-

Sting of the Scorpion

scription of the car was that of a large SUV, fairly new and black in color. Anyone with any information was urged to contact the Florida Highway Patrol, or call Crime Stoppers and be eligible for a one thousand dollar reward. One eye witness claimed to have seen an exchange of gunfire between the vehicles, insinuating road rage as the cause of the incident. At this time according to the news anchor, the gunfire claim had not been substantiated by the FHP investigators.

After turning off the television, San Peron leaned back on the couch, feeling much better now about the lack of information the police had released to the media. He knew exactly who had run the car off the road. He also knew that the car was Emilio's. Personally he didn't doubt there had been an exchange of gunfire and that the police were withholding that bit of evidence. Now he had to find out where Mister big shot Scorpion had gone. He would call his contact at the Hialeah Detective Bureau later and find out exactly what they knew and what they were not releasing to the news media.

Picking up the phone, he dialed another one of his men, ordering him to put word out on the street to find out where *El Scorpion* was now. If he was lucky, they would find him soon, but if the Scorpion had any common sense, he would be long gone out of Hialeah.

San Peron stood up and walked to the kitchen. When he entered he saw that everything was nice and neat, but he did happen to notice the broken dishes which had been deposited in the open trash can. He walked over to the fridge, pulled out a cola, flipped off the light and returned to the living room.

Earl Underwood

He dropped back down on the couch, pulled out his cell and dialed the private number of his contact at the Hialeah Detective Bureau. He wanted to know Jack Storm's status and where he was now. Emilio was completely gone from his thoughts, as if he had never been there.

Chapter 27

Full disclosure

AFTER SIGNING OUT AN UNMARKED LOANER from the motor pool, Stormy began the drive home. He was stiff, sore and tired. He knew Shaunie would be upset, but then again she was aware of the risks of his job. He had just pulled up to the traffic light on LeJuene Road by the station when a wrecker turned onto the service road to the motor pool. His smashed up Charger was on a flat-bed since most of the tires had flattened when the car rolled over.

To him it looked as if he would need a new car – the damage looked too great to repair. The roof was partially caved in, both sides of the car smashed in and the windows mostly broken out. He watched as the wrecker drove past him going in and took note of the bullet holes in the front fender, also the starred windshield from a round or two hitting it.

He suddenly realized just how lucky he and Dakota were to have escaped with mostly minor injuries. By all rights they should have been more severely injured if not dead, either from the crash or the bullets flying at their car. If he hadn't reacted as quickly as he had by hitting the brakes when he saw the gun, the end result could have been deadly. Stormy had been shot at many times before, but this time was close and he could have possibly lost his partner. That made it personal.

When he arrived home he saw that Shaunie's car was not in the garage. He figured she was probably tied up at work and would be home soon. He could call her, but he decided to prepare dinner himself tonight. It would give him time to do some thinking. He cooked on occasion and was fairly decent at it. Looking in the fridge he espied some lamb chops and mint jelly. He took them out and began preparing the meal.

By the time Shaunie walked in the door the meal was only minutes from being ready. He poured a glass of wine for the both of them and entered the living room. Shaunie had kicked off her shoes as was her habit when she arrived home and reached for the glass of wine. Stormy gave her a brief kiss, and they sat on the couch.

"Something smells really good, hon. What is it?" she asked as she took a sip of wine.

"Lamb chops, mint jelly and a few other fixings," Stormy said.

"What's the special occasion tonight?" She asked.

"Hey, what do you mean? I cook every now and then."

"You know what I mean, Jack. What's going on? Is there something about the accident today you haven't told me?" she asked, placing her glass with great deliberation on the end table.

"What have you heard about the accident?" he asked.

"Well, Captain Paradis filled me in a little about your getting run off the road. The news has their own speculations about what happened, but I don't know if I trust what they say. I know there is more to it, and you should trust me enough by now to tell me everything."

"You're right, honey, and I do trust you. I just don't want you to worry needlessly over something that is part of my job," Stormy replied.

"I'm a big girl and besides, I have been a part of your job. Let's not forget the Rolando drama."

"I'll tell you what. After we finish eating we'll have a cup of coffee, and I'll tell you everything, okay?" Stormy said, rising and heading for the kitchen to finish preparing the meal.

"Is there anything I can do to help in the kitchen?" Shaunie asked.

"Nope, just lean back, drink your wine and relax. I'll call you when it's ready."

* * * * * * * * *

Stormy started at the beginning when the Mayor had been shot and killed. He left nothing out and patiently explained who the Scorpion was, ending his dissertation with the call from Pablo about who the actual target was.

"Wow, you really know how to cap off a wonderful dinner, and it was an excellent meal, honey," Shaunie said, sipping the last dregs of her second cup of coffee. "What do you plan to do now?"

"I have to pick Dakota up in the morning, and then we'll meet with the Captain for a conference. I have a feeling he'll try to take us off the case, for our own protection of course. I'll do everything I can to keep him from doing that. I want to see this through to the end. You know I'm not one to run and hide, and I don't intend to start now. If I turn into someone who avoids confrontation, I may as well quit and take the job Alex offered me, although I would be bored out of my mind," Stormy said.

"The one question that hasn't been answered is why? What reason would the Scorpion have for wanting to kill you? You said you didn't know him nor had you ever heard of him. So why are you the target? Where does he know you from?" Shaunie asked with some concern in her voice.

"I don't think he knows me personally, honey. I'm a target because someone has paid him to kill me," Stormy replied.

"But who would that be and for what reason? What did you ever do to make someone want to have you killed? Don't answer that, I know you must have plenty of enemies from the past because of your job."

"Do you remember the bank robbery where I had to shoot the kid?" Stormy asked after a short pause.

"Oh, my God, and you think his father, San Peron, wants revenge, don't you," Shaunie said understanding dawning on her now.

"There's no viable proof that he hired the Scorpion, but I feel it in my gut."

"Aren't you going to confront him?" Shaunie asked.

"That's not the way it works, hon. Trust me, I would

love to confront him, but I need a lot more proof than I have right now."

"But there must be some way, or somehow to explain to him that you had no choice when you took the shot," Shaunie said, anxiety starting to show in her voice.

"Even if there was a way I don't think it would make a difference. When people lose their only child, they tend to react in different ways. I never want to be in that position, and in a way I do feel for his loss. I'm the one who took his child away from him, and I think he wants me to be punished for that," Stormy said somewhat compassionately.

"But surely he knows by now that you had no choice. It was you or him, right?"

"I'm sure he knows by now. But right or wrong, a life was lost. As a father, his reasoning will be blinded by the fact that his son is dead. Sure, it could have been me, but today it wasn't. It was a kid who for whatever reason decided to rob a bank. I was there and could tell he felt trapped when the bank was surrounded. He was in a situation that could only go downhill once the police arrived, and he knew it," Stormy said.

"I'm sorry, honey. I really am. But I'm still glad you came out of it okay," Shaunie said. "What are you going to do now?"

"I'm taking a shower and hitting the sack. I plan to try to get some sleep, but I doubt that will happen tonight," Stormy replied, rising and heading for the shower.

Stormy did manage to sleep a little, although fitfully. Shaunie lay awake with him for awhile before he finally dozed off. Throughout the night she would awaken to his moaning and tossing, rubbing his back until he calmed down. When morning finally arrived, she rolled over in bed and found his side empty. Slipping on her robe she went to the kitchen and saw that he was preparing breakfast for them, the coffee already brewing, a nice aroma filling the air.

"I have to eat and run, honey. Dakota will have my head if I don't pick her up first thing this morning."

"I understand, sweetie. If you need me or want to talk more, call me," Shaunie said, giving Stormy a goodbye kiss.

* * * * * * * * *

"Alright, what took you so long?" Dakota asked jokingly as Stormy walked into her hospital room.

She was sitting on the side of the bed, dressed and ready to go. She held out the release papers for Stormy to see, then stood and strode past him out the door. It seemed she couldn't get out of there soon enough.

Once they were in the car, she asked Stormy if he would stop by her house so she could shower and change. She still had on the same clothes from the day before and had refused to shower in the hospital.

Stormy sat idly in her tidy living room while she was in the shower. He casually looked all around the room, having never been inside before. He was not overly surprised to see that it was furnished very nicely. Everything was neat, clean and almost appeared as if no one ever visited her. He found it strange but then again, he had been a bachelor himself, and he imagined that some people who had visited him may have entertained the very same thoughts. When she finally entered the room clad in a short wrap around robe and her hair wrapped in a towel, he asked her how she kept it this neat all the time.

"I clean and dust often, but I spend most of the time in my bedroom, reading and watching television. Why do you ask?"

"Just wondering. It seems like this room is never used."

"Are you trying to say I don't have a social life, Mr. Storm?" Dakota said with mock anger.

"No, not at all…forget I asked," Stormy said, slightly embarrassed.

"Humm…okay, but just for your information, I do have plenty of visitors. We just like the bedroom better," she said, laughing as Stormy began to squirm uncomfortably. "Okay, I'm getting dressed so how about you go into my nice, clean pristine kitchen and make us some coffee. After drinking that hospital stuff I'm ready for some real coffee."

Stormy was more than happy to leave the room, feeling as if he was getting a little too personal about her life. Just as the coffee finished brewing, she walked into the kitchen, dressed for work and the faintest wisp of perfume wafting through the air. Stormy poured two steaming cups. He knew she liked a lot of cream, so he fixed hers the way she wanted. They sat at the kitchen table and sipped the hot coffee while she played back her messages on the phone.

While Dakota was occupied, Stormy made a quick call to Pablo to see if he had any further information on

Earl Underwood

the Scorpion. Pablo told him he was coming up blank, but if he heard anything concerning the Scorpion's whereabouts, he would call immediately. He also touched lightly on the accident and after being assured Stormy and Dakota were fine, ended the conversation.

"Okay, you ready to get to the station now?" she said when she had finished.

"Yep, we need to get moving and meet up with the Captain. We have a multitude of things to go over. Also I need to find out if I'm getting a new car anytime soon or if I'm forever stuck with a loaner."

Chapter 28

Deadly purchase

AT AROUND THE SAME TIME Stormy and Dakota were making their way to the office, the Scorpion was busy conducting some research on a computer at the Wilde-E-Library. He pulled up public tax records, and after entering San Peron's name he hit the jackpot. Thirty minutes earlier he had inquired at the front desk of the Hialeah Inn and was told that there was a library within walking distance. He had taken a leisurely stroll up West Eighteenth Avenue past the mall until he reached Fifty Fourth Street, where he found the library.

The jackpot he had stumbled upon was the home address for none other than Antonio San Peron, and it was within a few miles of this area. He would now have to find a car to use for an hour or so. First he wanted to scope out the area where San Peron lived before attempting to make any kind of invasion plan. He printed out the map for the property, remitted the small amount of change it cost to the librarian and began walking back to his room at the Hialeah Inn.

As he casually walked back to the Inn he racked his brain for an easily accessible yet safe place to get a car. He needed to find one that wouldn't be missed for a day or so and he needed it tonight.

When he reached his room, he spread the property map out on the bed and began to study it carefully, taking in every little detail, not wanting to miss anything. Finally he had what he needed to know memorized, and he carefully refolded the map, placing it deep into his rear pocket.

Next he needed to call a cab and take a little ride to the arms dealer in south Hialeah. He hadn't planned to return to that particular location again, but unfortunately he had no choice. He had a few more special purchases to make which would be vital to his plans later tonight.

He picked up the phone from the nightstand to call for a taxi but changed his mind. He didn't want to leave a possible trail where he was going if the phone records were ever checked. Instead he walked out to the lobby of the Inn and using the front desk phone available to all the guests, called for a taxi. Then he walked across the street where he had told the cabbie to pick him up. He didn't want the driver to know where he was staying in case it ever came down to that.

When he reached the location of the arms dealer several miles away, he told the taxi driver to wait for him. Walking around the corner of the dilapidated building and out of sight of the taxi driver, he approached the solid-looking windowless door he had used before and pushed the buzzer next to it. After about a ten-second delay, he heard the electronic click of the door lock.

He gently pushed the door open and cautiously entered the dank, dark and dirty hallway. He quickly spotted the poorly disguised video camera mounted on the dark ceiling at the far end of the hall. It had been spray painted the same color as the ceiling but failed to escape the sharp eyes of Victor as it had on his prior visit. He also didn't need to be told that he was being watched again. After passing three other doors he reached the end of the hall and quickly tapped on the fourth door with lightly curled knuckles. He absently noted again that it was made of heavy metal, probably steel, and was directly beneath the camera. Once again he waited for the click releasing the lock before he could enter the room.

"I didn't expect to see you again, *amigo*," the robust middle-aged Hispanic man behind the steel grille said.

"I didn't really expect to be back, but there are a few more items I need," Victor said.

Releasing the lock on yet another door the arms dealer motioned for him to enter behind the counter. The door closed and he motioned for Victor to follow him to another room, the same one he had been in before when he had picked up the sniper rifle. Neither had offered a name and hadn't really been expected to. In this line of business, the less you knew about who you were dealing with the better for all parties involved.

"What is it that you are interested in this time?" the dealer asked when they were situated in the secure arms room, his eyes visibly expressing his delight at another sale.

"I need a small but powerful dart gun, one capable of

accurately reaching a target at least twenty-five yards out, a dozen small reliable darts and a vial of the fastest acting tranquilizer cocktail you have. I'll also need a pair of night-vision goggles, preferably military grade, and a pair of ten-by-fifty binoculars," Victor said. "Lastly I'll need a 'slim Jim', one that is effective on power door locks."

"I have the Armasight NYX-17 Generation II goggles, but they are pretty expensive, probably run you around three grand." The arms dealer said.

"I only need the night-vision goggles for one night. You have anything less expensive?" Victor asked, aware his cash was starting to run low.

"I have a pair of Vega Generation One head mounts. You can have those for nine hundred."

"What about the dart gun and cocktail?"

"No problem with the dart gun and darts, but just how quickly do you want the cocktail to work?"

"No slower than four or five seconds," Victor said.

"Well, that rules out the Choral Hydrate based one. It will take at least ten to twenty minutes to work. I do have a new one, and it is extremely potent. So potent in fact that 1/100 of a gram will kill a human instantly. They use it to bring down six and a half thousand pound elephants for tagging," the dealer said in a serious tone.

"What is it called?" Victor asked.

"It's called Etorphine. It's five thousand times stronger than an equivalent dose of heroin which is why it's so deadly."

"Do you have a watered down version of it in stock?" Victor asked.

"I do, but I won't guarantee whether it will kill a person or render them unconscious instantly. You will have to take that chance if you want to use it. I'm sure you don't know the medical history of whomever you plan to use it on, such as a prior heart condition or any other conditions that would be a problem."

"I'll take the chance. It's not as if I haven't killed before," Victor said with only the slightest hint of remorse in his voice.

"You know that I only take cash and the tab comes to three grand. Are you good with that?"

"Don't try to gouge me. I figure the products are only worth two grand, take it or leave it."

"Twenty-five hundred, and we have a deal," the dealer stated.

"Nice knowing you. I'll find what I need elsewhere," Victor said, tiring of the haggling.

"Okay, okay! Two grand it is but cash only."

"I have the money, just get me the goods," Victor said with distaste, although he understood. He just didn't feel that the dealer needed to repeat his cash only demand since he had already been in several days ago and paid in cash.

The arms dealer, somewhat sullen now, left the room to gather the items Victor had requested, leaving him alone. Victor lifted his shirt and pulled open one of the Velcro pockets on the money belt around his waist. He counted out twenty hundred-dollar bills and then refastened the pocket, covering the belt with his shirt. He only had to wait ten minutes before the dealer returned with all the items he had requested.

"For two grand you can throw in some type of a

satchel to carry this in. I don't want to walk the streets with this stuff in my hands for everyone to see," Victor said, as he checked the goggles and mechanism of the CO2 dart gun to ensure it worked properly. The tiny vial of Etorphine was ensconced in a small padded steel box.

"No problem, *amigo*. Consider it done. By the way, you had better make damn sure you don't let this cocktail touch your skin. You could become a victim yourself if you do since it is readily absorbed through the skin. I suggest wearing latex gloves, even doubling them to be safe. The bottle is the same as a small medicinal vial. Just push the tip of the dart through the top to coat it and don't touch the dart, even when you think it's dry. You'll only need to barely wet the very tip, it's that potent."

"I'll remember that, and thanks for the warning," Victor said as he stuffed his purchases into the satchel, taking extra care with the Etorphine case.

Once he paid the dealer the two thousand dollars, he turned without a word and left the room. Out in the hallway he passed an elderly woman who was entering another room. She didn't even bother to look at him, just made her way into her room and quickly closed the door. At the exit Victor turned and gave a quick two fingered salute to the camera in the hallway, letting the dealer know that he knew the camera was there.

When he rounded the building, the taxi was still waiting for him by the curb, the motor idling and the meter still running. He figured it would be since he hadn't paid the fare yet. He entered the rear of the cab and startled the driver who was probably dozing. He told him to return to the location from where he had been picked up.

Sting of the Scorpion

The cabbie soon reached West Forty Ninth Street. As they neared the mall Victor glimpsed a hospital sign on the north side of the street, Palm Springs General. Now he knew where he could find a car to use. He instructed the cabbie to let him out in front of the mall, only about two blocks from the hospital. Once he paid the fare he got out with the satchel and waited for the taxi to pull away into the bustling traffic before turning and walking back towards the hospital.

Victor slowly wandered through the hospital parking lot, searching for just the right car. It had to be fairly common-looking to avoid standing out. He soon found what he was looking for. The car, a small sedan, white in color, was near the rear of the lot on the west side of the hospital. Trees were in abundance, and he saw that the car was covered with leaves, twigs and dust. That was an indication the car had been here for awhile, possibly someone who had driven themselves to the hospital for whatever reason and had been admitted. Looking around he scanned the area for any security cameras that would be in the visual range of the car. The only one he found was on the opposite side of a huge tree, effectively blocking out most of the car from view. It couldn't have been more perfect for Victor.

He turned and walked briskly to the front door of the hospital, in case he was being monitored on the security cameras. After entering the front lobby he spotted the cafeteria on his left. He went inside and selected a guava pastry and coke, even though he wasn't particularly hungry. He just needed to kill the right amount of time before exiting and the cameras began recording him again, giving the impression he was a visitor at the hospital. After wasting approximately thirty minutes, a minimal visiting time he guessed, he left the hospital, keeping his head slightly down as before, walking back to Forty Ninth Street and heading for the Inn only a couple of blocks away.

* * * * * * * * * *

With the door to his room firmly secured he opened the satchel and emptied the contents onto the bed. He stared at the small steel case for at least a full minute before gingerly opening it. He wasn't a stupid man so, he didn't attempt to take the vial out of the protected container without gloves. An idea popped into his head, and he suddenly left the room, taking the elevator to the second floor with a distinct purpose in mind. He quickly saw what he was looking for about halfway down the hall, a janitorial cart standing unattended by an open room. Confirming that the maid was busy making a bed inside the room, he swiftly scanned the cart and found what he was looking for on the bottom shelf. Making sure the maid was still engrossed in her duties, he deftly grabbed a box of latex gloves, turning his back to the hallway camera to conceal his actions, nestled the small box under his armpit and walked back to the elevator. Once he was back in his room and the door relocked, he checked the gloves to determine if the thickness was adequate. He felt they were but decided to use two pair as the dealer had suggested which should be more than safe enough to handle the deadly drug.

Very carefully he removed the glass vial from the

Sting of the Scorpion

small metal case. He gingerly sat it on the desk and then placed the darts in a row alongside the vial. Taking the clip from the dart gun, which bore a slight resemblance to his Beretta 9mm, he placed it by the darts. Taking one dart at a time, he gently pushed them into the spongy top of the vial, making sure only the very tip of the dart touched the fluid.

When he had finished coating all of the darts he began inserting them, ever so carefully, one at a time into the magazine clip. It was almost comical the extreme measures he used to avoid the dart tips as he handled them. But to him it was no laughing matter, nor would it be to the recipients later. Finally the clip was fully loaded, and he inserted it into the grip of the weapon, a soft click assuring him it was properly seated. He let out a gush of air, releasing his pent up breath.

Victor turned off the lights and made sure the dark drapes in the room were tightly closed. He donned the night-vision goggles and flipped them on. The darkness in the room wasn't total enough to really appreciate the effect, but they seemed to work fine for what he had in mind. The eerie green fuzzy glow engulfed the room allowing him to see everything, although it was not optimum conditions for this equipment. Once he was outside and away from the city lights he would really appreciate the quality of the goggles.

Now he needed to find a car for a recon of San Peron's property. He was saving the one at the hospital for use later tonight. While it was still daylight he needed to scout the property and determine not only it's layout but where the power lines were, if there were guards present and how many. He saw on the map that there appeared to be a wall around the property, so he needed to know what kind and how high it was. He was somewhat of an expert at performing a recon, but there were always unknown variables to contend with no matter how efficient you were.

The drapes were now slightly parted again, but the sheers obscured any outside view of the interior of the room. The goggles and loaded dart gun were placed inside the satchel and left on the bed. He pulled a black turtle neck and a pair of black cargo pants from his bag and placed them on the bed. As he left the room Victor placed the "do not disturb" sign on the door handle. He didn't need the complications resulting from a maid entering the room and possibly nosing around the bag containing the weapons. He had put the binoculars and jimmy in a plain paper bag to take with him. He walked across the busy divided street to the mall, the bag clutched tightly in his hand. He was in search of a car and planned to watch for a woman shopper, even better would be a pair of women shoppers, to park and enter the mall. Usually when there were two or more women it would be an indication they were going to be shopping for awhile, and the car wouldn't be missed.

Victor only waited a few minutes before observing a car pull up and park near the end of the lot, almost to the edge of the street. Three young women got out and began laughing and talking animatedly as they strolled towards the mall entrance. In all appearances it looked as if they were indeed out for a day of shopping. The car, an older light gray sedan, would be perfect for his needs. He wait-

Sting of the Scorpion

ed until the women had entered the mall and then walked casually to the car, slipping out the jimmy from the bag he had brought with him. He quickly popped open the door lock and jumped into the front seat, pulling the door shut behind him. He was about to lean over and pull wires from under the dash in order to straight-wire the car when he noticed a key ring lying in the console. On a hunch, he tried the keys and the second one started the car. *Some people are just plain stupid,* he thought to himself.

Chapter 29

Keeping Dakota in the loop

Captain Paradis paced the floor of his office, now and then looking at the two detectives sitting in front of his desk.

"You shouldn't be here, Dakota. I don't know why Stormy brought you here in the first place."

"I was released from the hospital, Captain. I'm fine and ready for work," Dakota responded, glancing at Stormy for vindication.

"No, you're not fine. You can't effectively do your job with two or more cracked ribs. Hell, you haven't even rested enough from the concussion. No, you need to go home and heal more before I can allow you to return to work," Captain Paradis said with some finality

"But, Captain…"

"No *buts*, Dakota. I'm not going to let you out on the road in your condition. One wrong move or even one wrong punch from some punk could cause a cracked rib to break and possibly puncture a lung, even your heart.

Sting of the Scorpion

No, I'm not taking a chance with your well being and that's final. One of the guys in the squad room will give you a ride home…now go!"

"Captain, may I say something?" Stormy asked.

"Sure, go ahead," the Captain said, figuring Stormy would plead her case.

"I could really use Dakotas input, so why couldn't she just stay here at a desk in case I need her for anything else? She can't get hurt sitting in here."

"If I have her word she will stay in the office. I don't want her on the road until those ribs have mended a lot more," Captain Paradis said after some thought.

"I would appreciate it if you let me stay in the office, Captain. I feel I can do a lot more here than at home, where I would slowly go bonkers doing nothing. Besides, my partner could use some extra help with this situation," Dakota said.

"Alright then, she can stay," the Captain said after deliberating the request for a minute.

"Fill me in again on everything that happened before the accident," Captain Paradis said, taking a seat behind his desk.

Stormy recounted everything from the time Dakota had woken him to the present. He replayed the interview with the two suspects that had been arrested and how the two sketches were almost identical. He told the Captain his feelings about how he didn't believe for one minute that the two kids had anything whatsoever to do with the shooting, even though the sniper weapon was in the trunk of the car they were driving. When he got to the incident on I-95, he relied on Dakota to help fill in some of the areas he didn't see. She was the one that recognized *El Scorpion* first from the sketch she was holding on her lap. When Stormy had finished, he looked to Dakota to see if she had anything to add. She just smiled, shaking her head and said nothing, so they leaned back in their seats and looked at the Captain.

"You said you had good sketches of this Scorpion guy. After seeing him in the car, do you think they're accurate enough in appearance to issue a BOLO?" Captain Paradis asked Dakota.

"I don't think the artist could have done much better. I recognized him from the sketch as soon as he looked over at me. I say put 'em out now so we can get as many eyes as we can on the road as soon as possible."

"Then get to it, Dakota. Make sure you state that he is armed and extremely dangerous. Have the shift supervisors put our guys on alert and not to try and be a hero. If they spot him, call for backup at once. This guy is no amateur, and I don't need any bleeding blues on my watch. Now, when you were in the hospital you said you knew who was responsible for this. You also said it was personal, very personal. Am I missing something here? Talk to me Stormy!" the Captain said.

"Do you remember when Pablo called me in the hospital?"

"Yes, that's what I'm referring to. What did you mean?" Captain Paradis asked.

"When Pablo told me that I was the intended target, I couldn't put my finger on it at first, but after hanging up with him it came to me…the shootout at the bank. San Peron would have the resources and connections to bring

Sting of the Scorpion

in a professional killer. The Mayor just happened to accidently take a bullet that was meant for me. It happened when he reached over in front of me to shake Dakota's hand. My money is on San Peron. After all, I did kill his son, so how much more motivation would he need?"

"That certainly sounds plausible, considering the timing of everything. Now, we need positive proof, so how are we going to obtain that? We can't just go after San Peron because we *think* he hired the assassin," the Captain said, frustration evident in his tone.

"If we could find the Scorpion and take him alive maybe he would hand up San Peron. What would he have to lose at that point?" Stormy said, not really believing that would ever happen. From what he had seen, he was dealing with a true professional, one who would never compromise his client. But stranger things had happened in the past, so it was not totally out of the realm of possibilities.

"Yeah, but we would have to find him and then take him *alive*. It would be a long shot at the least. I honestly don't think he would give up that easily, at least not without a good fight."

Before either of them could go any further, Stormy felt a vibration on his hip, a phone call coming in. He glanced down at the phone and could see that Pablo was calling again. Hoping he had further information for him, even more hopeful that he knew where the Scorpion was now, Stormy quickly answered the phone, holding up a hand to the Captain.

After a minute of silence on Stormy's side, he spoke. He asked Pablo to keep him updated, especially if he or his friends found out where the Scorpion was hiding out, if indeed he was still here and not on the run. Terminating the call, Stormy turned to the Captain with a forced smile on his face.

"Sorry, Captain, that was Pablo."

"Did he have any additional information for you?"

"Only that he had confirmation San Peron is the one who hired the Scorpion."

Now it was the Captain's turn to smile.

Chapter 30

Reconnaissance

AFTER TAKING THE CAR from Westland Mall, Victor drove out to 103rd Street and headed west, under the Palmetto overpass and towards Okeechobee Road. When he reached it he made a right turn, heading north until he approached his destination. On Northwest 104th Avenue he turned right and within a couple of blocks he saw San Peron's house, if you could call it that. It actually looked more like a walled compound, similar to the one Bin Laden was found to be hiding in. It was on the west side of 104th Avenue with no close neighbors. On the east side was a modest-sized subdivision with family homes, separated by the avenue.

Victor drove past without looking directly at the compound, making a right turn into the subdivision as if he lived there. He drove leisurely down the street past several houses before he made a quick turnaround in a driveway.

When he returned to the end of the street from where

he had entered he noticed that the northernmost house appeared to be empty. Then he saw the for sale sign leaning over in the yard. He deftly made the turn into the driveway and waited a minute or two, making it appear he was waiting for the real estate agent in case anyone was watching. With his binoculars around his neck and tucked out of sight under his shirt, he exited the car and began walking to the front door.

He tried one of the double doors and found it locked, just as he expected. He casually strolled around to the back of the house, glancing into the windows as he passed, checking for one that would possibly be unlocked. None were unlocked so he continued to the rear.

When he reached the back of the house he stopped and turned, looking at the compound without appearing to do so under the protection of his dark tinted sunglasses. At this distance and due to the height of the wall, he couldn't see anyone outside in the yard. He did notice that the wall encircling the compound was approximately eight feet in height and well rounded at the top, making it difficult if not impossible, to jump and secure a handhold. He had to figure out how he was going to scale the wall before he returned.

He turned back to the rear of the house and saw there was a privacy fence between this and the next house. He tried to make it appear that he was interested in the property as a potential buyer and walked to the back door. He turned the door knob and found it locked also, again not unexpected. Making sure no one was around he gripped the knob, turned it tight and slammed his shoulder into the door next to the jamb. To his satisfaction the door sprung open with the first blow, although with some damage where the lock partially ripped out, splintering the frame.

The closed up house was hot, stifling hot, since all the doors and windows were closed and obviously the air conditioner wasn't turned on. He could feel the expanded hot air silently rushing out the cracked door. It was okay – he was used to heat and didn't plan to be here very long anyhow. Still, it was really hot and muggy, and he immediately began to perspire.

He walked over to the window facing the west side of the road and being careful to not leave his prints, unlocked a window and cracked it open several inches, just enough to let some of the stale hot air begin to escape. With some deliberation he took the binoculars from around his neck and focused on the compound, which was now more visible from the window. Sweat was beginning to run down into his eyes, so he looked around for a paper towel to wipe his face. He finally had to use some toilet paper from the nearby bathroom. He was careful to tuck it into his pocket after he finished swabbing his face. Raising the binoculars once again to his eyes, he was pleased to see that they were more than powerful enough for his purpose.

He studied the compound very carefully, making note of many details that he would need to be aware of in the dark when he returned. Although his field of vision was somewhat limited due to the height of the wall, he could see that the area covered a couple of acres with the house located in the center. He was able to see a gleaming black Mercedes sedan parked in the circular driveway and assumed it must belong to San Peron. Slowly swinging the binoculars along the property line he mentally gauged the distance from the wall to the back side of the house. He could see that there were iron bars on the windows, so those points of entry were quickly dismissed.

He lowered the binoculars and took the toilet paper from his pocket. He once again wiped the rivulets of sweat from his eyes. When he put the binoculars back to his eyes he saw that a man had exited the house, walking around the side directly in his line of vision, slowly and with purpose. His head was swinging back and forth as he looked all around, a sign he was a pro and was scanning the property for anything out of place.

Victor suddenly observed another man coming from around the back of the house from the opposite direction. The two men stopped as they met and appeared to be talking with each other. One of the men lit a cigarette and offered one to the other. He took it from the pack, accepted a light, and blew a thick plume of smoke into the air which was quickly dispersed by the light breeze. They both laughed at something one of them said before continuing on past each other – an obvious patrol ritual they performed regularly.

The binoculars were powerful enough he could almost make out the brand of cigarettes they were smoking. He was also able to spot the telltale bulges under their jackets, an indication they were more than likely armed. Another factor he had anticipated, therefore the purpose for the drug-dipped darts. He also took note of the handheld radios carried in their hands, not on a belt, making for quick access. There was the presence of ear buds in both guards' ear, an indication that there were others listening

Sting of the Scorpion

in. Hopefully the potent drug on the darts would render them unconscious before they had the chance to use the radios to alert anyone. Victor wasn't under any illusions that they were the only guards present.

Slowly swinging the binoculars to his right he saw that there was a wooded area about forty yards behind the compound, outside of the wall. That would be the point from where he would approach the rear wall. Now he had to decide where to park his car tonight to keep it from looking suspicious to any nosey neighbors.

"Hello, anyone there?" A woman's voice suddenly called out, echoing throughout the empty rooms.

Victor jumped, so startled he almost panicked. He hadn't heard the woman drive up nor had he heard her come in the front door as he was concentrating so hard on his recon of the compound. Quickly he tucked the binoculars under his shirt and turned just as she walked in the room.

"Oh, you startled me!" Victor said with the warmest disarming smile he could muster. He was a little perturbed that he had failed to hear her car pull into the driveway. *Yep, definitely time to retire.* He was beginning to slip a little and that wasn't healthy. The only thing he could do now was to bluff his way out of this situation.

"Hi, I'm Juan Perez. I was looking around the outside of the house when I noticed the back door partially open. Did you know that it was open? I think someone must have kicked it in. The lock was busted, but I decided to come in and see if anyone was here or maybe hurt," Victor said, coming up with the phony name and story on the spur of the moment.

"I'm so sorry I startled you, Mr. Perez. I saw your car parked in the driveway and wondered how you gained entry. I was coming to turn on the air conditioner. We have open house this weekend, and it's been so terribly hot. Oh, I do apologize. I'm Martha Hunt, the broker for the house," she said, extending her hand.

"Oh, no need to apologize at all, Ms. Hunt. I tend to be a little nosey sometimes. It may be my downfall one of these days," Victor said with a deliberate nervous laugh as he shook her outstretched hand. "I suppose I should have called the police, but I don't have my phone with me."

She walked to the back of the house and examined the broken door.

"I'll call and report it before I leave," she said.

"Were you interested in the house?" she asked.

"My wife and I are looking to move out of our old house in Hialeah, but there's no rush at this time. I left her shopping, which I abhor, so I was just driving around killing time and saw the development from the road. Lovely area, it looks like a place we could be comfortable in," Victor said, embellishing the details as he went along, hoping he wasn't overdoing it.

"I would be happy to give you a tour of the house. In fact I have a couple other listings in this very neighborhood," Ms. Hunt said.

"Maybe we can make arrangements for another time, Ms. Hunt. I really need to head back to the mall and pick up my wife," Victor said, glancing at his watch for dramatic pause.

"I would be more than happy to show you and your wife our properties at any time that's convenient for you.

Sting of the Scorpion

Here is my card, so please, give me a call when you're ready," Ms. Hunt said, extending the card to Victor. "In fact, you should bring your wife this weekend to the open house if you're able."

Victor accepted the card, smiled as he shook her hand and assured her he might just do that as he walked to the front door. He didn't fail to notice she had repositioned the "for sale" sign once he walked outside and that she had considerately parked curbside in order to keep from blocking him in. He had parked in the middle of the double driveway not thinking someone would be coming. As he approached his car, he gave a sidelong glance at the compound across the way. Being at the lower end of the driveway he couldn't see over the wall from this vantage point. Still he had seen enough that he would continue with his plan to pay a little visit tonight.

When he arrived back in front of the mall, he carefully scanned the parking lot for any undo activity or any police units. He didn't know if the shoppers had came out and found the car missing or not, but he didn't see one marked unit, although there could be unmarked ones staking out the lot. He decided that there was no advantage for any surveillance since the car would be presumed stolen and the police would never be expecting the thief to return the car. Still, erring on the side of caution he drove to the easternmost side of the parking lot and parked the car among several others. He waited for a minute, carefully scanning the lot for any interest in him.

Seeing none he exited the car, locked it and taking the bag with him calmly walked away, heading for the hospital. He wanted to make sure the other car was still parked there.

From the entrance to the hospital parking lot he spotted the car, still next to the tree, still dirty. It seemingly hadn't been moved. He strode past the entrance and then crossed Forty Ninth Street, heading back to the Inn a couple of blocks away. He still had several hours before nightfall, so he decided to stash the bag in the room and wait until dark. He would get something to eat and then go fetch the car and pull it into the parking lot of the Inn. He planned to load his gear in the car and leave the "do not disturb" sign on the door when he drove out to the compound. By leaving the sign on the door, he hoped to buy himself another day before the maid entered the room. He had paid in advance for several days just in case he had to lie low for that long. His plan was to take care of business with San Peron at the compound, return to the room and stay the night. He figured he would find another vehicle the following morning and then after dumping the gear for which he would have no further use, he would head for the airport.

Chapter 31

Revealing evidence

Captain Paradis was still smiling when his phone rang. He answered and listened for a minute without saying anything, occasionally nodding his head to Stormy. He thanked his caller and hung up the receiver. He leaned back in his chair, still smiling and pointed a finger to Stormy.

"That was dispatch. One of the patrol officers found what he thinks is the car that ran you and Dakota off the road."

"Where is it?" Stormy asked.

"It's in the parking garage at the Hialeah Racetrack Casino. The patrol officer was following up on the BOLO Dakota had them issue with the rendering of the Scorpion and the car description. He was just outside the track when the BOLO came out. He swung into the parking garage on a hunch and may have struck gold. Head over there and check it out, Stormy."

"Okay, Captain, but can you please call dispatch and

ask them that if the officer runs the tag to *not* put it out over the air. I'll swing over to dispatch and pick it up personally."

"Done, but keep me advised on what you come up with."

Stormy rose from his seat and left the Captain's office. He stopped on the way out and told Dakota what he had just learned. She was visibly frustrated that she couldn't leave the office to go with him, but he promised her he would speak with the Captain when he returned.

As he drove the loaner out to LeJuene Road Stormy flipped on the grille blues and headed south to the racetrack, driving well over the speed limit. He had a feeling that this could be the break he needed to track down *El Scorpion*. He also knew that E*l Scorpion* was not a local and therefore the car wouldn't be registered in his name, otherwise he wouldn't have dumped it. It was probably stolen, but possibly he slipped up and left prints or some other evidence in the car that could be used.

When Stormy entered the parking garage, he drove up near the top level and came upon the marked unit with its blue lights creating a virtual light show inside the dark garage. The unit was parked in front of a black SUV backed into a parking space, nestled between two other cars. The officer had the presence of mind to tape off the vehicle and those parked on each side of it.

Parking behind the officer's unit, Stormy exited his car and walked over to the officer who was standing by the front of his own car. This officer was one he wasn't familiar with. Probably a newbie – definitely one he hadn't met before. When he reached the officer, he extended his hand and introduced himself.

"Officer Dixon, sir, and I've heard a lot about you. It's a pleasure to meet you sir," The officer responded.

"Just D*etective*, Officer Dixon, not sir, and you can call me Stormy."

"Yes, sir...I mean, yes, Detective. My name is Aaron."

"How long have you been on the force, Aaron?"

"Next week will be one year."

"Congratulations, Aaron, hope you like our little department," Stormy said, amused by the exuberance exhibited by the young officer. "Now let's see what we have here."

Stormy walked over to the SUV backed into the parking space. The first place he looked was at the passenger side front fender of the car, knowing that if this was the one they were looking for it would have damage from the collision. Kneeling down he saw there was a sizeable dent in the right front fender and evidence of a dark gray paint that had been transferred when the two cars had made contact. It looked to be the same shade of gray as Stormy's car, but CSI would make that determination later. Stormy had no doubt this was the car that ran him off the road, nearly killing him and Dakota.

"Did you run the tag yet, Officer Dixon?" Stormy asked as he walked to the rear of the car.

"No sir, I haven't yet. I didn't want to squeeze in behind the car and end up rubbing against it and possibly contaminating any evidence."

Stormy could see what he meant. The car was backed almost against the wall, making it very difficult to see the tag.

"That was very astute of you, Aaron. Keep thinking like that, and you may make detective someday," Stormy said, flashing a sincere smile to the rookie in an attempt to put him at ease.

Stormy pulled his cell phone out and called Linda Ward at CSI, not ready to broadcast what had been found over the air just yet. He asked her to arrange for a wrecker to tow the Denali to the garage in the back lot at the Detective Bureau and to meet him there. He wanted to go over the car with her even though he knew she was very thorough. Stormy figured that with both of them working on it he could speed up the process a little. The longer it took the better chance for the Scorpion to get away.

Stormy stayed and talked with Officer Dixon until the wrecker arrived. He wanted to make sure the tow truck driver was extremely careful about handling the car. He found Aaron Dixon to be likeable as well as knowledgeable. He told how he was from a family of law enforcement members, his late father being a retiree from the Miami Beach force. Their chat covered mostly family and goals in life. When the tow truck arrived and the Denali was hooked up, he told the driver he would follow him to the station. Giving a quick wave to Dixon he drove away, following the tow truck.

Once the car was unhooked from the tow truck and inside the city garage, Stormy walked to the rear and noted the tag number. Linda Ward wasn't present yet, so he strolled over to the communications center and had one of the dispatchers run the tag. It came back to one Emilio Sanchez, address in west Hialeah. Stormy took the printout and walked back to the garage to await Linda and her team. As he waited, he called Dakota on his cell and had her take down the info from the printout to see what she could come up with on Emilio Sanchez. He had barely hung up from the call, when he spotted the CSI van rolling into the lot, continuing on to the garage.

"Stormy, I see you may have found the car that almost did you in," Linda said as she exited the van, another tech following.

"I'm hoping it's the one. The damage is consistent with the point of contact and there seems to be paint transfer on the damaged fender. Hopefully you will be able to tell me that it came from my car."

Linda walked over and gave Stormy a brief hug.

"I'm glad you weren't seriously hurt. How is Dakota doing?" she asked.

"She's doing fine so far, just sore and frustrated at being confined to her desk."

"Let me guess. John Paradis benched her until she is better."

"Bingo! And she's not one bit happy about it. You know Dakota, she wants to be in the thick of things, but her cracked ribs are still on the mend so therefore, desk bound."

"Well, let's see what little secrets we can find on and in this behemoth."

The first thing she did was instruct the tech to take the license plate off, using latex gloves of course, and bag it. Later they would print it and possibly lift some prints. While the tech was taking the tag off, Linda approached the damaged fender and examined the paint smear. She took a thin scraper from her work case and began carefully scraping flakes of the gray paint off, gently placing them into a plastic evidence bag. She would take it to the lab later and subject it to analysis in order to determine if it was the paint from Stormy's Charger. Once she completed that chore, she instructed the tech to take extensive photos of the entire car, with particular focus on the damaged fender. Tread patterns on the tires were photographed, door handles were printed and finally it was time to open up the car to see what was inside. While Linda concentrated on printing the steering wheel and driver's door, Stormy opened the passenger's side door.

"Well, well. What do we have here?" He said with a big grin.

Linda looked over at Stormy and then down to the floor on the passenger's side where Stormy was staring. On the floor mat were several shell casings, lying in plain view, only inches apart. The tech was still photographing the damaged fender next to where Stormy was standing, so Linda had him take several photos of the casings, a six-inch metal ruler placed within the frame of the shots. Once enough photos were taken Linda walked around the vehicle and using a thin plastic rod, lifted the casings and placed them into an evidence bag. They would be printed back at the lab later. Stormy knew that if the Scorpion hadn't donned gloves when he loaded his weapon, which didn't seem likely, there would be prints on the casings. At last there was a glimmer of hope that he was going to obtain some prints and possibly be able to tie a name to the Scorpion.

"I want a priority rush on these casings, Linda."

"I'm finished enough that you can drive me to the lab now. My tech can finish up the rest and meet us there," she responded.

As Stormy and Linda were getting into his car, Dakota walked up. She stopped at the driver's side and waited for the window to roll down.

"Aha...I see I've been replaced by another beautiful woman."

"No chance of that, Dakota. Stormy would never let it happen, he likes you too much," Linda said with a hearty laugh.

"Yeah, he says that to all the girls," Dakota said laughing also.

"I found something on Emilio that you will be interested in Stormy," she continued.

"What did you find?"

"It seems that Emilio Sanchez is connected with San Peron. Either he is or was an employee of sorts."

"Do we have an address on Sanchez?" Stormy asked.

"An apartment in Hialeah Gardens. Here's the printout."

"Thanks, Dakota, hopefully you'll be able to get back on the road tomorrow," Stormy said.

"God, I hope so. I'm going bonkers sitting at this desk."

* * * * * * * * *

An hour later Stormy was cooling his heels in the lab at CSI awaiting the results on the casings. Linda was being overly cautious in her attempts to lift prints from the casings. She was aware of how important this could be to

Stormy's investigation.

Walking into the outer room, she approached Stormy, who was sitting in a chair, apparently dozing while he waited.

"Wake up, Detective. I have some good news for you," she said as she nudged Stormy's leg.

Stormy had in fact been dozing but became alert instantly when she touched him. Shaking his head, he straightened up in the chair and looked up at her expectantly.

"Sorry, Linda, I didn't get a very good night's sleep. You said good news?" He asked as he stood.

"I managed to get one partial and one full print off of the shell casings. Luckily for us there were enough whirls and points to make it usable. I took the liberty to run it, but so far nothing has come back."

"My CI told me that he is sure the Scorpion is from out of the country. We need to run them through AFIS," Stormy said.

"You're a little behind, Stormy, It's now being called IAFIS."

"What are you talking about, Linda?"

"NGI, the Next Generation Identification system has been slowly replacing AFIS and is now called IAFIS, the Integrated Automated Fingerprint Identification System. It will soon simply be called NGI."

"What benefits will the new upgraded system afford us?" Stormy asked.

"A much more defined data bank with faster search times. Now a search will either be almost instantaneous or a max of only a few minutes. It should be a big improvement over the previous max search time of fifteen to twenty minutes."

"Well, let's try out the new and improved system, shall we?" Stormy said with a grin.

Linda entered the prints into the system and waited for a response. After approximately four minutes they received a response, but not the one they wanted. The prints weren't on file with any of the agencies in the United States. Either the Scorpion had never been arrested, had never served in the military nor had ever been printed for a government job, at least in the United States. That was another clue supporting his suspicion that the Scorpion was from out of the country.

"Is that it? Or do we have another alternative?" Stormy asked.

"We can run it through Interpol, but you'll have to get FDLE to do it for us."

"I think I can manage that. I just happen to have a friend in the Orlando office that should be able to arrange it. I'll call him now and see if he can run it and how long it'll take," Stormy said as he pulled his cell phone out and began dialing.

When the phone was answered at the FDLE office, Stormy said, "Could I speak with agent Thomas Moore, please. Tell him Jack Storm is calling,"

Thomas answered the phone almost immediately. After exchanging a few pleasantries, Stormy got down to the purpose of the call. He told him about running the print through IAFIS and coming up empty and that it was entirely probable his suspect was from out of the country. He asked Thomas if it was possible to run it through Interpol's database and how long it would take. He added that time was something he didn't have a lot of right now. Thomas asked him to fax over the prints, and he would contact the Fusion unit and run them immediately. He said he would call back just soon as he received the results. He promised that it shouldn't take much more than fifteen minutes once he received the fax.

It was closer to thirty minutes before the call finally came. "Stormy, there was a hit on the prints, from both Cuba and Russia, but not an over abundance of information since the last entry was back in the eighties. I do think there's enough for you to use, so I'm faxing the results as we speak. You need anything else, pal? Or maybe you want to fill me in on what you're working."

"I'll bring you up to speed later, Thomas. Right now I can tell you that it has something to do with the Mayor's murder."

"Oh, I heard about that. Kind of hard not to have since it was all over the news. Keep me informed, and please, don't hesitate to ask for some help," Thomas said. Stormy cut the connection after assuring him that he would.

He turned to Linda and told her to take him to her fax machine. Once the printout had finished its clattering and came to a stop, he ripped it off the machine and began processing the information it contained. Thomas was a little off on his estimate of how much info was there. There was more than enough to proceed with. Now he had a name for the Scorpion and confirmation that he was indeed from out of the country, or at least had been at one time.

After giving Linda a quick hug and thanking her, he

headed for the door with the printout, asking her to make sure to let him know the results of the paint test as soon as she received them. For now, he needed to get back and share this information with Dakota and the Captain.

Chapter 32

Identity revealed

CAPTAIN PARADIS, DAKOTA AND STORMY sat around the conference room table at the Detective Bureau. When Stormy had returned to the Bureau he made copies of the printout for each of them. As they digested the contents of the document, the revelation that they finally had a name for *El Scorpion* was, to say the least, exhilarating. The printout revealed that the last activity noted on the Scorpion was in 1983. The further they read the clearer it was why there was no other mention of his activities.

They learned that his birth name was Juan Castro and he was born in Matanzas, Cuba, in 1964. He was serving a mandatory hitch in the National Revolutionary Police Force in Cuba when he had been sent to Omsk in the Soviet Union, for some unknown reason. The data indicated that he had also been photographed and printed in the Soviet Union, and once his mission was complete, he was put on a plane and sent back to Cuba. He never arrived back home. It was assumed that he walked off the plane

Sting of the Scorpion

and defected in Colombia during the last stop on the way to Cuba. That was the last anyone heard of him, even though agents of the PNR made a few unfruitful trips to Colombia looking for him. The lack of any further information on his whereabouts was a clear indication that the PNR had given up on finding him many, many years ago.

Captain Paradis was the first to break the silence. "Well, we now have a name and the photograph of a teenager. I would imagine that he has changed considerably over the years. He should be what, in his early fifties now, if I'm doing my math correctly? I'm sure in his profession he's deliberately changed his appearance many times. The only reliable guess as to what he looks like presently is the one we just put out on a BOLO."

Stormy replied, "So far we haven't had one single sighting, so we may have to consider that the Scorpion, or should I refer to him now as Juan Castro, is a long ways out of Hialeah by now."

Dakota turned to Stormy and asked, "Have you heard anything more from Pablo?"

"Nope, but I'm sure he's doing all he can for us. We'll just have to carry on until we do hear from him, if we do."

"I think you should call Pablo and give him the Scorpion's real name. Since they're both from Cuba he may be able go in a different direction with his inquiries. Just tell him to be discreet. This guy won't hesitate to kill in order to cover his tracks," the Captain said.

"I'll call him now, and then I need to go check out the apartment for the owner of the Denali we recovered. Any chance I can take Dakota with me? I could use her help canvassing the neighbors in case Emilio isn't there."

283

"I don't see why she can't go with you. Just make sure she doesn't get involved in any kind of altercation. It's getting late, so when you finish just drop her off at her place on your way home," the Captain replied.

Dakota arose from her seat with a smile and thanked the Captain. As she and Stormy started walking out of the office, his cell rang. Glancing at the screen he saw that Linda Ward was calling, so he stopped and answered.

"Watcha got, Linda?" he asked.

"I just now received the results on the paint comparisons. It *is* the vehicle that ran you off the road," she said.

"Great, now let's see if I can find Emilio. He needs to answer some questions, such as how the Scorpion came into possession of his car. Thanks, Linda. I'll catch you later."

"That was good timing. Linda just matched up the paint transfers, and the Denali is definitely the one that ran us off the road. Hopefully we'll find him at his apartment," Stormy said to the Captain and Dakota.

* * * * * * * * * *

Dakota used her feminine charms to persuade the building manager into opening the door of Emilio's apartment when no one responded to the knocks. Inside they found a neatly maintained living room, the appearance of one not having been used very much. There was no television and only a long sofa and plush easy chair complimented by a wrought iron coffee table, which had a thin layer of dust on the glass. Neither photos nor paintings adorned any of the walls, and there seemed to be little incentive for anyone to sit there. In the kitchen there were a few unwashed dishes in the sink. A roach scurried down the drain as Dakota moved a dish, causing her to step back in disgust. It appeared from the old caked food on the plates that no one had been here for several days. The sole bedroom was as sparsely furnished as the living room, only a bed and chest of drawers, although there were some clothes hanging in the closet.

The few available neighbors they questioned couldn't provide much information on Emilio. They all said that he was seldom there and that he kept mostly to himself, so they left him alone. They did confirm that he drove a black Denali and that he lived alone. One older man they talked with said that Emilio scared him, that he looked like a "gangster." Everyone they talked with agreed that they hadn't seen Emilio or his Denali for several days now.

"We're getting nowhere here, so let's call it a day," Stormy said.

"You need to give Pablo a call and give him that name. Or did you forget already?" Dakota replied.

"Thanks for reminding me. I'll call him while I'm driving home."

When Stormy dropped Dakota off at her place, he placed the call to Pablo and filled him in on the Scorpion's real name. Then he called dispatch and explained to the supervisor that he needed extra patrol in the complex where Emilio lived. He gave her the apartment number and a description of Emilio from the driver's license he had pulled up earlier. He asked her to make sure that if the patrol officer did see any activity at the apartment or the subject, to call for backup and make the arrest. He asked that he be notified as soon as an arrest was made.

As he pulled into the driveway at home he saw that Shaunie was not home yet. But then again, he was home a little earlier than usual. He mentally inventoried in his mind what was in the fridge and what he could prepare for dinner.

Chapter 33

The assault

SEATED IN THE FOOD COURT at the mall, Victor tried to remain inconspicuous while he ate. The fast food was bland, probably not real chicken anyway and certainly not very appealing to him. It lacked any flavorful spices that could have bumped it up a level from its present state of tastelessness. Still, he ate all of it, knowing he would need his energy in just a few hours for his assault on the compound.

He used his time while eating trying to decide if he should kill San Peron or not. After all, the man had sent a hit team to take him out at the motel. He really wished he could just get out of here and make his way back home. This contract had really been the deciding factor in his decision to retire. In his profession, a man couldn't make the mistakes he had made this trip and expect to continue on. That would be pushing lady luck to the extreme.

Victor decided the last bite was destined for the trash where it really belonged, so he picked up the tray and walked to the trash receptacle where he dumped everything. Glancing at his watch he saw that the mall would soon be closing, so he headed for the exit. It was still too early to go to the compound, but he needed to get the car from the hospital parking lot, drive back to the Inn and load it up. He also needed to change into some dark clothes for his foray tonight. By the time he accomplished all this it would be close to midnight and that was around the hour he had planned to pay his visit.

He wasn't even sure that San Peron would be home this evening, but he had no way of knowing unless he tried. If he made it inside and San Peron wasn't home he had already decided he wouldn't make another attempt. Time was one luxury he didn't have.

The parking lot at Palm Springs General was dark, even though there were some pole lights. The fringes of the lot were the darkest, the scattered pole lamps struggling to penetrate that far into the darkness. The car Victor planned to take was on the western side, under a large tree and shielded from the nearest light. He walked around the lot carefully glancing up at the cameras on the building, aware that there could be others mounted in the lot. He doubted that a decent image would be obtainable in the darkness, so he wasn't too concerned about the security cameras.

Pulling the jimmy from his waistband, he stood next to the tree to block any vision of him from the cameras or passersby. He slipped it between the door frame and window on the passenger's side of the car and after a quick up and down motion he was rewarded with the click of the lock opening.

Sting of the Scorpion

He opened the door and quickly put his finger on the button inside the door jamb to turn off the interior light. Reaching up he hit the overhead lens with his fist, shattering the thin plastic into several jagged pieces. He unscrewed the bulb and dropped it into his pocket. Only then did he release his finger from the button. Now he could work in darkness without being illuminated during the process of straight-wiring the ignition.

As a result of hours of practice he had the wires pulled from the dash and stripped within thirty seconds. He connected the two that would start the car, hoping to hear the sweet sound of the engine starting. Instead he heard the heart-dropping sound of a dead battery, the sound he hadn't considered. Evidently this car had been sitting here for a very long time. He would have to find another car, and he couldn't chance walking around the lot too much since the cameras were bound to notice him loitering.

He sat in the darkness of the disabled car and looked around at the parked vehicles nearest to him. At this time of the night there weren't nearly as many cars as during visiting hours. He spotted a dark colored Subaru SUV nearby and decided it was close enough that he would be out of sight of the cameras. He exited the car and scanned the parking lot for anyone that would be walking around, such as security guards.

At the exact moment he began to approach the SUV, a golf cart with a security guard rounded the corner of the hospital from the front entrance. He quickly stepped back into the shadows of the tree and waited, hoping he hadn't been seen. The guard drove past his position, actually going between him and the SUV and heading for the back of the hospital. He apparently didn't notice Victor, just drove with his eyes straight ahead.

Would he be returning anytime soon? That was the dilemma he was facing. Victor decided to give him a few minutes before making any further move. Luck was with him as the cart and guard returned in about two minutes and parked back in front of the main entrance, the guard dismounting and entering the hospital.

Once Victor was in the SUV, it took less than a minute to straight-wire the vehicle. He drove slowly out of the parking lot, keeping an eye out in the side and rear view mirrors for any indication that he had been observed taking the car. He finally released his pent up breath once he made a right turn at the light on Forty Ninth Street.

He drove carefully until he was back at the Inn. He found an empty parking space two rooms down from his which was actually what he was hoping for. If the owner of the SUV came out and reported his car stolen, a patrol unit could possibly drive through this lot and see it. This way it wouldn't be directly in front of his door and would enable him a better chance to slip away. He still had about an hour before midnight, so he would wait until the last minute before loading his gear.

* * * * * * * * * *

When Victor arrived at the street the compound was located on he turned in and drove slowly up the street to recon the area. There were outside lights burning on the four corners of the house within the compound, probably low wattage since the lights weren't overly bright. His guess was that to keep the neighbors from complaining about the brightness San Peron made sure the lights were aimed down to illuminate the interior of the compound only.

He managed to get a glimpse through the front wrought iron gates and saw that the Mercedes was still in the driveway. There was also a guard standing by the front door. He was sure that there would be at least one more outside, possibly roving or stationed at the rear of the house. From his viewpoint he couldn't see any lights on at any of the windows. San Peron was most likely in bed by now and that would fit his plans nicely.

As he passed the compound he looked at the subdivision on his right. A few of the houses had lights on inside and the street lights, one about every block, were burning. Most of the neighborhood was in darkness, and there didn't seem to be anyone out walking around. He continued on about a block past the development and made a quick u-turn. He turned in at the development and parked in the driveway of the empty house he had been at earlier and switched off the headlights.

Sitting in the car he carefully watched out for any other vehicles coming down the street as he began putting black makeup on parts of his face. He would need to be almost invisible to make it inside the wall. That was another problem he faced now, getting over the wall. Attempting to go through the gate was out of the question. Then it hit him! He could pull the car, headlights off, between the tree line and the back wall of the compound. From there he could stand on the roof of the car and clamber over the wall. The more he thought about it the better he liked it. The car was dark colored, the wall was painted fairly dark and with his dark attire he would blend in, at least from a distance.

After driving across the intersecting road with his headlights off, he eased onto the grassy area and slowly pulled up to the rear wall, making sure he was far enough away from the road to avoid detection from any cars that drove past. He had parked so close to the wall he had to exit the Subaru through the passenger door.

He put the night-vision head goggles around his neck. He couldn't use them until he had either killed the outside lights or made entry into the darkened house, but he was sure he would need them at some point. With the loaded dart gun hanging from a strap over his shoulder, he gently climbed up onto the hood of the vehicle, and then scampered up onto the roof, careful to keep his head down and below the top of the wall. If he stood up he would be visible to anyone that happened to be looking in that direction from inside the compound.

Cautiously, he inched his head above the top of the wall, his dart gun in hand and at the ready. Just as he expected there was a guard stationed at the rear of the house, standing just beneath the overhead light which was casting its soft glow over the back yard. The guard had his head down and was looking intently at something glowing, most likely his cell phone.

Suddenly, he raised his head when he heard the soft whoosh of the dart gun firing. He still hadn't seen Victor as he wildly grabbed his neck, attempting to pull the dart out. Before he could sound an alarm, his eyes rolled back and he slumped to the ground, his hand still on his neck

Sting of the Scorpion

and the cell phone falling from his grip onto the grass. The cocktail worked fast just as promised, but Victor didn't know if the guard was just out for the count or dead. Scrambling over the wall and dropping softly on the plush grass below, Victor bent over and quickly made his way to the downed man. He took a quick pulse and although weak, the man was still alive. Either he would make it and have one hell of a headache when he came to, or he would die.

Victor reached for the portable radio on the guard's belt and stuck it in his rear pocket, careful not to trigger the transmit button. Reaching up and barely making it, he tried to unscrew the light bulb, burning his fingers in the attempt. He looked around for something to cover his hand and then saw a trash can by the corner of the house. Lifting the lid he picked up a used paper napkin lying on top of the trash. Using it he once again attempted to unscrew the bulb enough to break the connection, this time succeeding. The darkness was immediate, enveloping and certainly welcomed.

Now he had to draw the guard from the front of the house to the rear. Walking to the far corner of the darkened yard Victor considered donning the night-vision goggles but ruled against it, there was still the light from the front interfering with its function. In the darkness the guard would have to really look hard to see him, giving Victor enough time to take him down.

Extracting the handheld from his rear pocket he lifted it to his mouth and pressed the button. He deliberately muffled his voice and said, "I need you at the back. The light just went out."

"I'll get another bulb and be there in a minute," the front guard responded, sounding tired and bored.

Victor knelt to one knee to minimize any view the guard would have of him when he came around the house. He aimed the dart gun, visualizing approximately where the head would be when he came into view. He didn't have to wait long before the radio crackled, "Alright, Jorge. I'm on my way so take out the old bulb."

The guards bobbing shadow became visible seconds before he arrived. The front light against his back was casting his shadow well into the back yard. As he rounded the corner of the house he began talking to the guard he thought was waiting for him.

"Alright, take the bulb so I can get back to the front."

Suddenly he espied the guard lying on the ground and grabbed for his handheld. Before he could pull it from his belt the dart found its way into his arm. Evidently the first guard went down so quickly because it was in the neck and the blood flow was right at the brain. The guard with the dart in his arm still managed to pull his radio and trigger the transmit button, "I've been sh……..." That was all he managed to get out before he succumbed to the fast acting drug and collapsed on the ground. Victor had to worry now that more guards would be spilling out to find out what happened.

He didn't have to wait long. Within ten seconds two more men came running out the front door and headed to the rear of the house when they didn't see the guard at the front. As they neared the rear of the house they stopped running and approached slowly, guns outstretched, looking for any threat.

Sting of the Scorpion

When Victor heard the partial radio transmission he quickly dropped prone on the ground. He didn't know how many more would be coming, so he reloaded the dart magazine. He also took his 9mm Beretta out and placed it on the ground next to him, just in case. He hoped he wouldn't have to fire it because the lack of a suppressor would wake the entire neighborhood up. If that were to happen he could only escape the compound through the front gate. Climbing back up the wall was not an option now. He kept the dart gun aimed upwards from his prone position.

When the first head peeked around the corner, he was tempted to take the guy out immediately, but he held back. If the first guy went down and one or more behind him saw it, there would be a standoff, and he wouldn't have any advantage then. The man that peeked around the corner must not have spotted the downed guards because he called out and then stepped into plain view, another man just behind him. Victor didn't have much choice now – it would only be a matter of seconds before the two men on the ground were seen.

In rapid succession he pulled the trigger of the dart gun, getting off four shots, three of them finding their targets. The two men slumped to the ground, their weapons falling from their hands, the deadly cocktail once again doing its job quickly.

Victor continued to lie still, watching and waiting to see if more guards would appear. After a minute and no others showing he slowly stood, picked his Beretta up and walked over to the men on the ground. Taking all of their weapons and tossing them into the darkness near the wall he then sidled over to the corner of the house and quickly peered around the edge.

He didn't see anyone else coming, but he wasn't a fool. There would likely be at least one or more if they knew what they were doing, and he had to assume they did. That meant there would be at least one man inside guarding San Peron.

He inched down the east side of the house until he reached the front corner. Reaching up, he tapped the bulb with the butt of his Beretta, breaking it with a soft popping sound. That left one light still burning on the west side of the house. He could either go back around the entire house or he could take the chance and cross in front. Not being foolish and risking his life, he chose the route around the house and began to make his way back and around.

* * * * * * * * * *

Humberto stood quietly, as still as a statue, waiting in the darkness inside the front room of the house. He had heard some of the last transmissions from the guards and instinctively knew in his gut that something was going on outside. At this time of night, his men rarely used the radio unless absolutely necessary.

He removed his weapon from his waistband holster, chambered a round, and waited quietly in the dark room. He knew someone was planning to make entry into the house, and he had the patience to wait for them. He didn't know why or what their purpose was, but it couldn't be good. He would shoot and ask questions later.

Humberto was still watching when the east side light

on the front of the house went out. He was sure now that someone was coming, and he was torn between waking Mister San Peron or staying where he was to block an entry. If he left to awaken him, the intruder could possibly enter the house and be hard to find in time, and he couldn't allow that. If the intruder had taken out his four men already, that made him a formidable foe. Humberto made the decision to stay in place, confident that he could handle the intruder. He knew the windows were not an option for the intruder to use since they were heavily barred, so that left the main entrance.

He stepped back deeper in the shadows at the far end of the room, slightly spreading his legs and turning a little sideways. He extended his weapon with a two-handed grip, his aim unwavering at the front door. From his view he was able to see the outside light on the west side of the house through the living room window, which was still burning. Suddenly, as if on cue, that light was extinguished and darkness enveloped both inside and out at once.

* * * * * * * * * *

Victor stood at the west corner of the house, the darkness embracing him like a blanket, waiting for any sound from within. The hair stood on the back of his neck, giving warning that one or more men could be waiting for him once he entered the front door. He lowered himself to his knees and crawled beneath the front window, until he reached the main entrance, a massive pair of double doors. He was banking on the guard that had fetched the light bulb to have left it unlocked. Otherwise, he had to figure a way to breech the doors. As solid as they appeared nothing short of a vehicle ramming them would work if they were locked. He could return to the rear of the house and search the downed guard's pockets for keys, but he had no way of knowing how long the drug would be effective. They could be out for another hour or more, but also they could come to at any time. He needed to make a move and he needed make it fast.

Standing up between the window and the doors, he slowly reached across to the door handle, a lever type that he only needed to pull down. He gently pulled on it and felt the bolt disengage, a barely perceptible click which sounded loud in the stillness of the night. He was in luck! The door had been left unlocked.

Victor refrained from pushing the door completely open, instead stepping back and waiting again for any movement inside.

* * * * * * * * *

Humberto heard the soft sound of the door mechanism when it clicked. Now he was sure that someone was preparing to enter the room. Whoever it was would be in for one big surprise. He kept his aim on the center of the door, his finger slowly tightening on the trigger. Suddenly the door flung open and without hesitation Humberto squeezed the trigger, firing several rounds. The flash temporally blinded him, and he had to wait a few seconds to see if he had hit the intruder.

* * * * * * * * *

Sting of the Scorpion

Victor pulled the night-vision goggles from his neck and strapped on the head band. Dropping the optics down over his eyes he waited for ten seconds to adjust. Lowering himself to his knees he reached up and pushed the door open, rolling into the room at the same time, continuing the roll to his left to keep from silhouetting himself in the open doorway. Knowing that if someone were waiting and fired a weapon that he would be blinded by the flash, he closed his eyes at the moment he made entry. Sure enough, there were several retorts from a weapon, the noise deafening in the confined room. He was hoping the shooter would be temporally blinded from the flash of the gunfire. Opening his eyes and looking through the night-vision goggles, he quickly spotted the eerily green shimmering image of a tall robust man standing at the far end of the room, his gun outstretched, and his head moving back and forth looking for the threat.

* * * * * * * * *

Humberto tried to quickly adjust his eyes to the room, after the flash from his gun blinded him for the moment. He didn't know if he had hit the intruder or not. He couldn't see anyone lying in the doorway. They should have been hit – there was no way he could have missed.

Suddenly he felt two stings on his neck and one in his gun hand. He knew instantly that he was in trouble, big trouble. Swinging his weapon, he began emptying it by spraying gunfire all around the room. He never heard his last shot as blackness suddenly closed in on him, the gun falling from his lifeless hands. The triple dose of the cocktail was too much for his heart to take. He was dead before his two hundred and fifty pound body hit the marble floor.

Chapter 34

San Peron meets *El Scorpion*

THE PUNGENT SMELL OF CORDITE filled the room from the freshly fired gunpowder. The smoke from the dozen or more rounds that had been fired by the man hung suspended in the air like a thin curtain. Once the ringing subsided in his ears, Victor stood and stared at the man's body lying on his side several feet away. He waited for a few seconds to make sure the man was down for the count. He had fired several darts tipped with the potent cocktail but wasn't sure how many had hit the target. It was definitely overkill but he had to make sure the man went down.

Wending his way through the room he quickly reached the shooter and bending over, took his pulse. The man was dead, no discernible pulse could be found. Victor then saw two of the darts sticking out from his neck and knew that the potency of the cocktail had been more than a human could survive.

Victor walked through the doorway leading from the living room to a hallway and stopped, listening for any sound that could signal another guard nearby. Taking a quick look through the doorway he could see that there was no one else waiting for him. Now he had to find the room that San Peron would be sequestered in, aware that the man would most likely also be armed. If he was here and had been asleep he certainly was awake now. The gunfire would have wakened the dead, much less a sleeping man. Victor just hoped that the sounds didn't spill out onto the open yard, echoing into the neighborhood across the street. If it did someone was sure to call the police, and this would have all been for naught. He doubted San Peron would call the police, thinking his people had everything under control. Being reasonably sure that there were no other guards in the house, Victor began slowly walking down the long hallway.

There were four doors in the hallway, two on each side. Two of the doors were standing open and a quick inspection revealed no one inside. The next two doors were closed tightly, no light creeping from under or around them. Most likely one of these was the bedroom that San Peron was in.

Without standing in front of the door Victor reached over and tried the knob on one, it was unlocked. He stood quietly with his ear pressed against the wall, not really expecting to hear anything, but he had to at least try. Once again he reached over and turning the knob, pushed the door open. There was absolute silence. He saw that there was a large mirror on the opposite wall, so he moved over

Sting of the Scorpion

a little closer without exposing himself to the open doorway. Looking at the interior of the room reflected in the mirror he could see there didn't appear to be anyone inside, the bed still made up. To make sure he dropped down on his stomach and slithered into the room. Once he was sure no one was inside he rose up and looked around.

Satisfied the room was empty he walked softly back into the hallway and slowly approached the last door. As he touched the door knob he heard a soft voice from within ask, "Humberto. Is that you?"

Victor removed his hand from the door knob and answered, "*Sí*, it's safe to come out now, sir."

Removing the goggles from his face Victor watched as the door slowly opened. As soon as San Peron stepped into the hallway, Victor grabbed him by the neck and shoved him against the wall, his drawn Beretta pressed against the man's temple.

Surprised and shaken San Peron asked in a quivering voice, "Who are you? What do you want?"

"I think you know who I am. As to what I want, I want some answers," Victor said.

Gripping San Peron by his neck from behind Victor half pushed and half walked him back down the hallway to the living room. When they reached the room, Victor flipped a light switch, illuminating the room from several lamps scattered about. He shoved San Peron onto the couch and stood in front of him, his Beretta still in his hand, aimed at the shaking man in front of him.

"If it's money you want, just take it and go," San Peron said, beginning to muster some courage.

At this moment San Peron glanced over to the side of

303

the couch and saw Humberto lying on the floor, not moving, probably dead. He was furious and scared at the same time. Humberto had been his personal bodyguard and confidant for many years. He was, or rather had been, a very loyal and competent man whom he had trusted more than any other he had known. Now, to see him lying on the floor like a dead dog infuriated San Peron beyond words. He suddenly stood and faced the man holding the gun on him.

"You didn't have to kill him. You probably killed all of my men. You may as well kill me now because I won't stop until I have your head!" San Peron said with renewed bravado. He hadn't been killed yet, so he figured the man wanted him alive for some reason.

"I didn't want to kill your men and actually the ones outside are still alive. This one wouldn't stop shooting at me, so I did what I had to do. As for you, I'm still undecided. You sent men to kill me at the motel earlier. Why?" Victor asked calmly.

"Oh… so you're *El Scorpion*. You were supposed to be the best and you screwed up. You missed the target I paid you to kill. I don't tolerate mistakes, not to mention that you took a million dollars of my money and for what…nothing. You missed!"

"And I planned to stay and finish the job, but you made a move against me before I could. Now I can't get to your target with all the heat you've caused. I just want to get out of here. How much money do you have on hand?" Victor asked.

"Now you think I'm giving you *more* money? Are you some kinda nut job?"

Sting of the Scorpion

Victor aimed the Beretta downwards and pulled the trigger, the noise deafening in the confines of the room. San Peron screamed in pain as he fell to the floor, holding his leg where the bullet had struck his thigh.

"Now, you can open your safe and I'll be on my way, or you can say a final prayer to whatever God you believe in because I don't have the time to waste on you and I definitely won't leave you alive. Do you understand?" Victor said.

"The safe, it's in the bedroom. I'll get you the money, just take it and leave," San Peron said as he rose in pain and began to hobble down the hallway towards his bedroom, averting his eyes away from his bodyguard and friend lying dead on the floor.

Victor followed close behind, not taking his eyes off of the man as he hopped on one leg down the hallway. Passing a light switch in the hall, he flipped it up turning the light on. San Peron reached the bedroom and looked back at Victor before entering.

"Don't even think of trying anything. Just get the money, and I'll be gone," Victor said, waving the gun for emphasis.

San Peron turned on the light and walked to a closet next to the bathroom, Victor right behind him. He reached up and moved a cardboard box which was covering the safe and dropped it on the floor. Carefully he punched in the numbers to open the safe and Victor heard the soft click. San Peron opened the door and reached in, handing a bundle of hundred dollar bills back to Victor.

Taking the money, Victor watched as San Peron reached into the safe again, this time coming out with a small handgun in his grip. As he turned Victor grabbed his wrist and slammed it against the safe. The gun fell to the floor, San Peron's shoulders slumping as his last gambit failed. Now he was sure that he was going to be killed and mentally said a prayer, the images of his wife and son flooding his mind.

"That was a stupid thing to do," Victor said as he pushed San Peron deeper into the closet.

Reaching into the safe he pulled out several more banded packets of hundred dollar bills. He estimated he had approximately twenty or thirty thousand dollars and that was more than enough for what he had in mind. He knew he would be taking a big risk if he attempted to fly out of Miami International, so he had changed his escape plans.

"I probably should put you out of your misery now, but I'm going to let you live," He said to San Peron.

"You know I'll be coming for you, so why are you being so generous with my life?" San Peron asked, slightly puzzled.

"I don't kill just for the sake of killing. I don't want to kill you even though my gut tells me I should. But, you can take it to the bank that I will kill your miserable ass if you do try to find me. I won't be so considerate the next time, so I suggest you get on with your life and forget you ever heard of me."

Victor picked up the gun from the floor. He unloaded the cartridges and put them into his pants pocket. It was a tight fit but he was able to stuff the banded bills into his money belt and pockets. Then he took the dart gun from around his neck and aimed it at San Peron.

"What are you doing? I thought you weren't going to kill me," San Peron said, holding out his hands as if to ward off the shot he knew was coming.

"I'm not going to kill you. Good night, San Peron," Victor said as he squeezed the trigger, the tipped dart striking him in the chest. San Peron slumped back, leaning against the shoe rack in the back of the closet. He looked with pure hate at Victor but the look faded almost as fast as it had appeared. His eyes rolled back in his head, and he was out.

Victor strolled quickly to the living room and was almost at the door when he spotted a set of Mercedes car keys on a table by the entrance. He picked them up and looked at the fob, then clicked on a button that said, "Unlock gate." He looked out the door and watched as the massive wrought iron gates began to swing open at the end of the driveway. The car he had arrived in was probably already reported stolen, so he would take San Peron's Mercedes. It would be awhile before it could be reported stolen, if it ever was. It was less than a couple of hours before the sun would be rising, and he wanted to be well out of Hialeah by that time.

As he drove out the open gate he looked back at the house. The only visible lights were in the living room, and there was no sign of the outside guards he had taken down, the darkness masking their unconscious bodies.

When he reached Okeechobee Road he turned and headed east, but not to the airport. He had a plan of escape now, and it didn't include returning to the Inn either.

Chapter 35

Sleepless night

STORMY TOSSED AND TURNED throughout most of the night. He was so close to catching the Scorpion he could almost taste victory. Glancing at the bedside clock he saw that it was nearly five in the morning. He decided to get out of bed since he couldn't sleep. After taking a shower he tried to dress without waking Shaunie, but she must have heard him because she was awake when he reentered the room.

In a sleepy voice she asked, "Why are you up so early, hon?"

"I couldn't sleep so I decided to head on in to work. I have a lot to do, so I may as well get to it. Sorry I woke you. Go back to sleep, and I'll give you a call later."

"Okay, be careful and don't forget to call me," Shaunie said as she plopped her head back down on the pillow. Almost instantly she was fast asleep.

Stormy made a pot of coffee. After pouring a cup he dialed Dakota's number. She answered on the first ring,

Sting of the Scorpion

evidently awake also from the clear sound of her voice.

"You couldn't sleep either, huh?" she said, knowing who it was.

"Nah, I bet I didn't get a total of two hours all night."

"Me neither. You want to head to the office? I can be ready as soon as you get here."

"I'll pick you up in thirty minutes," Stormy said as he hung up the phone.

* * * * * * * * *

When they arrived at the Detective Bureau, the night shift detectives were wrapping up their reports and getting ready to head home. None of the day crew had arrived, so for a few minutes they had the squad room to themselves.

Dakota went to the back and made a fresh pot of coffee. She seemed to live on the stuff. Stormy didn't dislike the taste of coffee, but he usually drank it out of politeness or habit. He didn't think he would really miss it at all if he quit altogether.

He waited for Dakota to return and then began reading the dispatched calls from overnight. Nothing of interest caught his eye, so he began going over the incidents of the day before, trying to ascertain if they had overlooked anything of importance. Dakota returned and took a seat, blowing on her steaming mug of coffee.

"Sure you don't want some?" she asked.

"No, I'm sure. I had a cup before I picked you up."

"There's no mention of any activity on the BOLO. It looks like he must have gotten out of Dade County," Stormy said.

"Let's go over what we have and see if we missed anything that could steer us in the right direction." Dakota said, still trying to cool her coffee off.

"Good morning, people."

Looking up they saw that Captain Paradis had just walked in.

"Why are you here so early, Captain?" Dakota asked.

"I could ask you the same thing, Dakota," He replied.

"I guess none of us could sleep," Stormy said.

"I stopped by dispatch on the way in, and they said that Hialeah Gardens had a call from an anonymous caller who claimed to have heard gunshots in his neighborhood. A patrol unit responded, but nothing was found," Captain Paradis said as he went to the rear to fetch a cup of the freshly brewed coffee.

"What's so unusual about that? We get gunshot calls all the time," Dakota said.

"The neighborhood is across the street from San Peron's home. I thought you might want to know in case you were planning to go out that way later," the Captain said as he poured his coffee.

"We had planned to go check him out this morning. We'll see what's up when we get there," Stormy said.

"There were no sightings at all on the BOLO, huh?" the Captain asked.

"No sir, none at all. The longer it goes the more likely the Scorpion is long gone from here."

"Did you call Pablo and give him the name?"

"Yes sir, but I haven't heard back from him so far," Stormy replied.

"Well, follow up on the San Peron thing and be careful."

Stormy looked at his watch and saw that he still had a couple of hours before it would be a fit time to pay San Peron a visit.

Chapter 36

Beginning of the end

VICTOR DROVE THE SPEED LIMIT even though it was still early in the morning. There were several cars on the road, and he knew it wouldn't be long before the morning rush hour traffic began. He made sure he stopped at all traffic lights, not taking a chance of going through any caution lights. He didn't want to be stopped by a patrol unit at this stage of the game.

He had rolled his window down to enjoy the fresh morning air and had just stopped for a red light when a patrol unit pulled up alongside him. Not wanting to draw attention to himself by rolling up the window, he just stared straight ahead, trying to appear nonchalant. He could feel the officer's eyes on him and willed the light to change.

Once it turned green he pulled away and noticed that the officer had dropped back, falling in behind him. *Just great*! he thought to himself. Getting stopped now was something he didn't need. It was not possible the car could have been reported stolen this quickly. Barely ten minutes had passed since he had left the compound. Hopefully it was just a minor traffic stop. Even then, he would have to present his passport for identification, and not having a driver's license would put him at risk of arrest. He was determined that would not happen.

Although he expected he was going to be pulled over by the police unit he was hoping against hope it wouldn't happen. The overhead blue lights suddenly lit up the early morning, the reflections from his rearview mirror splaying over his face as he glanced up. Victor knew he had to do something, but panic was not in his makeup. He carefully looked for a side road that he could pull off and stop. In case things went south in a hurry he wanted as few cars as possible to witness what could happen.

He spotted a side road on the other side of the canal and turned across the small bridge to reach it. He saw that he was on South River Drive. Few houses were in the area so he pulled over. Still, he was in sight of Okeechobee Road, but he doubted any cars passing could see him in any detail, although the blue lights from the patrol unit would naturally draw their attention.

The marked unit pulled in behind him leaving about ten feet between the cars. The front end of the police car was deliberately turned slightly towards the street, the headlights on bright, effectively blinding him in the side and rear view mirrors.

* * * * * * * * *

Ileana Fernandez, called Lena by her friends, was

slowly making her way back to station, her shift soon ending. She had put up with an unusually slow night, the boredom of patrolling a zone not helping her to stay awake and alert. She had caught up on the few reports she had taken on her shift and only had to turn them in and go home. It was to be a three-day weekend for her, and she was looking forward to spending most of it at the beach with her boyfriend.

When she pulled up to the traffic light, she was taking one last look at the BOLO sketch that had been issued at roll call. As she casually turned to look at the car idling next to her, she did a double take. The man driving the Mercedes looked almost identical to the artist's rendering in the BOLO. She also observed that the man deliberately kept from looking in her direction, his gaze straight ahead.

When the traffic light turned green, she waited until the Mercedes pulled away, then she changed lanes and fell in behind it. Picking up her radio mike from the dash and her adrenaline beginning to rise, she called and advised that she was making a traffic stop, that the driver resembled the suspect in the BOLO. Lena proceeded to read off the license tag number and advised she was making the stop at this time. By the time the Watch Commander could break in to have her wait for backup, she had already pulled the car over.

* * * * * * * * * *

Victor had left the dart gun and night-vision goggles at the compound after determining he had no further use for them. He still had his Beretta and a couple of loaded clips with him. He slowly took the 9mm from his waistband and held it by his right side, out of sight. The bright headlights in his side view mirror were suddenly blocked by an officer walking up to the rear of his car. He did a double take when he saw that it was a female officer. He had a steadfast rule when it came to harming women and children, but this was a different situation. The officer continued on to his open window and stopped just behind the door jamb.

"Sir, could you please switch the engine off and show me your driver's license?" she asked politely.

"Yes, officer. What was I doing wrong?" Victor asked, buying time.

"Sir, please turn the car off and show me your driver's license," she asked again, her flashlight shining in the driver's side window.

Victor reached over and turned the key to the ignition off and then opened the door. As he started to get out of the car, the officer stepped back, her hand moving to the grip of her holstered weapon, and told him, "Sir, please stay inside the car."

"I have to stand, so I can get my license from my rear pocket," Victor said smiling at the officer, holding his hand with the gun behind his back. By that time he was out of the car and pretending to reach in his rear pocket. The officer not seeing any threat, waited as he took a step towards her, watching in shock as he suddenly pulled his Beretta from behind. Before she could react he was in her face, the gun against her chin. He could see the fear in her eyes and almost felt sorry for her. She had been lax, and it was going to cost her dearly, unless she did as she was told.

"We're going back to your car, and you will turn off those flashing blue lights. I'm not going to hurt you, but you must do as I say if you want to keep it that way. Do you understand me?" Victor said grimly.

Nodding her head and taking a deep swallow, the officer walked back to her patrol car, her legs wobbly and mentally cursing herself for being so careless. Victor followed her, so close he could smell the perfume she wore. He had taken the weapon from her holster and was now in control. He sincerely hoped she wouldn't do anything foolish as he really didn't want to hurt her. She was only doing her job, but he would not allow himself to be brought in.

When they reached the patrol car, the officer reached in and flipped a switch, the sudden lack of flashing lights disarming her for a brief moment. Then he had her turn off the headlights. Before he could say or do anything else, the radio in the car and on her hand-held suddenly came to life. The dispatcher reading back the registered owner of the tag she had run. Victor heard it all, and the name of San Peron came up.

"Answer her back and acknowledge receipt. Don't even think of trying to call for help. I'll be long gone when they get here and find you on the ground. Do you understand?"

"Yes, I understand," she said, feeling helpless.

The officer reached up and pressed the mike on her lapel, acknowledging she had received the transmission. Victor could sense she was on the verge of saying some-

Sting of the Scorpion

thing else, so he pressed his gun harder into her neck. That was enough for her to reconsider and quickly take her hand away from the mike.

"You don't have to do this, mister. Just get in your car and drive away," the officer said, assuming she was going to be shot regardless of what she said or did.

Victor took the handcuffs from the case on her gun belt and put her hands behind her back. He snapped the cuffs on her wrists, snug but not too tight. Gripping her arm at the elbow he walked her to the Mercedes, put her in the passenger seat, and strapped on the seat belt. He wasn't overly concerned for her safety – he was just placing another obstacle in her path in case she tried to escape. As he began to close the passenger's door her radio blared once again, a man asking her if she was okay, wanting a status report.

"That's my Watch Commander. He knows something's not right. You need to let me go…get out of here while you can," Lena said with a burst of bravado.

"Answer him back and make sure you convince him you're okay," Victor said calmly.

Since she couldn't press the transmit button Victor unclipped it from her lapel and holding it in front of her mouth, pressed the button. Even with a quiver in her voice, she managed to relay that she was fine. Victor took her portable radio from her belt and carried it with him as he walked around the car to the driver's side. Once he was inside, he glanced over and saw that she had tears welling in her eyes, her chest heaving as she struggled to breathe.

"Hey, I'm not going to hurt you. Calm down and continue to do as I say. I'll let you out of the car once I get further down the road," he said in a calm voice as he reached over and patted her shoulder in an attempt to calm her down. She simply nodded and turned her head away, looking out the window, wondering if she would ever see her family or friends again.

Chapter 37

Missing officer

STORMY AND DAKOTA WERE HALF LISTENING to the radio as they sat at their desks. When the officer came on and advised she was making a traffic stop on a suspect from the BOLO they both jumped up. They heard the Watch Commander order her to wait for backup to arrive, but his call went unanswered.

Fearing the worst, he and Dakota gave a heads up to the Captain and headed for the car. Dakota quickly changed channels and asked dispatch the location of the officer. Stormy told her to have dispatch send every available car to that location immediately. He and Dakota jumped into his loaner and screamed out of the parking lot, heading for Okeechobee Road several miles away.

Traffic was beginning to get heavy with the morning commuters heading for work. With siren blasting, all lights flashing, Stormy drove like a madman, desperate to get there. He had a bad feeling about the fate of the officer.

Then he heard her on the radio assuring dispatch and the Watch Commander she was okay. From past experiences Stormy could recognize fear in a person's voice, and this female officer definitely was scared, although she was bravely trying to mask it.

Stormy and Dakota weren't the only units heading for Okeechobee Road. He caught up with a marked unit trying to cross the intersection at LeJuene and Forty Ninth where traffic was at a standstill. Weaving in and out Stormy jumped the median and crossed ahead of the marked unit. Drivers began pulling to the side as much as they could in the bumper to bumper traffic, but it was still slow going.

"Call dispatch and have them attempt to raise the officer again," Stormy asked Dakota, as he kept changing lanes.

Dakota made the call, and in a few seconds she was advised that the officer wasn't responding. This wasn't good and Stormy knew it. He had a feeling of dread and began driving even more aggressively. Even Dakota, who knew that Stormy was a great driver hung on with white knuckles.

At the intersection of Okeechobee and LeJuene, most of the heavy traffic was heading east-bound. Stormy took a quick right turn, the car almost fishtailing in the intersection as he kept his foot on the pedal. He pushed the accelerator even more, the speed odometer now flashing eighty miles per hour. It was precarious driving because there was still moderate traffic on the road heading west, and you never knew which way a driver would go when he saw blue lights behind him. Stormy could see a marked

Sting of the Scorpion

unit several blocks ahead of him and two others pulling out from side streets. The word was out that an officer was in distress, and all other calls were secondary.

The location of the traffic stop was on Okeechobee near South River Drive, but when they reached that area they couldn't see the officer's unit. There were no flashing lights to indicate a traffic stop; there wasn't even a stopped car. Without knowing it, most of the units flew past the car parked on the opposite of the canal, looking in vain for the unit on the main roadway.

The sun had just begun creeping above the eastern horizon, daylight replacing the fading darkness. Stormy was the first to see the unit parked on the far side of the canal, canted slightly on the edge of the southernmost shoulder of the road. He had sped just past the bridge and quickly made a u-turn, causing several cars to hit the brakes. Dakota keyed the mike and advised the units that the officer's car had been spotted across the canal on South River Drive. Police units that had flown past the location began making turns and heading back to the scene.

Pulling up behind the patrol car parked on the shoulder, Stormy and Dakota swiftly exited their car, their weapons drawn and ready for any potential threat. They split up and began walking up behind the patrol car, which appeared to be empty. When they reached the driver and passenger doors, they could see that there wasn't anyone inside.

As a precaution Stormy hit the release button for the trunk, hoping he wouldn't find the officer inside. After lifting the trunk lid, Stormy breathed a sigh of relief – there wasn't anyone inside. But where was the officer?

Was she in the canal or did the suspect take her with him?

Several more units began arriving, officers bailing out of their cars. Stormy told several of them to search the bank of the canal for any clue of where the officer was.

"He must have taken her with him Stormy," Dakota said.

"Leave the uniforms to scour the area. We'll drive further down the road and pray we can catch up with him," Stormy said as he headed for the car.

Chapter 38

Al Lawrence

THE A-1 CAR PARTS AND JUNKYARD had been in the Lawrence family for over fifty years. After his father had passed away in the seventies, Al had taken over the family business. Although many acres larger now than it had been in the past, the junkyard was still manageable for Al and his two longtime employees. He had two car crushers and three heavy-duty forklifts. These days the vast majority of his business was selling used auto parts. Due to the ever-increasing advancements in engineering and computerized engines, the only car parts he would soon be selling would be body parts. The everyday wanna-be mechanic couldn't keep up with the car manufacture's complicated engine parts now. It almost seemed by design that the car manufacturers were designing engines that only highly qualified mechanics could work on. The days of replacing your own water pump, carburetor, radiator or any of a multitude of parts under the hood was past. Still, he had a respectable business and it allowed him to live a moderate lifestyle.

Al, called "Strawberry" by most everyone, had lived in Medley most of his life, and until his wife had passed he had lived in the same house. It had been so long since he had acquired the nickname "Strawberry" that he couldn't even hazard a guess where it came from. Although he still had the house he and his wife had shared until her death, he had put a single-wide trailer in the back of the junkyard, and that's where he spent most of his time now. The house in Medley contained too many memories, and he didn't like being alone with those memories now. Still, he couldn't bring himself to get rid of the house.

He had one son who was an attorney in Ohio, but other than that he had no one to leave the business and house to. He knew that his son wouldn't keep the junkyard, and he could appreciate that in his own way. He even considered selling out and taking a long extended vacation, but when that was over, then what. No, he harbored no intentions of retiring, and this was the only thing he had ever done. He would stay with it and probably die on the job as his father had before him.

The one thing he had been thinking about lately was setting up the business to be passed on to his two faithful employees. They would benefit from it, and he knew they would continue to operate it long after his death. He doubted his son would even care, so he made up his mind to contact an attorney soon to draw up the necessary papers.

Al sat in his small kitchen in the single-wide, sipping a cup of coffee as he watched the morning news on the thirty-two inch television. He had a restless night and had risen early. He had finally shrugged off the chains of his old-fashioned habits and subscribed to cable television, ditching the outside antenna. He was amazed at the number of channels he had access to now, but in his mind he smiled at the thought that you could still only watch one at a time, the difference being that you had more choices, and with more choices you paid more.

Just as he raised the cup to his lips again, a loud crashing noise came through the half-open window. Quickly setting the cup down, he jumped up and ran to the bedroom to put on his pants and shirt. Once he was dressed, and as an afterthought, he grabbed his shotgun from beside his bed and raced out the door, heading for the front gate. As he turned the corner of the aisle that led to the front gate he saw a female police officer running towards him, eyes wide and hands fastened behind her back. He knew she was in trouble so he ran and met her halfway, pulling her to a side lane, out of sight of the front.

"What's happening officer? Are you in trouble?" Al asked.

"Yes, I've been kidnapped, and the man responsible is behind me. He's very dangerous and will probably come looking for me," Lena said, breathing hard.

"Don't you worry, officer. I'll handle him," Al said as he hoisted the shotgun.

"NO! Please, mister! He *will* kill you. He's a professional killer who we've been looking for. I have to get to a phone and alert the department where we are and that he is here."

"I have a phone in my house just behind us. Come

with me, quickly," Al said as he turned and helped the officer race to the house.

Within seconds they reached the trailer and entered through the front door. Lena told Al to reach into her front pants pocket and retrieve the spare handcuff key she had on her key ring. Retrieving them he unlocked the cuffs, and the officer stood rubbing her sore wrists for a few seconds, trying to restore circulation.

She grabbed the phone on the table and quickly called dispatch. After advising them she was okay, she explained where they were and that there was a civilian living on the property and she was in his home. She advised that she had been disarmed by the suspect, and he had also taken her hand-held. That was important because the suspect could actually listen in on the calls and monitor where the units were at any given time.

"Take the shotgun and wait here, officer, I'll be right back," Al said as he headed for the door.

"Where are you going? You'll only get yourself killed. Hang on, I'm going with you," Lena said, hefting the shotgun and walking to the door also.

As they walked out the door, the first shots rang out.

Chapter 39

End of the line

VICTOR WAS HOPING TO FIND A WAY back across the canal and onto Okeechobee Road, but so far he hadn't passed another crossover. In the distance he could see a patrol car with flashing lights speeding towards him, on the same side of the canal. He had just passed a small white sign that read "Medley City Limits," but he had no knowledge of the town or how it was laid out.

Coming into view was a junkyard surrounded by ten-foot high concrete walls and a closed double gate adjacent to the road. He had little choice and no time, so he turned and drove the Mercedes directly at the gates. The officer, even though seat-belted in, turned her head and uttered a small scream. At thirty miles an hour the gates stood little chance when the two thousand plus-pound car made contact. Impacting the gates dead center the two wings were flung open with enough force to rip one off the pole that held it. The massive chain that had held them together was now swinging freely from the right one, several heavy links stripped away as easily as buttons popped from an overly tight shirt.

Victor brought the car to a stop just inside the yard. Both air bags had deployed, so it took a few seconds longer to exit the car. He rushed around to the passenger's side and opened the door. Jerking the air bag aside, he unfastened the seat belt holding the officer. He quickly dragged her from the car and holding her arm tightly rushed over to the nearest aisle of stacked automobiles.

Peering around the twelve-foot high tower of crushed vehicles, Victor watched as the police car sped past the junkyard, lights flashing, and the officer intent on the action further up the road. He evidently hadn't seen the Mercedes swerve off the road and crash through the gate.

Once Victor could no longer hear the siren he hustled back to the car, the female officer in front. He told her to stand by the front of the car. He entered the driver's side and grasping the blown airbag, tried to rip it from the steering column. It was more firmly attached than he figured, and he had no knife. So he kept jerking and pulling. Victor was so intent on getting the spent airbag loose that he failed to see the female officer running from the car and disappearing around the row of crushed cars, fleeing down the long dirt path to put distance between the two of them.

Where the hell had she gone? Victor asked himself when he exited the car with the remnants' of the airbag in his hand. He couldn't waste time to look for her now – he needed to take out the other airbag and get out of there.

As he began walking around to the passenger's side, he heard a car approaching from the direction he had come from. Pulling his weapon, he quickly darted back to the corner of the pile of crushed cars. Plastering himself out of sight against them he carefully turned his head and peered around the corner. Just as he looked he saw an unmarked car slowly roll halfway into the opening where the gates once stood.

Things were not working in his favor right now, and Victor knew it. He couldn't do anything until the unmarked car left, if it did. They must have seen the crashed gates and decided to investigate. He needed to move deeper into the yard, and quickly, to avoid detection. Staying close to the columns of junk cars, he ran deeper into the junkyard.

The place was huge, covering acres and the several paths between the rows ran for a hundred yards or more. He came to one path that intersected the row he was on, so he turned into it and stopped. Looking intently back the way he had come, he couldn't see anyone following him. He didn't think that would last too long once the people in the unmarked car spread out and started canvassing the yard.

Victor stood in place as he watched for pursuit and at the same time scanned the area. He couldn't see any way out other than the front gate. But there had to be one, so he decided to search further into the yard.

As he began to turn and walk towards the rear of the yard he saw the doors to the unmarked car open. His eyes widened as he watched Jack Storm and his female partner get out of the car. Evidently he was going to have to deal with those two once again.

****

When Stormy pulled into the yard through the gates that had obviously been forced open, he killed the engine, stopping a few yards behind the Mercedes just inside. Immediately Dakota ran the plate, and it quickly came back as registered to Antonio San Peron. Stormy knew that San Peron wasn't driving the car, so it had to have been taken by the Scorpion. But from where and how was the question now.

They both exited the car cautiously, never taking their eyes off the yard, their weapons drawn and at the ready. Risking a fast glance he looked inside the car. He didn't see the female officer, or anyone else for that matter. He did note that the airbags had been deployed and assumed that they had deployed when the car had struck the gates.

Spreading out, he and Dakota began inching towards the first lane of stacked automobiles. As they glanced around the corner of the pile a hail of bullets pinged off of the junked cars, some buzzing uncomfortably close to them.

Standing with their backs to the metal tower of junk they quickly leaned around the corner and let off a burst of shots, hoping to either hit the shooter or throw him off-balance enough for them to get down the aisle. Several shots were fired in their direction once again, causing them to duck back for cover.

Stormy caught Dakota's eye and motioned that he was going to jump over another aisle and try to head the shooter off. She was to stay in place and give him covering fire. He held up his free hand and silently ticked his

Sting of the Scorpion

fingers off, 3...2...1...and then he ran down the far aisle as Dakota began firing again.

* * * * * * * * *

Victor now knew there were two of them. He fired his weapon in their direction to keep them from advancing any further. He was, for the moment, pinned inside the junkyard with no visible way out. He needed to buy a little time to give himself a chance to find another way out. Putting himself in the two detectives' shoes, he knew that they would soon split up and come after him. In this situation divide-and-conquer was the only way they could get to him. Unless, of course, ample backup arrived before he could get out. He knew that would be only a matter of time.

He felt confident he could handle Storm and the female, but if a dozen or more officers arrived, and especially the SWAT team, he would be screwed. He had to move fast because he knew that at any moment he could expect to find one of the two detectives trying to cut him off from behind, which is what he would do in this situation.

Turning down the next adjacent side lane, he sprinted to the end as gunshots rang out from the front again. He saw that there was nothing but an oversized forklift and more crushed cars when he reached the end of the aisle. Even though the ground was packed dirt, Victor could still hear the muffled footfalls of one of the detectives coming in his direction. The detectives didn't live in his world where announcing your arrival, no matter how hard you tried not to, could mean the difference between life and death. As far as he was concerned, Detective Storm was choosing death, and Victor was going to have to oblige him.

Victor could almost hear Detective Storm breathing as he made his way down the side lane behind him. The forklift was huge, and the tires were tall enough for him to kneel behind, completely out of sight.

* * * * * * * * * *

Stormy turned the corner cautiously, expecting to see the Scorpion either waiting for him or moving further down the aisle. He was puzzled about where the captive officer was. Was she here with the Scorpion or had he killed her and dumped her body along the way? He wasn't in view so Stormy quietly stepped around further, his eyes and head jerking in several directions, his weapon held out in front ready for action. All he saw was a huge forklift and a car crusher in front of it. Beyond that there were piles and piles of more junk cars waiting to be crushed. He walked slowly along the side of the forklift, his back to the tires, ever watchful for the Scorpion hiding among the junk cars.

Then, almost as fast as he heard the sudden whisper of movement behind him, he knew he had made a huge mistake. As he whirled around he caught a glimpse of a hand clutching a weapon descending on him, striking him in the temple before he could evade the blow. A kaleidoscope of stars exploded in his vision, a dull pain suddenly emanated from his head and then blackness as he slipped

Sting of the Scorpion

to the ground, still clutching his weapon.

* * * * * * * * *

Victor hadn't really wanted to kill Detective Storm, and now he had no need to. He dragged the limp body of the detective over to a stripped out car in front of the forklift. Dropping the body to the ground, he opened the door of the car and hoisted the body of Detective Storm into the front seat. He quickly found the detective's handcuffs tucked in his back waistband and swiftly cuffed both of his hands to the steering wheel. He saw a wadded up orange work towel lying on the floor of the car. He grabbed it and folding it into a smaller size he stuffed it into the detective's mouth, effectively prohibiting him from calling out for help.

For now, he had solved one problem, but the female detective was still out there. He didn't plan to underestimate her. Also the officer he had cuffed was hiding in the yard somewhere. He wouldn't waste time on trying to find her. Instead he would look for a way out of the junkyard before more officers began arriving.

As Victor turned the corner heading for the back of the junkyard, he was surprised to see an older man and the female officer coming his way. The man, probably in his late fifties or early sixties, was carrying a shotgun. As soon as the man spotted Victor, he raised it, aiming it in his direction. Victor jumped back just as the blast of the shotgun reached his ears, pellets striking the junked cars all around him.

He felt a stinging sensation in his gun hand. Looking

down, he saw that one of the pellets had grazed him. It almost looked like a rope burn and hardly any blood was coming from it. He instantly dismissed it.

Holding his weapon around the corner of the car, he fired off several rounds. He watched through a crack between cars as the man and the officer turned and ran back the way they had come. By now he was at the back wall. At one side he saw a mobile home and adjacent to it, leaning against the house, was an extension ladder.

Victor approached the home cautiously. When he saw there was no one there, he grabbed the ladder and placed it against the wall. After scanning the area again and still seeing no one coming in his direction, he scampered up the ladder and quickly jumped over the top, landing unharmed in a soft boggy area on the other side. It was at that moment he heard the wailing and chirps of sirens moving in the direction of the junkyard. He breathed a big sigh of relief. He had found a way out and not a moment too soon. But he still needed to put a lot of distance between him and the manhunt he knew would be forthcoming.

Chapter 40

The days after

THE FOLLOWING TWO DAYS were very hectic. Linda Ward and her crime scene technicians spent one full day processing the scene of the abduction of Lena and the showdown in the junkyard. There was no sighting of the Scorpion. It was later determined he had used a ladder to scale the wall at the rear of the property and had simply vanished.

When the first units had arrived on the scene they were met by Dakota and briefed on the situation. SWAT was the first to invade the yard and quickly found Strawberry in a junked box truck. He was standing in the cargo space in the rear of the truck and had placed himself in front of the abducted policewoman, Ileana Fernandez, cradling his shotgun. She called him her hero and Al was beside himself with pride.

It was two weeks after the junkyard drama that Ileana Fernandez turned in her resignation from the Hialeah Police Department. She didn't list her true reasons for resigning. Rather than admit that police work was not for her, she stated that she was leaving for personal reasons.

Dakota was beside herself when no one could find Stormy. SWAT along with patrol officers and detectives scoured the yard searching for him. When he couldn't be found, it was assumed he had been taken hostage by the Scorpion. Just as all hope of finding him was beginning to fade, Al found him cuffed to the steering wheel of a car when he climbed onto the forklift and looked inside the car.

Stormy was still unconscious and was transported to the hospital for treatment. He spent the following two days in a hospital with a concussion. Since it was the second concussion in as many days, he was placed under extreme observation. When Dakota was finally able to bring him up to speed on everything that happened, he was at first quiet, almost pensive. Then he looked at Dakota and promised her that it wasn't over, that he would never stop looking for the Scorpion.

* * * * * * * * * *

In the following two weeks things gradually began to return to normal, or as normal as they could if you considered all the events that had transpired in the weeks before. The funeral for the Mayor was full of all the pomp and regality that he deserved. The Governor as well as other dignitaries from around the state attended. Stormy, Dakota and a delegation of officers from several agencies were in attendance also. The HPD honor guard performed the ceremonies culminating in the twenty-one gun salute.

Sting of the Scorpion

The citizens knew they had lost a Mayor that truly cared for them and their city. It was unlikely they would see the likes of him anytime soon, if ever.

Captain John Paradis announced his retirement, and a party was in the planning stages for him, honoring his thirty-three years of service to the city. He advised Stormy that he and his wife were planning to take up scuba diving lessons, and they were going to take him up on the offer of going to the Keys together for a weekend, and soon.

Antonio San Peron had been investigated in reference to his activities surrounding the Scorpion debacle. Nothing that could tie him to the Scorpion was uncovered, so the investigation led to a dead end. He was questioned about his vehicle which was used by the Scorpion and abandoned at the junkyard. He claimed to know nothing about it but would file a stolen vehicle report. After all it was a Mercedes, and they didn't come cheap he said. He claimed to not have heard the burglar that Humberto had died trying to stop. San Peron stuck to his guns about not knowing the Scorpion and what had happened at his compound the night gunshots were reported by the neighbors. For now there was no ongoing investigation into the activities of San Peron, but if Stormy had his way there would be, and soon.

As for the death of Humberto…the report stated that another employee told them he had attempted to thwart a burglary in progress and was killed by an unknown assailant. That case was still under investigation.

Dakota had just recently begun dating George Von Hartman, the analyst at the FBI office in Miami. She and

George had gone out to dinner with Stormy and Shaunie once already. Stormy noticed her demeanor had changed a lot, and he attributed it to her infatuation with George. He was happy for her and hoped that the relationship would continue to be a fruitful one – she really deserved some happiness in her life.

Strawberry received an award for valor from the Hialeah Police Department in recognition for his part in the junkyard standoff. The newspapers had all printed articles about how he rescued the police officer that had been kidnapped. He bought over a hundred copies of the newspaper plastered with his awards ceremony and a photo of him accepting the award. Nothing this exciting had ever happened to him in his entire life. Anyone and everyone he knew were sent a copy of the newspaper. He was especially proud that his son had flown in for the ceremony, and he advised him about his plans for the junkyard and the two employees. His son had no objection and told his dad how proud he was of him. He tried to persuade Al to move to Ohio to live with him and his wife once he turned over the junkyard to his employees. Al promised him he would think about it, but deep inside he knew he would never leave Medley. This was his home and he had no desire to leave, although he would take more trips to see his son now.

Shaunie announced to Stormy a few days after his release from the hospital that there was going to be a little Stormy in their lives, evidently a gift from their vacation in the Keys. The pregnancy was a total surprise to Stormy but his happiness was obvious from the smile plastered on his face, one that refused to go away. He couldn't stop talking about becoming a father.

He also presented Shaunie with a present that he had promised her when they were in the Keys, something he had ordered a week earlier. It was a CD of "Our Winter Love" by Bill Purcell. She told him that it was probably the second best present she had ever received, the first being with child.

Alex Krane made a trip to the hospital to visit Stormy when he was aware of what happened in the junkyard. The offer for a job with Wells Fargo was still open. Stormy told Alex he was honored by the offer but was still content working at HPD, but that he would never totally close the door on the offer. Who knew what the future held. They shook hands and Alex returned to Iowa with the promise to stay with Stormy and Shaunie whenever he was in town again. Stormy felt that it was going to become a great friendship between the two of them, as he really liked the guy.

* * * * * * * * *

Out of the blue, the call came. Pablo told Stormy that he had information on the whereabouts of the Scorpion. He met with Stormy at the Hialeah Racetrack and Casino where he gave him all of the details on where *El Scorpion* could be found.

Chapter 41

Paradise found – Paradise lost

WHEN VICTOR WENT OVER THE WALL at the junkyard, he quickly hitched a ride with a road worker on his way to Okeechobee and near State Road 84 in Broward County. It was going the opposite direction that he needed to go, but he would be safer from apprehension if he took his time and went south in a roundabout way. Through a series of bus rides, taxi rides and even some hitchhiking, he made his way to the Homestead area in south Dade County.

There he was able to use a burner cell he purchased at a local Wal-Mart and contact his broker. Using as few words as possible, he explained to the broker what he needed and that he needed it now. He was told to sit tight and he would get a call back within thirty minutes. When the call came in, it was exactly thirty minutes later. It was with a sigh of relief once he terminated the call.

Sting of the Scorpion

He made his way to a small airport on the outskirts of Homestead and upon arrival he asked for Randall Fulmer, a frequently used asset of his broker. He was told that he would spend the night in a back room at one of the bays and at sunrise they would fly in a small Beechcraft down to Key West. When they reached Key West he would be put in touch with another pilot who would take over from there.

The next morning at sunrise Victor made his way out to the tarmac where he boarded the small plane. He hadn't had any breakfast or liquid yet but he didn't care, he was getting out of the State finally. He paid the pilot the two thousand dollars he owed, and within two hours of boarding the plane he had landed at Key West. He was told by his pilot where to go next and the name of the person he was to ask for.

When he reached the west side of the Key he found a seaplane docked and the pilot waiting for him, lounging in a chair on the dock, a wide brimmed straw hat keeping the sun at bay. No names were exchanged although Victor already knew the pilot's name.

He boarded the plane and they were soon airborne, Key West quickly receding behind them, the mid-morning sun climbing high in the sky. This plane was much larger than the Beechcraft he had flown in from Homestead, and it would take him on a multi-island hopping trip until he reached home.

Before he reached home he touched down in Cancun, Mexico, Jamaica and then finally Colombia, where it was home sweet home. He was fairly close to having used all of the money he had taken from San Peron at the compound. His new plan for getting out of Florida and making it back home had worked due to the fresh influx of San Peron's money.

Victor used the next eight days to tie up loose ends and arrange for an agent to sell their home. He didn't need to be here for the sale, the money was going to be deposited in his account directly.

All he had left to do was arrange for passports for him and his wife Marta. He had his, but he had to explain to Marta why she needed a new one. Over dinner one night he carefully explained to her, without going into details, that he had gotten into some trouble and that they had to leave Colombia for awhile. She didn't ask any questions as usual because of her love and trust in Victor. Before long they were flying to Costa Rica under new identities.

The plane landed in Tortuguero on the Caribbean side of Costa Rica. Within a few days Victor had leased a house for an indeterminate length of time on the beach midway between Tortuguero and Cano Blanco. His plan was to eventually make his way to a country without extradition and spend his life and retirement there. But there was no rush just yet. For now he would stay here in Costa Rica basking in the tropical sun, walking the white sandy beaches feeling the fine sand squirting between his toes and taking long swims in the beautiful turquoise waters of the Caribbean. At last he would finally be spending some long overdue time with his wife. Life was going to be good for both of them from this day forth.

* * * * * * * * *

Sting of the Scorpion

Two lounge chairs sat in the sugary white sand side by side, the sparkling multi-shaded blue water softly lapping within yards of their feet. The man and woman were not young by any means but neither were they really that old. They appeared to be just two people enjoying life and didn't seem to have a care in the world. Their cottage was only fifty yards behind them on the beach.

"Would you like another beer, honey?" Marta asked her husband, Victor.

"I would love one and when you return we'll take a quick swim to cool off, if you like," he said to her with a loving smile.

"I would like that very much. I'll be back in a few minutes with our drinks," she said as she rose and began gingerly walking across the hot sand to the cottage, happy with her life now. She had never once stopped loving her husband, and now she loved him even more that he was finally going to be spending all his time with her. It was all that she had ever wished for and now it was happening.

Victor turned and watched her for a minute as she walked across the sand to the cottage, admiring her youthful figure which she had kept up all these years. He turned back and watched a dozen or so boats sailing with the ocean breeze. An occasional fish leaped out of the water, trailing streams of wet droplets that formed a mosaic rainbow in the air.

He was so entranced with all this beauty that he almost dozed off, his relaxation beginning to put him in a hypnotic state. He couldn't remember a time in his life he had felt this relaxed. He should have made this move to retirement a few years earlier and would have if he had known how glorious it was going to be. His reverie was broken when a shadow suddenly blocked off the sun he was basking in.

Thinking Marta had returned with their drinks, he smiled and with his eyes still half closed held out his hand. When she failed to hand the drink to him and the persistent shadow was still there, he sat up and slowly turned around with an unexplained shiver suddenly coursing through his body. He had a gut feeling that something was amiss.

Standing to the side of him and blocking the sun were several uniformed and plain clothes police officers of the Fuerza Publica, an arm of the Ministry of Public Safety for Costa Rica. As if in slow motion the row of policemen parted in the center and a lone tall figure stepped forward.

Victor gasped in disbelief, his eyes widening.

"Hello, *El Scorpion*," Jack Storm said.

Sting of the Scorpion

Earl Underwood

AUTHOR

EARL UNDERWOOD WAS BORN AND RAISED in a small town in North Carolina. In 1961, at the age of 20, he and his family moved to Miami, Florida. He served in the United States Army Corps of Engineers from 1964 to 1966 and did a tour of duty in Viet Nam.

Upon returning home, he married Linda Susan Albert and pursued a career in law enforcement. He retired after serving the public for many years. Most of his police career was that of a homicide detective where he received many awards.

After retirement he relocated to Grand Island in Central Florida with his family. Earl enjoys spending time with his four children, Shaunie, Scott, Michael, and Dejah, and his four grandchildren, Victoria, Erica, Zachary, and Mikaella. Family is the most important thing to Earl and his wife Sue.

Earl came out of retirement and served another fourteen years in law enforcement in Central Florida before finally retiring for good in 2003 with a total of almost 32 years. He now spends his time golfing, painting and pursuing his lifelong passion of writing.

Earl may be contacted at Underwood914@yahoo.com.

Other Books by Earl Underwood

Austin Steele Space Adventures
Austin Steele's New Life on Xova (**2013**)
The Scourge of Alpha Centauri (**2015**)

Detective Jack Storm Mysteries
The Cold Smile (**2014**)
Sting of the Scorpion (**2016**)

Autobiography
This Is My Story and I'm Sticking to It (**2012**)

The above books are published by Shoppe Foreman Publishing. For more information go to www.ShoppeForeman.com/Underwood. To purchase a book in softcover or e-book go to www.Amazon.com.

Made in the USA
Columbia, SC
09 October 2023